WALLACE
LEGEND OF BRAVEHEART
BOOK 5

# BRIGAND CHIEF

## SEORAS WALLACE

1ˢᵗ EDITION

Published in 2020 by Wolf and Wildcat Publishing

Copyright © Seoras Wallace 2020

Seoras Wallace has asserted his right to be identified as the author of this
Work in accordance with the Copyright, Designs
and Patents Act 1988

ISBN Paperback: 978-1-8383470-0-0
Ebook: 978-1-8383470-1-7



A CIP catalogue copy of this book can be found
in the British Library.

Published with the help of Indie Authors World
www.indieauthorsworld.com

www.facebook.com/InDiScotland

Wolf & Wildcat publishing
Associate: Jade Macfarlane
+44(0)7766 584 360
www.wolfandwildcat.com
www.facebook.com/Wallace.Legend
Clan Wallace PO Box 1305 Glasgow G51 4UB Scotland

Dedicate to the memory of a great clansman…

RIP

**Wee Graham**

*- A Wallace -*

Dedicate to the memory of a great clansman…
RIP
**Auld Tam (MacDermott)**
*- A Wallace -*

# Acknowledgements

Big thank you for the writing support from
my hard working family and friends

# About the Author: Seoras Wallace

After a career in the film industry spanning over thirty years, in such films as Highlander, Gladiator, Rob Roy, Braveheart, Saving Private Ryan and many more. In 1997 following a serious horse riding accident, Seoras turned his valuable experience to becoming an author, and parallel to his professional life. Seoras has also served as acting chief executive of the Wallace Clan Trust for Scotland.

"An experience like no other," said Seoras, "One of the constants in my vocation has been the revelation of private or secretive documents and accounts from many unusual sources that gave me a wholly different perspective of William Wallace, that shaped him as a man who became a nations Iconic patriot and world hero in the eyes and hearts of many. At first I used to think that the information I witnessed was too incredible to be true, but when certain parts of that narrative repeated from different sources, another story from the academic norm began to emerge. Growing up in a remote west coast village, that was extremely patriotic and nationalist, I was taught from the clan elders at an early age the family legend of Wallace, but that too did not match the publicly available narrative. On my many travels around the world, especially after the release and success of the film Braveheart, people would often say upon hearing my account, "You should write a book about the Wallace." "I have always replied that no one would ever believe it, but following my accident, I decided to leave the family legacy as a fact based fictional narrative for my family and future generations, almost as a historical bloodline diary. The epic account I have written about the Life and Legend of William Wallace has been an inspiration and brought to me a newfound love for the man, the people and the country he fought for. Many who have been test reading the epic series as it developed, have a constant response that stands out more than any other comment, "Seoras, I've researched what you've written, and it's true…" My reply has always been… "Naw… it's just fiction!"

# Amulets of the Aicé

**W**alking the horses slowly through Comunnach gatehouse and across the drawbridge of the Castle, William pauses and looks to the heavens and sees a clear and beautiful still night sky blissfully illuminating the familiar drove road, well enough for him to travel at a reasonable pace. He frees Warrior's reigns to follow-on then leans forward slightly; Fleetfoot immediately breaks into a gentle canter, loyally followed by a free and unbridled Warrior. William's mind is lost in the thoughts of what has happened at Ach na Feàrna and Glen Afton and It's not long before he realises he is approaching the imposing Loudoun hill, scene of his uncle Malcolm and Sandy's murder. Suddenly Fleetfoot pricks his ears forward and pulls back. William doesn't think as he presses the flanks of Fleetfoot to walk-on… but Fleetfoot refuses to budge… suddenly a gruff voice calls out to him from the darkened tree line at the side of the road, "HALT…" William curses under his breath as armed English soldiers emerge from the woodlands with pole-arm weapons pointing directly at him; then he notices another two soldiers coming at his back with cocked crossbow's… then another two appear with halberds who approach him head-on.

"Dismount Scotchman." commands a burly looking soldier who appears to be in charge. "Fuck…" curses William under his breath, caught unawares because of his distractions.

Reluctantly he dismounts, his grandfathers sword is securely tied down and stuck through his night-pack behind his saddle. "You…" commands the burly soldier to one of his men. "Take his horses, and you Scotchman… you follow me."

William looks around with urgency and sees there are six more armed English soldiers pointing their weapons at him. A soldier prods him in the back with the sharp point of a long pole-arm; then they lead him over a high bank, down into the glade and past the oak tree where he had found Malcolm's body hanging a few days earlier. He focuses on the tree as the soldiers lead him into an English camp at the foot of Loudoun hill. "Move Scotchman…" barks the soldier as they escort him through the English camp towards a large pavilion, there they come to a halt. "Wait here." demands the burly soldier. He then walks towards two guards standing outside a smaller pavilion and briefly talks with them. The burly soldier turns and calls over to William, "Do you speak English Scotchman?" William stares at the soldier momentarily; then he replies, "Aye, that I do." At that moment, two English knights come out the door of the small pavilion and approach him. The lead knight enquires, "Well then, who do we have here?" the second and younger knight enquires, "Do you have a name Scotchman?" William glares at the English knights in pure defiance; then he replies, "Aye… ah do, my name is William Wallace."

The two knights share a furtive glance, completely unnoticed by William as he stands under a secure guard in the middle of the English army encampment surrounded by tough looking English soldiers, their faces grim with determination and focus while continually training their weapons on him. Their armour, halberds and helms are of highly polished well-worn steel that briefly glints from the campfires and moonlight.

The two English knights scrutinise William thoroughly as they sup their wine and feast on boiled swan legs. William, his mind racing, prepares for what may happen next, knowing he's trapped in a fraught and uncertain situation. The elder knight steps a little closer and looks menacingly into William's eyes, then he raises his hand towards the guards and commands, "Leave us." William is surprised at the knight's command, he studies the knight, a tall young man, well built and not much older than himself, with short black hair fringed high above his eyebrows. It's obvious this knight is an experienced soldier by his scarred complexion, authority and confident manner in which he carries himself.

"Sit, William Wallace." says the knight. He turns and calls out, "Squire…" Immediately a squire jumps to attention, "Yes my Lord?" The knight replies, "Bring refreshments right away for master Wallace, by m'lady, if anyone needs the taste of fine Burgundian wine and some good English fare, it's this young man."

The younger knight slowly circles William while the elder knight watches him closely. Moments pass in ominous silence, the strain pulling at William's nerves, his troubled thoughts are interrupted when the squire soon returns with a tankard of wine and a large platter full of food, but William is wary of the fare. The elder knight comments, "Eat Wallace… for you look starved." The younger knight laughs, "By God sir, you stink as though you have not bathed in a lifetime." The elder knight laughs too, "You do stink Scotchman… So tell me this, what is your story, why do you travel at night, are you a thief or perhaps a brigand? Maybe you're an erstwhile assassin that has come to our camp here to kill us? My guards tell me that you arrived here on two valuable mounts that are beyond the wherewithal of someone like you, are you a horse thief?" Both knights laugh… a little.

"No sir knight, I am none of those things, I…" says William, then he focuses directly into the eyes of the elder knight before continuing with his answer. "I am William Wallace, son of sir Alain Wallace, former lead hunter to the late King Alexander; I'm from the lands of the King's Kyle, Black Craig, glen Afton and the Wolf and wildcat forests. I return with great urgency to be with my family in Ach na Feàrna up near Paisley town in the Barony of Riccartoun." The elder knight replies sullenly, "Do you really?" Then he looks curiously at William; he sees something about William's demeanour that makes him extremely suspicious. "Not very skilled in the hunt are you my friend, not looking as you do… and by the way you are tearing at that food." William hadn't noticed he was ravishing the vittals, for he hadn't eaten in nearly three day's. He pauses as the elder knight continues, "Well master Wallace, perhaps you may be of assistance to us?"

A moment passes as William ponders over what assistance he may be to these English knights, he enquires, "What d'yie mean sir Knight?" The elder knight gazes menacingly at him then he says, "Earlier today we found the bodies of dead English soldiers just a little way in the woodlands up there… murdered by some of your countrymen no doubt. You wouldn't know anything about this incident would you?" William says nothing, the question has caught him off guard; suddenly he feels a surge of uncontrollable nervous tension pass through his entire body like a rash. He thinks 'Fuck… that must be those English soldiers who tried to kill me a few days ago'. "Curiously Wallace…" continues the knight, "it appears as though they were foully murdered in a scurrilous ambush. At first we considered it may be by a group of renegade Scotch felons, but what defies this particular scenario is that the bodies were left where they fell, none were robbed nor were any of their monies, weapons or horses taken. They had been shot with arrows and then their throats had been cut. I believe that those killings were the result of some misguided fool's personal lust for revenge, not robbery. A strange state of affairs, don't you think?" William begins to panic and tries desperately not to show it as the two knights continue to scrutinise him closely. With each passing moment, the atmosphere is becoming extremely tense. For a little while, no further words pass between them. The long silence is crushing William's spirit. He's becoming desperate in his search for an opportunity to escape the fraught situation. He knows if he could just make it to the edge of the dark woodlands, he may have a chance, but it feels as though the English knights know what he's thinking and they also know it was he who had killed the English soldiers. He's now convinced they are simply playing with him, like two fat cats toying with a doomed mouse. He also believes that if he even blinks, it will appear as an admission of guilt...

The elder knight leans close to William's face then he speaks quietly, "If we were to examine your quivers and find that you have the same number of Arrows without heads as there are holes in the bodies of our dead soldiers, do you think those numbers will match up Wallace? For I know you Scotch do like to use loose heads for a flight." William's mouth begins to dry and he feels the panic prickling his brain. He needs only a one lapse of concentration from the elder knight and he'll smash him in the face with the heavy wine jug, all he has to do is wait... Suddenly he sees his opportunity when the elder knight looks over Williams shoulder, he tightens his grip on the jug readying himself to strike, when a voice in a heavy Scots brogue calls out from the darkness behind him, "Aye, it is you young Wallace... so what brings you here?" Turning to see who calls out to him, William peers into the darkness and notices a religiously dressed man walking directly towards them. "Young Wallace…" says the stranger, "I know the elders of your family well." William nods his head as the stranger makes introduction. "I'm Prior Abernethy from the Mount Lothian Cistercian priory, on the western gate of Ballentradoch."

The Prior casually walks past William towards the makeshift table and pours himself a drink from a flagon of wine. He turns and looks back at him. "William Wallace you say?" William nods again in acknowledgement as Abernethy continues, "I know your father Sir Alain and your uncle, Sir Malcolm." Abernethy strolls over and stands beside William while diffusing the tense atmosphere with his pleasantries; then he makes another introduction…

"Wallace, this here knight before you is my good friend sir John Seagrave, a knight of King Edward, and this good knight beside him enjoying his fare is Lord Robert de Clifford, the Sheriff Westmorland." Seagrave looks thoughtfully at William, then he says, "You do not appear to relish our company so very much Wallace, do you?"

William replies "Begging your pardon lord Seagrave. It's not your company that ails me, I travel with great haste to reach my home in Ach na Feàrna, for my grandmother is gravely ill and my presence there is urgently required." Seagrave replies brusquely, "Then feast yourself Wallace, and do take some food for your travels, for your appearance does appeal to the needs of fortification, otherwise you could be easily mistaken for a miscreant by your sullen appearance and be dealt with as such." De Clifford approaches William, he says, "You should bathe soon too Scotchman. It is not becoming a son of even a lowly knight to be in such a wretched condition as you are, and to present yourself thus in our company, I ask you, is this worthy of your rank?" Before William can reply, de Clifford continues, "Though it would appear you are from a lesser breed, nonetheless you are reputedly of higher station than a peasant, and as such, you must always maintain a standard becoming." William replies by way of explanation. "Begging your pardon sir, but I am just returned from a long arduous summer hunt." Abernethy picks up some bread while keeping a fixed gaze on William, "I can vouch for his name lord Robert, and that of his family. He's from good stock my lords, a family of God fearing honour."

Seagrave and de Clifford appear satisfied upon hearing Abernethy's account and they soon lose interest in William as they begin to converse between themselves about more pressing matters. Abernethy winks, "Come with me young Wallace, tell me all about your father and how he fares." Abernethy walks towards the horses as William follows him cautiously; very much relieved to be taking this opportune moment to escape the predicament he's in. Seagrave and de Clifford acknowledge their departure then they return to their own pavilion deep in conversation. William walks warily with Abernethy, who continues talking.

After a few moments, when they are out of sight of the two knights and a short distance to where William's horses are tethered, Abernethy says, "Quickly Wallace, we must get you on your horses now then you must leave this place with much haste. I have already heard what has happened at glen Afton... and also the grave news of your father and uncle." William is taken aback, he exclaims, "But how..." Abernethy is curt, "Hurry Wallace, we'll discourse another time, for these knights are newly arrived in Scotland and I know they have not yet scrutinised the list of families to be put to the sword." William gasps, "A list?" he stands momentarily dumbfounded. Suddenly a voice behind them says, "You should do as the good Prior bids you Wallace." Startled, William spins round to be met by Seagrave staring at him from just a little distance away. The piercing eyes of Seagrave and his relaxed attitude perplexes William. The three men stand in silence; the tension of the moment is becoming virtually unbearable for William. Seagrave speaks, "I am a Chivalric Knight Wallace, I am not a murderer, now go you to your family, before I change my mind." Seagrave immediately turns and walks away. William looks on in disbelief, Abernethy quickly ushers him away, "Go now like he says Wallace, for there is to be no mercy to be shown to any of the peasantry who does not bow and scrape to the English army, nor any mercy to be shown to those with any direct links to our beloved Alexander's rule..." Abernethy calls out, "Soldier... Bring this man his horses, by order of Lord Seagrave." William is stunned at the opportune intervention of Abernethy and by that of the English knight Seagrave, who has so obviously spared him. William stammers, "I don't know what to say."

"Say nothing," replies Abernethy, "when you get to Ach na Feàrna, please convey my condolences and deepest sympathies to your grandmother and your uncle Ranald." The soldier soon returns with Warrior and Fleetfoot. William mounts and is about to leave when Abernethy grabs his reigns, "Go carefully Wallace, soon we will have a true King back on the throne of Scotland, then we'll gain redress for what's happening at this time. Heed my words... we shall meet again, of that I have little doubt." William could scarcely believe he is free, then Abernethy says, "And Wallace... I sorely grieve for your father and sir Malcolm, and I'm deeply sorry for your loss." William exclaims, "I don't know how to thank you..." Abernethy replies, "I do, stay alive Wallace." William looks at the prior with curiosity. Abernethy steps back and slap's Fleetfoot on the flank. William acknowledges Abernethy then canters out of the English camp with his heart pounding in his chest like a great drum, he knows he has just passed a moment in time when his life could have been so easily ended, he thinks, I don't understand these Englishmen…

As he travels onwards and through the long night, William carefully avoids any further contact with English patrols and sentinel guards. When he approaches the magnificent and regal Ruther's glen Castle, he remembers true Tams advice, *'Hide in plain sight Wallace'*. He rides on past the castle and soon passes the busy link bridge that crosses the Clyde and leads up to Grey Rock Castle and Glasgow Cathedral. He rides on to the smithy villages of Gobhain and past the Templar's chapel on the Kings Ynche, till finally, as dawn breaks, he rides through the gates of Ach na Feàrna, where he's utterly dismayed at what he sees. The Balloch appears derelict, abandoned and empty of life, yet it had been only days before it was full of laughter and the sounds of people going about their business, even the incessant sounds of the livestock making their barnyard noises is deafening in its absence. Ellerslie Ach na Feàrna is like a ghost village as he walks Fleetfoot and Warrior cautiously towards the main house.

He sits awhile on Fleetfoot, observing the dereliction surrounding him, the chilly silence reminds him of the ruined villages, Ballochs and sheilins he had seen during the fighting between Brix and Baliol in the southwest civil war a few years ago. He vividly remembers the brutal slaughter and destruction of Coinach's clan; then he thinks of his own family, seeing their faces, both in life… and in death. He thinks *'What if…'* But he can't think the worst here, it would be too much, he begins trembling, puts his hands to his eyes then hangs his head as tears begin to well up inside of him. His emotions are raw; suddenly, his thoughts are disturbed hearing a noise behind him. He turns quickly, this time his sword is drawn at the ready as a character he recognises comes walking out the kitchen door to greet him…

"True Tam…" exclaims William. Tam smiles, then he enquires, "Are you all right there Wallace?" William stares at the strange looking knight, he swallows hard while trying to compose himself as true Tam approaches. William has still not got used to this odd characters appearance nor his nuances, but he's drawn to him and his peculiar mannerisms. William dismounts and rushes towards the doors to seek his kinfolk, as he brushes past true Tam he says, "Naw, I'm no' all right…" True Tam says, "they're all on the mend Wallace, so you bide yer time and let them have peace." William realises his arrogance towards this man who has shown him and his family nothing but kindness, is unwarranted. He enquires, "Have you've heard the news from Glen Afton?" True Tam replies, "Aye son, Ranald told me everything. Ahm so sorry for yer loss." William enquires anxiously, "How fares my family here?" True Tam replies, "Safe and as well as could be. Come away into the kitchens and ah'll tell yie all."

True Tam follows William inside the house and watches him frantically rushing from room to room. "Calm yerself Wallace…" says True Tam, "They're all away to places o' safety." William stops and looks into the face of true Tam, he enquires desperately, "Where are they Tam, for I've got to go to them." True Tam sits down on a chair beside wee Maws throne, "Your uncle Richard has taken Margret, Uliann and Aunia to your kinfolk near Dunipace. Ranald has taken young Andrew and Malcolm óg over to Crosbie, all for their safety and protection." William enquires, "So where's wee Maw?" True Tam points outside the house in the direction of the clan burial grounds, "Bheitris is away up at the old yew tree yonder, aye, she sits there by your grandfathers sweet ground talking and singing to him all day long she does."

William rushes to the door and looks over to the burial grounds of his people. He sees the figure of wee Maw huddled with brat and plaid to keep her warm. She appears happily lost to the world, sitting beside Billy's Sweet ground and rocking gently back and forth. William begins to walk towards her when true Tam catches his léine sleeve…

"Not now Wallace." he says firmly. William stops and looks into the brown speckled eyes of true Tam, this odd character with the thin grey face, wispy beard and unkempt greasy hair who wears ill-fitting black armour that almost mesmerises him. True tam says, "She knows you're here son, but she's also in her own world now preparing herself, so it's best to leave her awhile, she'll come to us in her good own time." William looks over at wee Maw, then he looks again into the eyes of true Tam as though he understands something in his words that in any other circumstance he would have ignored or questioned. True Tam says, "Now young Wallace, you come wie me and we'll strip the tack off Warrior and Fleetfoot, for it looks like they be needin' our attention too."

They walk over to the horses where true Tam loosens the harness and tack from Fleetfoot while William unclips the girth belts, saddle and leathers about Warrior. Throwing the tack over a post, William enquires, "How did they all take the news about Glen Afton?" True Tam shakes his head mournfully, "The girls are still in painful humours and they grieve deeply Wallace, but they are young and strong, their bodies will heal, but their heads will need a great deal of nurture and understanding. Margret, well, I fear that she is too ill to fully understand, caused by the violations meted out upon her by the English soldiers. I fear for her too that her mind is broken at the loss of dear Malcolm. I believe that your elder brother Alan said he will take Margret up to your uncle Alex's family near Kilspindie, for Margret's sister Elsie is a goodwife up there and best suited to aid her ailments." William punches his saddle in anger, he angrily pulls it from Warrior's back and hurls it at the house door then he curses and kicks over a large water barrel, screaming out in sheer anguish. "Why… why the fuck would they do this to us Tam…." True Tam reaches out, "Make easy there Wallace, for their time will surely come, believe me that." William turns aggressively towards true Tam and glares at him, he's about to curse and rage, but something in this strange knight's gaze calms the explosive pain that wells up within his heart. Tam says, "Rest easy Wallace like ah said, and finish yer chores." William compliantly picks up his saddle and sets it on the tie bar; then he glances across the yards to see that his grandmother is still contentedly rocking back and forth.

"Why does wee Maw remain here Tam?" True Tam shakes his head and smiles, "Wee Maw wouldn't leave till you were back here safely. Yie should know by now that no-one and nuthin' can budge her mind when it's made up." William smiles then looks to see that wee Maw is still sitting content-edly, as though somehow she has heard Tam's reply.

True Tam strokes the face of Warrior and mutters, "So tell to me, what's happened to you my bonnie fella?" He begins fussing about Warrior, gently stroking all the wound edges while talking in some olde tongue. Warrior instantly reacts in an almost human manner as though both he and Tam are conversing in the mystical language of the olahm magh meall; (Otherworld plain of joy) William watches intently as true Tam examines the wounds on the flank and neck of Warrior. "English arrows…" mutters True Tam. He shakes his head and continues to converse quietly with Warrior in the olde tongue. William enquires, "Are yie talkin' to me?" True Tam replies, "Naw boy, don't be stupid… ahm askin' Warrior where all his inner pains are." William laughs to himself while he studies with great curiosity the way the old knight touches and prods about and below the neck of Warrior, then pressing his fingers about the horse's neck and shoulders. William enquires, "What are yie doin'?" Suddenly Warrior jerks his head up as true Tam probes deep into the neck wound with two thin strips of wood then he quickly removes the arrow shaft with the head still affixed. "Hmm…" sighs true Tam, "That was lucky the head came out se' easy." William too is relieved, "I didn't think the arrowhead would have came out without tying Warrior to the rutting posts and cutting the flesh deep." True Tam replies, "Och Wallace, don't yie know that both man and beast all have wee buttons to press to take away the pains and make yie feel the way the button presser wants yie to feel?"

"What the fu…" William doesn't finish his exclamation as true Tam quickly reaches up and presses his thumbs firmly on each side of William's chest; then he touches him on the forehead and runs his thumb down the centre, stopping between his hairline and his eyes. Before William can react, True Tam smiles and turns his attention back to the care of Warrior. William is utterly bemused by this odd action from his peculiar acquaintance. After a few moments, True Tam enquires, "How are yie feeling now young Wallace?" William's mind is experiencing a pleasant lightheaded giddiness while simultaneously an inner-warmth ripples throughout his entire body, a warmth that glows from deep inside of him as though emanating from his very core.

For a moment, William begins to relive all and every horrific detail of Glen Afton, he sees the macabre tortured faces of Alain, Mharaidh, Caoilfhinn, Malcolm and all of his murdered kinfolk, but then, the anguished faces seem to sense he is thinking of them and pleasantly begin to morph into faces with features so full of love, health and vitality in his thoughts; happy faces he knows and loves, faces that smile and alleviate his pain and innermost torments, confirming to him they're now safe and in a better place. He tries to steady himself, dismissing his feelings and thoughts as that of simply fatigue. "I think that I'm feeling very feckn tired Tam." They both know William is experiencing an effect from the Touch, but are content not to mention it, not till curiosity gets the better of William. He enquires, "What the feck did you do to me?" True Tam grins, "Nuthin son…" William smiles, accepting that he really must be tired from his experience and lack of sleep, but he feels extremely contented and greatly comforted by the simplicity of true Tam's reply. He watches as true Tam runs a bony finger ever so gently over the open wound in Warrior's neck.

"Dyie think his wounds will heal Tam?" True Tam replies, "Aye… His wounds are scabbin' and that's a good sign. Just you keep bathing all his wounds with warm salty water and a dab of flongeur a few times a day, keep the wounds clean then gently rub some o' this balm liniment on the scabs to keep them soft." True Tam holds out a little wooden bowl filled with a buttery looking substance. William dips his fingers into it then carefully he runs his fingers over the wounds on Warrior's neck and flanks. Warrior pins back his ears, responding to the soothing connection of William tending to all his wounds with the healing balm.

True Tam observes as William meticulously applies the balm to Warrior with great care. He smiles seeing that William is lost in these Elysian moments of peace and serenity, then he grins when William puts his arms around the warm neck of Warrior with his head resting on his horses shoulder. After a while, true Tam says, "I'll make up some feed mix that I want you to remember Wallace, It's for keeping your horse fit and healthy… and if you ever have a need of it, you can eat it too if you want." Smiling at the thought, William feels as though he is waking from a peaceful and serene dream, yet he knows he hasn't been asleep. "Are yie with me Wallace?" The voice of true Tam is sharp, yet soothing to William's soul, then he notices that true Tam is delving into a large flaxen bag, "I've some fine horse-scran here, made up from young Beet roots, Burdock, Chickweed, Dandelion, Nettle, Slippery Elm, Yellow-dock… and remember this too Wallace, always make sure yie carry a few bunches o' dry sphagnum moss and linens in your saddlebags, they're to be mending any horse's wounds they may have about the legs, otherwise a horse could bleed out pretty damn quick from any innocent wee cuts. And mind you this too what I say next, most healing balms for horses will see you right as well should yie be ailin." Mumbling by way of reply, William says, "Fuck's sake Tam, I'm feeling like I've had one nip o' craitur too many. What have you done to me auld fella?" True Tam ignores William's comical belligerence.

"Wallace?"

"Wha… eh?" splutters William, "Aye Tam, what is it?" True Tam laughs then says, "I want yie to watch what I'm doing, so don't be fallin' asleep on me just yet."

William concentrates on true Tam as the quaint old character mixes even quantities of herbal remedies while humming little melodies. After a while, true Tam administers the elixirs and poultice balms to Warrior as he had done previously to the wounds of wee Maw and the family. William thinks of something that his father had once told him about true Tam being a seer, a man with the sight of the future, a magician, or something of that description. Finally, they tend to the horses by brushing and washing them down, then they take the horses over to the grazing paddock and release them to feed on the lush thick green grass, now overgrown without the stock animals to feed on and crop down. They both lean on the wooden fence spars watching the horses play and canter about the paddock. True Tam looks at William and sees deep lines of stress and grief etched in the young mans face. He also knows the ordeal William has endured in seeing the slaughter aftermath of glen Afton, he knows it will take its toll on him for a long time, likely a lifetime.

True Tam is concerned and thinks about what William may do next to exact revenge or find justice. He puts his hand on William's shoulder but says nothing. William, without taking his eyes off the horses, enquires, "You haven't asked me the detail about what happened down at Glen Afton." True Tam replies, "I already know son, Ranald and Richard have told me of what they witnessed and all of what they know."

They stand awhile longer watching the horses, both lost in thought, then True Tam says, "C'mon back to the big house Wallace, I've some fine stovies simmering on the fire. Get yourself a good meal and bathe and ah'll make yie up a real fine toddy too, then you can try and get some sleep for you've done so much these last few days young fella, more than most I'll wager." William looks into the eyes of true Tam. As he studies true Tam's features, he laughs to himself, even looking at true Tam gives him a feeling of peace and good humour. It seems that being in true Tam's company dispels the nightmarish pain of what he has seen, but never to be forgotten. "Aye Tam," replies William "Yie could be right." True Tam and William both smile as they l wander towards the main house...

Suddenly William cries out, "WEE MAW..." True Tam looks to the burial grounds and sees wee Maw slumped on the ground. William runs over to her as fast as he can. By the time true Tam reaches them, William is cradling wee Maw in his arms. True Tam kneels beside them and gently holds wee

Maw's hand; then he notices there's a trickle of dry blood at the corner of her mouth and a heavily bloodstained kerchief lying on the ground beside her. William cries out desperately, "Is she gone from us Tam…?"

True Tam replies, "Quickly Wallace; you take her inside the big house and get her into the warmth, for her skin is the colour alabaster and she's as cold as winter ice, we must get her warmed up and quick. I'll go on ahead and get a hot toddy and some hot broken gruel ready wie plenty o' spices in it, for she must be eatin' to fill her with warmth and fine healin' nourishment."

William gently cradles the frail body of his beloved wee Maw in his arms as true Tam rushes ahead of them to the main house to prepare sustenance and comfort beside the great fire for his old dear friend Bheitris. William is relieved when he hears wee Maw groan as he walks with her, then she puts her arms around his neck. He exclaims, "Granny…" Wee maw opens her eyes and smiles, "Oh my dearest Billy, you've come for me at last." She closes her eyes, hugging tight to William like a child, she whispers, "I've been so very tired Billy and I've missed you for so long, now all I want is to go home with you and the family passed, don't leave me alone this time Billy… take me with you…" William fears for wee Maw's health; but he's relieved to be seeing her open her eyes and to see her bonnie wrinkly smile. He carries his wee Maw into the main house and over to the inglenook fireplace, where True Tam has already made up a warm crib.

As William kneels to lay her down, wee Maw struggles, "Naw naw Billy, I want to be sitting in my own auld chair beside the fire, just you get me a thick plaid and a wee nip o' honey craitur and I'll be fine, now put me down ah say." William looks at her, "Are yie sure Granny?" Wee Maw shrugs her shoulders as she tries to find her way to her throne.

"Stop fussing me about Billy and get me my wants, for it's terrible cold and I'm thinkin' a wee drop o' the honey craitur will see me fine, now be away with yourself I'm telling yie." William helps wee Maw into her throne beside the big fire just as true Tam comes back in with hot vittals, then he too fusses about wee Maw, he says, "Get that plaid off the arm o' the chair Wallace and wrap it around her shoulders." William helps true Tam to comfort wee Maw, then he pours some honey craitur into her horn jug while True Tam hands her a bowl of hot boiled corn and broken spice gruel. Wee Maw looks up, "William… Your back already son?"

"Aye Granny." Wee Maw begins supping her gruel then she stops to speak, "Oh William, I'm so glad your back home with us lookin' safe and well." He replies, "I'm well enough Granny." Wee Maw spoons some more hot gruel, then, without taking her eyes from the food, she enquires, "Did you see my Billy?" She glances at him with a crinkly cheeky smile and winks. "He's coming for me yie know…"

"Come on now Billy," says wee Maw, "be getting the obhainn-pipes out to play me some fine tunes for auld lang syne, Its been too long since I heard yie playin' the bonnie chanter, even if it is badly yie play, yie know it's still music to ma auld ears." William smiles, it doesn't matter any more what she wants to call him, he's just happy she seems to be in fine spirits, despite her forgetfulness.

True Tam enquires, "Do yie play the obhainn-pipes boy?" William replies, "Aye that ah do Tam… badly though as yie may gather from wee Maw's comments." True Tam laughs, "Aye, me too… I've got ma whistles and bone claves with me. You go git yer obhainn-pipes then we'll play some fine auld tunes together this eve, all for the soothin' o' the soul and bonnie heart o' our dearest Bheitris." William gets up quickly and goes to another room. He soon returns with his uncle

Malcolm's obhainn-pipes, meanwhile, true Tam is playing some beautiful haunting flute melodies for wee Maw. After fixing on the bellows belt and tuning-in the small drones on the pipes, they begin to tune their instruments together. Once they are musically in harmony, Wee Maw sits back in her chair, staring intently at the flames of the fire; she pulls up her plaid and shawls and nestles into her throne then she says, "This will be our very own wee wake me fine boys…"

True Tam and William smile, for the keen wit of wee Maw has made sure that their own small wake is to be a big part of the bereavement healing they all so desperately need. William feels relief, thinking, She's back with us.

Tam and William begin playing familiar tunes sitting in front of the glowing fire of Ach na Feàrna, while wee Maw hums along. Time passes as the tunes sooth the heartbroken souls of William, true Tam and wee Maw. They play and sing many old tunes and songs along with the distinct contra-harmonies of the ancient bellows-pipes and flutes; then a while later, William notices that wee Maw is fast asleep. He glances at true Tam then they finish their tune and lay down their instruments. True Tam sighs, "Aye son, music sure soothes the soul right enough." William watches true Tam put some more wood and peat on the fire, the scents from the burning peat and wood resin contributes to the feeling of wellbeing in William's heart.

"Tam?" he enquires, "Ma father once told me of how people ignorant of your ways want to kill you or harm you, yet when they need help or solace, they would always come to you. He also said you are a seer, though some I have heard callin' you a sorcerer or warlock, what are yie really…?" True Tam laughs, "Well," he sighs, "First of all, a Warlock is from an ancient Cruathnie word that means an oath breaker to Christ, so that only applies to any Christians who have broken their oath with their church and returned to the old heathen ways. So a warlock it is I'm not, for I've never given my oath nor faith to Christianity." William smiles as true Tam continues, "And the Norsemen… aye well, they call me a Varth-lokkr, which sounds a wee bitty the same, so me being neither Norse nor Christian young Wallace, then again… it's a Varth-lokkr I am not." William looks at true Tam and grins, "Well you're sure something different, that's for sure Tam."

"Me…?" Laughs true Tam, "I'm just an ordinary wee fella trying to make sense out o' what this world has to offer, it's everyone else that's different son, no' me." William laughs, "You may be a lot of things Tam, but ordinary just isn't one o' them." Tam smiles at William, thinking that this young man could possibly understand more about his gifts than most. Perhaps if he were to part with William some of his thoughts and experiences, if even a single solitary grain of understanding passes between them, then this may help him deal with his grief and his pain. True Tam thinks to himself… *'This is a brave heart young man, he's worth at least that…'*

"Well?" Enquires William, "Wee Maw sez you've got the gift of the sight and that you're a person who can influence good and evil spirits, she also said you can access the other worlds to influence ours here." Tam laughs, "Wallace me boy… everyone can do that, it's just a matter of your own attitude to personal discipline, believing in your own truths and believing what you may say and do is only ever intended for the betterment of others."

William frowns as True Tam continues, "You've heard your grandmother calling you Billy haven't you? You've seen her sit beside his sweet ground talking and singing to him haven't you? And didn't she just say a wee while ago that Billy has come for her?" William stammers, "Well, aye…" True Tam grins, "You think she is losing her mind don't yie boy?

William replies, "I don't know?" Sitting forward, Tam gently clasps wee Maw's hand, "Your granny is of the olde blood son, not just from the Morríghan, but from the divine sisters Scáthach and Aofin, the twin Aicés." William is enthralled hearing of his bloodline. True Tam continues, "It's not that she's losing her mind son, it's simply that the walls that divides the realms becomes thinner as she gains closer to the door o' a better place. What she sees and feels is very much her reality, and who are we to deny its existence?"

Finding these words refreshingly enlightening, William understands what true Tam is saying, but he also knows that folk who speak as wee Maw does is often cast from Christian society, yet revered by the likes of true Tam. William says, "But you're different Tam, you see things that no one else does, and many say you see the future... wee Maw sez it's because the Sídhe favours you."

"Wallace, the Sídhe favour everyone, its just so sad that most don't feckn accept it. In the auld days the ancients believed that everything had a spirit, be it Welsh druids, the Céile Aicé, Cruathnie healers or Breitheamh Rígh... they're all individual trees evolving from pre-Christian roots. And down through the generations for some of us, the knowing, the Touch or the gift has been passed to us with appropriate and necessary skills, even to this very day, I just happen to have been passed my beliefs from my own influential Wee Maw as yie like to call her." William laughs out loud, "You had a wee Maw too?" Tam grins, "Och aye boy, of course I did. When her time was near she used to dress in a bull hide gùn mhòr (Long dress) inlaid with white swan peann feathers. She would also like to wear a bleached ram skull headdress and a great mantle brat made from a thousand of the most beautiful blue-black and crimson raven feathers... blessed by the old Anam fitheach (Bird spirit). Aye, she used to dance about our auld hoose at Ercildoune to be scarin' away the evil spirits or any malicious folk that would wish to do us harm. I mind that long before she departed us to a better place, she would always say to me, anyone might put love or fear into another's head, it's how you do it that's the trick, aye me boy, there are many wee Maws all over Scotland that still have those particular gifts." They both laugh at that thought; then William enquires, "So why do the Christians fear you in particular Tam? Why do they say you can influence the spirit world that makes them so full o' fear?"

Shaking his head almost in futile despair, True Tam replies… "Son… folk like me, the Christians would rather we didn't exist. Think about it, those religious fella's use the power of fear and punishment to have folk do their bidding, Do as I do, do what I say, or you will suffer hellish torment for eternity, this is their fact. And most folk like to think that we are all supposed to be one faith, which is fine on occasion, the problem comes when you're dependent solely upon one person's teachings, then you become a mere shadow o' that person, which usually means that you never fully reveal or understand your own potential for the benefit of others. Wallace me boy, experience life on your own two feet and yie can still have faith and hope, that's no' things that are just exclusive to the followers of the one true God as they say."

William nods in understanding as true Tam continues, "Us folks o' the auld faith son, we see the Anam Álainn in everything and everybody… we don't fear these Christian threats of hell as they see and understand it to be. In our faith there is no hell, only the otherworld. Those Christian fella's feel threatened by any individualism because they have no control over how we as free spirits like to live our lives, they don't like that at all. Their religious hierarchy insists that we must all believe in their one true God for there is no other…

fuck that, of course there is." William says, "Me Dá used to tell me there was an Anam Álainn in everything too when we hunted together, I really began to believe it and could feel that his belief is so much more important and relevant to us out there in the wilds than to be on my knees mumbling away to myself in a feckn monastery mesmerised, like most o' the masses."

True Tam sighs, "Christians don't fear me son, what they fear is losing control of the masses caused by one single solitary free thought. For them, if someone like me passes across one single individual idea, thought or course of behaviour that doesn't give them silver, gold or power by return, then they see that individual as a thought plague carrier, which if considered by other minds can reproduce itself as an evil manifestation to be jumping from mind to mind, then where would they be in the scheme of things if no one fears their threats of damnation." William laughs, "Free and happy souls said me Dá." True Tam notices a look of sad reflection descend upon Williams face.

"Ah your father…" sighs true Tam "He was a great believer in the Grecian Eudaemons." Curious, William enquires, "The Grecian what?" true Tam replies with a grin. "Ha, the Grecian Eudaemons, the Anam Sonna…" William enquires, "Isn't that the Greek version of our Anam Álainn or our Anam Áciamhach (Elegant spirit) and isn't it the same for the Genus that the Romans believed in too, that a soul or spirit inhabits all objects? I remember wee Maw telling us about the similarity of the early Roman, Moorish and Mithras faith's and that of our Cruathnie beliefs not being so very much different in many ways."

"Ha, near enough," says True Tam, "Daemons like the Sídhe Nanígan, are malevolent, or simply wild energies o' nature, either mortal and deity. Sometimes folk will call them happy spirit guides or chthonic heroes of the otherworld, other times they may even appear to some religious folks as revelations from the deities themselves, it depends in what yie believe in, but the Christian folks use the word Daemon malignantly in order to eliminate any of the ancient faith beliefs from the individual by fear. Take for example that place away over by Camelon near Falkirk, exactly centered between the Forth River and River Avalon, there used to be a big feck-off sized Roman temple over there, dedicated solely to the Emperor Claudius, that's who those Roman fella's considered to be a living God of their very own empire. Well son… the old Cruathnie Ardeaglais bán naofa rosnachan, (Cathedral of sacred white stones) near Camelon was our particular faith centre, that's why the Romans took the stones away from there and the great auld roundhouse at Stenhousemuir to construct their very own temple, for they believed those same stones in particular contained the Anam Áciamhach or Genus Loci o' the three worlds."

"Aye," says William, "When I was studying in Cambuskenneth abbey, I read about the Cruathnie belief in the Anam Áciamhach, in that, every tree, rock and flower has a spirit, every river, hill, mountain, Glen and spring has its own genus loci as the Romans used to call it." William enthusiastically continues. "I also read somewhere in the legends of Scáthach, that she had a lethal hot spear that held a powerful Sídhe Daemon called an Bás luath, the swift death, and how it had to be kept drugged all the time because of its temperamental spirit, for it was said that it would kill any folks who would harm Cruathnie beliefs." True Tam laughs, "Ach Wallace, yie have to remember that these books you read o' legends or supposed fact, were written after Christianity became the dominant religion here. What yie must always mind is that Christian scribes are awfy hostile to the Cruathnie faith and so very ignorant of it too. Sure they would write these fabulous stories they picked up when they first came here, but Instead of treating our Anam Áciamhach as deities of enlightenment, they reduced them to mythical demons who have evil magical powers of the dark who would oft' spread a plague of the mind."

Appearing puzzled, William innocently enquires, "You mean like you?" True Tam laughs out loud, "Naw, no' like me… well I hope no'" William says, "Only men who acted like Christian demons could have visited such brutality upon glen Afton, here, the Corserine and many other homesteads…" True Tam shakes his head, "Wallace me boy, I don't need to tell you your life will never ever be the same again, but ah will, all the acts that a man can inflict on another man from love to barbarism, you will encounter it more and more, so yie must be prepared son…" William enquires, "How can yie prepare for what I have witnessed Tam, nobody could." Tam nods in agreement,

"You're a man now Wallace, so yie must act as one, but don't lose the child within you or yie will lose the special powers that Magda mòr has granted you, for then yie will surely lose yer way in life…"

Suddenly a voice calls out, "William is that you?" He jumps up and leans over wee Maw, pulling up her shawl to keep her warm and comfortable, "Aye its me granny, are you all right there, for yie have been sleepin' a long while now?" wee Maw replies, "I'm so very, very cold William. Will you be stoking up the fire for me? Ma old bones have got the chills to the core." True Tam reaches over to wee Maw with a drink of the craitur and places it in her hand. He says, "I'll go and get more peat and some logs for the fire Bheitris, then I'll be leaving you both awhile as I want to be looking to the needs o' the horses." Wee Maw reaches up and clasps true Tam's hand,

"Yie've been a good friend to me true Tam o' Ercildoune, but I'm thinking that our time is near all but done here..." True Tam smiles, "Ach, maybe we have a wee while to go yet before we're to be getting the calling Bheitris. Now you just keep yourself warm and I'll get all the chores done." As True Tam leaves, William sits on the floor and holds wee Maw's cold hands.

For a long time they both sit watching the small blue flames gently flicker upon the peat fire. William looks up at his wee Maw and sees the fire reflecting in her eyes, then she speaks, "I hear the sound of much sobbing and wailing when I sit beside your grandfathers sweet ground son, like many spirits are all passing above us on their flight away to Tír na nÓg. I also feel a great host of evil wraith's gathering around us too, watching, waiting... biding their time for any signs of weakness in our spirit, so that they may take a hold of our fears, our loves... and they're sure set to be causing us the greatest of earthly pains when they do strike, more than any of us have ever seen afore in our lifetimes."

Wee Maw gazes into the fire as though mesmerised. The darkness of the room causes the reflection of the fire to dance gently on her face. William studies the old wise features of his grandmother, occasionally getting a glimpse of her youthful beauty. What impresses him most is the crystal clarity of her steely blue eyes. Then he notices a slight filling of tears.

"William son, intentionally and by ma own choices, I've lived a good life... and almost all of those I have ever loved have now passed away to a better place. And even though we have all made mistakes in anger or in the ignorance of youth... I say this to yie William, never have we deserved this wretched visitation that's been placed upon our family, nor that o' the good people o' the forests." Lovingly, William clasps wee Maw's hands as she continues, "When I walk the woodland paths to be fetchin' in the field vittals son, everywhere I am sensing these wretched wraiths watching and stalking me, as though they're presence here is to collect a debt for some great misdeed I've past committed, or something I have done that has angered the Goddess beyond my redemption. William, I tell yie, I've never designed to be the cause of hurt to others… yet a punishment that tortures our souls and eats ravenously at the spirits of the young is fast approaching us like never before. An evil comes to us with a hunger to be feastin' and gorgin' on all our pains and grief, and I fear this great evil will bide its time patiently to savour many thousands more morsels of human flesh and frailties before discarding our empty hearts and worthless bodies to be eaten by the worms."

The morbid words of wee Maw dismay William, he doesn't know how to respond or what he could say as he listens to his her. The dilemma of her soothing voice comforts him, but her mystical thoughts are a frightening revelation. Her words appear to be to herself, yet she shares them with him as though he's also a close friend of a lifetime's experience. Wee Maw looks at him and clasps his hand, "William son, I see yie are worried about ma thoughts ma bonnie boy, but I'm at a loss as to why everything has now come to this… yie know, once I was young, strong, fearless and so joyously independent of mind and thought, but now I am humbled by my fears and now my visions."

"Your visions?" exclaims William. He looks at wee Maw and sees the lustre and sparkle in her eyes dimming as a melancholy expression descends. She says, "I often sit in a mind-numbing empty darkness son, though I try to escape that emptiness by resurrecting the ones we have both loved in my thoughts and in my heart, but too often the effort is in vain, it's then that the visions come to me." William enquires,

"I don't understand?". Wee Maw shakes her head then settles back in her chair watching the flames make their merry dance, "Ach it's nothing William, you pay no heed to me, its just an old woman ranting." she looks down at William and can see the expression on his face is a mixture of sadness, disappointment and concern. She can also feel his hearts pain and his grief, "Come here son…" as she reaches down and pulls his head to her bosom, he puts his arm across her knees and they sit gazing at the fire as tears of grief come to both.

Sitting under the nurture and protection of wee Maw, William enquires "Granny?" Wee Maw enquires, "Aye son, what is it?" William continues, "True Tam… is he a sorcerer or a seer?" Wee Maw strokes William's long hair and thinks awhile; then she replies, "True Tam is gifted son, though your right, many do call him a seer."

"What exactly is a seer granny?"

Wee Maw smiles, "Well, it's someone who sees things that others don't. Ach son, some things are so very difficult to explain as yie know, like the Cruathnie faith, where we are all so close, yet we see things differently. Like at this very moment, we both watch the same fire as we sit together, we would agree upon this wouldn't we?" William replies "Aye." Wee Maw continues, "But should we give an exact written or oral detailed account of how we see the fire to another, then each of our descriptions would be close, yet so very different. And in describing to you of what a seer is would only be my own opinion and possibly no' one held by others of the same faith." William persists, "So what of true Tam then Granny, is he a seer, what is he… can he really see into the future and predict what's going to happen?"

Wee Maw continues stroking William's hair and thinks long before she answers. "William son, True Tam has been a good friend to me and mine for my whole entire life, and

I know he is gifted with the sight of what things might be, though he would call himself a clarifier or a voice of the Anam Áciamhach, but he is also greatly cursed with the pain that comes with it.",

"What dyie mean," enquires William "he's a clarifier, what's that all about?" Wee Maw smiles then tries to explain, "When you see leaves fall from a tree, that's what most of us see, but Tam also sees those same leaves as letters or numbers, they fall for him in an order that makes words or passages of information that he can read, as you or I would read a codex. When you look at the stars, it's infinite how many stars you see, when true Tam looks at the stars, he knows how many are up there." William laughs as Wee maw continues, "It's true son don't you be laughing…" Wee Maw chuckles.

"Right enough though, it does sound a wee bitty funny and unbelievable, but I tell yie this William, it may also sound like a madman's curse. The bonnie man out there understands that for him to see these things where others don't is a gift of an nochtadh diaga, the divine revelation… but in equal and opposite measure it near drives him to despair and madness, for he also suffers the pains of persecution from non-believers. True Tam has only ever used these gifts for the well-being of others."

"Is that like what you do with your wee bag of Oghamic (Ohmik) stones, read the future Granny?" Wee Maw smiles, "Aye William, the sight… that's something I have learned, where true Tam does see these things by his very nature of simply being. His discipline of honesty or truth regardless of the consequence to him, is in stating the interpretation as he sees it, be it good or evil, and that is the curse he must carry as well as the blessing, that's why we call him true Tam."

Intently watching the fire, Wee Maw continues, "Tam perceives a meaning from things that are obscure to others.

He also sees what the future could be from readings of the past, then he makes known to us all the truth of what he sees regardless of how good or bad it is, be it a certain truth or a definitive truth… And by true Tam conducting himself in an honest and open harmony with Magda Mòr and nature herself, he has sworn and is known to never ever lie, he's also capable of receiving divine messages on behalf of others too. Though a curious thing is that he nearly always makes his seeings known in songs or rhymes, that's why some folks call him Thomas the Rythmer."

William sighs, "Its easy now to understand now why he's called true Tam or Thomas the Rythmer." William reaches out and throws some more peat blocks on the fire; then he turns to wee Maw. She immediately sees in his eyes that he's disturbed and showing to her an underlying anger and deep frustration. "What's agitating yie son, tell me?" enquires wee Maw. "Granny, if true Tam really has the gift of the sight, then why did he not see what has came to our family, why did he not warn us if he is so fuckin' knowledgeable…"

Wee Maw growls, "WILLIAM…" while giving him the infamous 'Look'.

"I'm sorry granny, but I need answers, my mind is running hot and mad with anger and vengeance rings loud in ma ears so much so, I cannae take the pain much longer without doin something." Wee Maw clasps his hands tightly, "I know William… I wish I had answers too. True Tam did see divine messages warning of a great catastrophe, but he didn't relate them to us, for he has a greater foreboding for all of us in Scotland and it has him near to madness trying to understand what he sees." William exclaims in despair, "Why granny? Why if he is so true, why did he not see this coming to be warning us? If his is a divine gift, then surely what's happened merits that truth. Or is this need to believe just a load o' horseshit for weak minded people to believe in something, anything?" Wee Maw feels anger well up inside her at his remark. At first she thinks his anger is directed squarely at her, but she knows all faiths when challenged does not always reward the good when it is desperation seeking an answer.

"William, ah will tell yie, this gift of true Tam is as I said, is balanced by a curse. True Tam has only ever wanted to be normal, just like everyone else, and while his gift is good when it helps folks, it tears his mind and heart apart when he sees hurt and harm." Wee Maw looks at the fire and thinks to explain true Tam's pain, "William, when good king Alexander was killed, true Tam blamed himself for being too drunk in the Leith taverns to be warning the King of his seeing. Now he frequently drowns his sight in the craitur, but such is the greater power of his gift, the messages keep coming even stronger than before, now his dependence on the craitur causes him to lose his faith as a divine messenger. After awhile, the messages no longer make any sense to him, so great is the continual messages of catastrophe. I know true Tam believes that he has somehow violated his divine agreement with the Anam Áciamhach and thinks nothing of natures gift of seeing will ever respond to him again."

True Tam has quietly entered the room and overhears part of the conversation. He says, "It's the truth you speak there right enough Bheitris, I have lost my way… and my faith." True Tam sits beside wee Maw, then he continues, "I climbed the tree of the great elder Yew away down in Huntley bank, who's roots are fed from the underworld, there I sat a long time on a bough of the middle-world looking through the branches that cradles the stars, the sun and the moon, yet I could find no answers to the questions of which we all now ask. I fear that I have lost the precious gift." wee Maw replies,

"Nonsense Tam, we are both Céile Aicé, and all of my life I have respected and loved you as a friend, companion and a fellow Breitheamh Rígh. Haven't we shared the most private o' intimacies of our lives both you and I? Never you fear ma auld friend, you'll find the gift that sleeps but is never lost." She turns to William "And you ma bonnie boy… in the bonnie lass Marion, you both have found your Anam Álainn with each other, she's your spiritual partner and someone you may share your innermost heart and soul with. You both have joined in an ancient and eternal union that's without limit of time and space upon your conjoined souls. That's a real rare gift son, believe me, there are many in this life who may never find that loving friendship nor that belonging of the heart, now you be telling me otherwise if that's not true?"

Thinking about Marion, William feels a sadness and misses her touch, her scents, her beautiful smile and warm, soft, svelte-like skin. He smiles thinking of when he makes her laugh and seeing the wonderful sparkle in her almond eyes when suggesting something cheeky or risqué. How he wishes that she were here now. He looks at wee maw and smiles, "Aye your right Granny, I really am lucky to share love with one so beautiful in mind, body and spirit as the bonnie Marion."

"Then you must soon put behind your pain and grieving son." says wee Maw, "Good thoughts of those who have passed will always be with us, but you must think of the good times and happy times to come with those who are with us now. Our departed loved ones no longer feel earthly pains of life or death, they're free now and wait for us in a better place. What purpose would it serve to seek vengeance and perhaps lose the love of Marion, when love is there to be nurtured and lived to the fullest?" William looks at true Tam who simply smiles in acquiescence. William replies, "If life and death in nature is all about balance, should I not seek out vengeance on those who perpetrated these murders of our family? If I don't, where is the balance should these people continue unbridled to inflict their evil upon others?" True Tam wags his finger, "You Wallace, which should you choose… your love for Marion and your unborn or claiming vengeance and retribution for the dead? Don't be destroying your soul and wasting your life seeking out the perpetrators, for you'll only create your own prison from which you will never escape."

"What?" William is amazed and taken aback to hear wee Maw and true Tam's revelation of an unborn child.

"Aye William…" says Wee Maw, "The wain is coming because of the deep awakening and companionship in the love you both share, the wee soul will allow your grief and pain to heal. Yie can believe true Tam and me when we say these things. Understanding and forgiveness surely allows true love to flourish. And the love you both share is so very precious son for it contains within its light the Anam Áciamhach so many seek, but sadly never find… but you have found it in each other, like two golden cords becoming one as they intertwine, that's what a child is, making both your lives stronger and the better for it."

True Tam continues as William listens intently, "Bheitris is right in what she tells to you Wallace, trust in our experience and old age, that we are a long time passed where you are today. Indeed, we share and consider everything you feel, true love is the only path to happiness. You have to leave the pain of grieving behind if you want a peaceful loving life, to achieve this you must use peaceful loving means as your way of life, and the first key to that is forgiveness."

Shaking his head, William sighs, "I don't know about that Tam, isn't it just so that my father and Malcolm enjoyed the harmony of a peaceful loving life, yet look what has happened to them, now you tell me not to be seeking revenge? I don't understand, it sounds like the Christian philosophy of turning the other cheek, and that I cannot do, that I wont do, for my experience of the English has well taught me this." Wee Maw says, "And that is what you must do son. Would you let the child of your loving union with Marion be born to a life of misery, ills, poverty and an early cruel death? Are you really that prepared to be risking Marion and your unborn for the sake of what… bloody vengeance?"

True Tam speaks, "Wallace, you're no' a cruel man by any means, nor do you have the willingness in your heart to be a killer of men… yet I see a greatness all around you. You must resist the understandable hunger you have in your soul for retribution, so be heeding your grandmother's words of wise council."

Wee Maw yawns, then says "William son… It's to my crib that I must be going now for I'm very weary and need to be sleeping, will you help me up and take me there, for me heart is aching to be resting and my auld bones are already sleeping." William helps wee Maw to her feet. As he walks her through to her crib, she speaks with him, "While I get settled son, I want you to go fetch my wee wooden box from up in my old crib chamber and bring it back here to me. Will you do that for me son?" William enquires, "Is that the one I saw glen Afton when Marion and I pledged betrothal?"

"That it is ma boy, but mind and hurry up now and come back quick, for am sure to be sleeping very soon."

While William rushes off, Tam enters the room and helps wee Maw get settled into her crib. William bounds up the stairwell towards the bedchambers of the great house, then he stops abruptly, becoming acutely aware of the emptiness of the home, he feels loneliness then a great anger well up inside of him, threatening to overwhelm his senses.

Ignoring as best he can these chilling feelings, he enters the small bedchamber and sees the box wee Maw insists be brought back to her. Picking up wee Maw's box, William quickly returns to her crib.

"I have your box granny."

She smiles then says, "Tá son, now come and sit beside me and give to me the wee box." Wee Maw sits up, pulls a shawl around her shoulders and pats the crib beside her; true Tam stands up and holds her by the hand. Curiously, William senses a bond between the elders he has never noticed before. Wee Maw and true Tam look at each other with a deep affection, akin to secretive lovers. His thoughts are broken when True Tam says, "Ahm away to sleep wie the horses Bheitris, ah need ma sleep too bonnie darlin'"

Tam leans over wee Maw and carefully strokes her hair back from her brow, she looks up lovingly and closes her eyes then true Tam leans forward and kisses her gently on the lips. William is taken aback and surprised at this display of intimacy, yet something is very right in his understanding of how they both exude a love of life. True Tam turns to William and puts a hand on his shoulder, "You look after our bonnie Aicé here young Wallace."

True Tam smiles then he turns and leaves the room on his way *'To sleep wie the horses.'* Wee Maw is grinning as William turns back to look at her, she pats the bed at her side and says, "Come William, come and sit beside me."

Sitting on the crib beside wee Maw, he hands her the little box, she takes it carefully then places it behind her and holds him by the hand, "William, there is life after death for us all, can you understand… do you understand?" He doesn't know what to say as she continues, "I truly understand how you feel about our loss, believe me I do. There has been many times in my life I've seen death and I've sure felt the pain of losing loved ones, but to lose your children, it's not the way nature intends for a parent to outlive their wains. I cannot be telling you what that pain is like. But what I have learned in this auld life is that nature has its own way of letting you live and master the pain." William sighs, "I don't know, how can I walk away granny? I mean… I cannae get my thoughts away from revenge and justice. It's tearing my heart apart so much, if I give up the thoughts for just a moment, the pain is so cruel my head feels as though it will burst if the murderers of our family escape justice. The only calm I get is when thinking to seek out those who are responsible."

Wee Maw squeezes his hand, "Do yie remember young Coinach when he spoke then as you do now? Weren't you the one who kept his wits whole with your wise advice?" William shakes his head, "Then I admit truthfully Granny, I think Coinach was a better man than I, for I've no-one to stop or keep me from seeking justice in my own way." Wee Maw replies, "I'm here William, Marion is here, Margret and the girls, little Andrew, Malcolm óg and true Tam? And what about your friend Stephen of Ireland…?"

William thinks of wee Maws words; although they make sense, he is still undecided. She clasps his hand tightly; "Think about your unborn child then son?" William has heard her say this before and it does give him cause for thought. Smiling curiously, William then enquires, "Granny, how could you and true Tam know about the wain?"

"Ach William…" sighs Wee Maw, "when you get to our age and have a lifetime experience, then it's for us wee Maw's and elders to know and you youngblood to be finding out." Leaning back against the headwall, William smiles as wee Maw rests her head against his chest. He puts his arm around her shoulders and comforts her as they lay awhile. He feels and hears wee Maw's breathing grow heavier, then, just when he thinks she's fallen asleep, she speaks quietly in a sleepy voice, "I have something precious here for you William, but you must promise me that you will let your uncles Ranald and Richard bring the law to bear on the evil doers… do yie promise me?" Sensing the fear in wee Maw's voice, William looks around the darkened room, lit only by a single tallow lamp and the glow from the peat fire. He smiles hearing her call him Billy. He gives her hand a squeeze and replies, "I promise yie granny… I promise."

Wee Maw smiles then she sits up and reaches behind her, she brings forward the little box and opens it. But before she takes anything out, she looks at William with a happy demeanour in her expression. He smiles at the holy terror of wrongdoers and transgressors, armed only with the infamous "Look." William glances into her cobalt-blue eyes, conveyors of so much love and motherly nurture. She gazes back at him awhile, till he feels he has to enquire, "So Granny, what is it yie want to show me?" Smiling, she shakes her head, "Nuthin' I was just looking at yie son… Anyways William, I want you to have these." Wee Maw looks down into her little box and pulls out what appears to be two little amulets; one gold the other appears silver, then she presses them into his hand. William studies the detail on the amulets then holds the silver one close to his eyes and examines it; then he examines the gold amulet.

"They've both got the same symbols on them granny… what are they?" Wee Maw watches William with a look of satisfaction on her face, delighted in seeing his examination and curiosity, she replies, "Those are the magical talisman of the first Aicé and Artur's of our people, Scotia and Oengus, passed down each generation for nigh over a thousand years. First to Aicé and Artur, then on down each generation o' the Garda, till finally, they came to me and your grandfather

Billy… they're the amulets of the Aicé." Looking at wee Maw in awe, William exclaims, "You're giving these to me?" Wee Maw smiles, "Aye son, one's for you, the Orchy gold one. The other is pure white Strathclyde silver, that's for bonnie Marion. In turn, you may pass these down the generations as those who have gone before you have done."

William studies the amulets intensely and sees that both are identical, save they are in the two different colours of differing precious metals. On the obverse side of both are small emblems and marks, but the major impression is a curved bow and straight arrow, like a crescent v-rod and moon, with five arrows clustered at the flights, spreading like an arc at the heads, following the curve of the bow. When he turns the amulets over to the netherside, both have a naked faceless woman with arms outstretched and a flowing mantle draped as angel's wings.

In awe of these two ancient and fabulous amulets, he enquires, "What's this all about with the crescent bow and the arrows Granny?" Wee Maw replies, "The Aicés favoured weapon has always been the bow and flights William, and the five other flights represent Aofin, Scáthach, Gwydoddan, Devorguilla and your matriarchal mother of our bloodline, the Morríaghan. Now you be looking after them son and take great care of your Aicés and they will always look after you, for a happy woman makes for a happy family. These two amulets were struck on the four magical forges o' Carlibar, long before the Romans came here, and they shall be worn long after these English invaders have left, so you and the bonnie Marion, uze wear them with pride."

Sliding his fingers over the smooth faces and tails of the talisman, William thinks of all the people who have ever worn these two particular symbols down through the centuries. It amazes him to think that they had been worn around the necks of the Aicés and their consorts for over a millennium. He looks to ask wee Maw another question, only to see her silently sobbing as she gazes at the fire. He immediately drops the talisman as he reaches out to her, "Wee Maw…"

48

# Blood of Heathens

Weeks have passed into months since William's return to Ach na Feàrna to remain faithfully by the side of his wee Maw. He sits idly by at the gatehouse of the homestead as a chilly morning mist rises over the river Clyde, while he continually looks eastward along the great meandering river as though searching desperately for something or someone. He rubs his eyes and yawns, for he has slept and ate little since his return, caused by the vivid nightmares from memories of the slaughter at Glen Afton and Loudoun hill, memories kept at bay as long as he stays awake. But even his waking moments are relentlessly challenged by his need to do something... anything that will bring some kind of justice and closure.

Irreverently, he notices the soft white flowers have long since fallen from the Blackthorn bushes, deliberately planted long before he was born to flourish and form many dense impenetrable thickets around the enclosures where his familie's livestock used to graze. He focuses on the density and shapes of the Blackthorn roots that old men would occasionally select to make their walking sticks and infamous hot butter-seasoned draighean cudgels. The emerald green winter blackthorn leaves are beginning to broaden, sprinkled liberally with thousands of little sloe berries, ripening and coated in a pale blue powder coat to grace the dark purple skins of the swollen fruits, so noticeably unpicked by the absent women and children of Ach na Feàrna. No longer will they use the bush fruits for baking medicinal sweet-loaves, cloth dyeing and distillation into winter beverages.

The crops of other bramble fruits are also un-harvested and hang in over-abundance for nightingales, Robins, Speughs, Corby's, Widoos and local wildlife to gorge and feast. William turns his focus to the vast Clydeside willow fields that front the sprawling Shaw lands and Shields forests surrounding the Balloch's and Toun's of south Glasgow. He peers towards the rolling hills beyond that eventually lead to his father's homeland of glen Afton, the northern gateway to the notorious Wolf and wildcat forest.

A shudder wracks his body as he imagines the desolation of glen Afton and the barbarous acts of inhumanity and murder visited upon his kin there, a heinous cruelty that has destroyed almost everyone he loves with such evil intensity, from which he now lives in constant torment. He clasps his face with his hands in futile exasperation at the recurring images etched eternally into his memory, then his thoughts turn to his bonnie Marion, and how she had came to him as he lay sentinel beside the funeral pyres of his loved ones. He can see her beauty in his minds eye and imagines her gorgeous smile, the bright sparkle in her eyes… he laughs thinking of how clumsy she is for such a delicate and caring soul, then he realises how much he misses her and his unborn, but it's vital to stay with wee Maw and protect her till Ranald considers what they may do next, and that would not be settled until a safe place for her and the surviving family members is securely established.

Rumours abound of English death squads actively afoot in the realm, and the recent experience with the English soldiery by the Border, Galloway and Kyle clans have made it vital for all to be cautious of the English. William glances back at the empty stockyards and vacated little obhainn's, waiting and hoping in vain for everyone to rise, but they wont, for now they are all gone, all he sees is the absolute desolation and emptiness of this place he once called home. His heart burns to leave, he is getting more desperate to leave, for every moment he tarries reminds him of the happiness of a life once spent there. He imagines his loved ones and hears their everyday noises and chatter. Their laughter and banter echo in his head as he views the heart-wrenching emptiness. It's painfully obvious the old family Balloch will soon fall to eternal disrepair, he knows none of the surviving family would want it… not now, not ever. He certainly didn't want to remain, had it not been for the presence of wee Maw, he would now be with his love maid Marion in Lammington, beginning a new life in new surroundings as far away from the heart pain and anguish he must endure while remaining still at Ach na Feàrna.

Shaking is head in despair, he glances across to the sweet grounds and notices wee Maw is happily tending to his grandfathers grave. Elm and Alder trees frame the peaceful scene, evergreen leaves of the ancient Yew trees with a bright blue morning skyline behind them illuminates natures canvass around his wee Maw. He watches as she carefully nurtures and fusses about the burial mounds and smiles. He thinks she's right when she advised him to open his heart and embrace his love with Marion, she said it would help heal his pain, though the murders and killings of his family still cause him to wrestle with his thoughts of seeking vengeance and retribution. '*Maybe I am a coward and don't have the courage to seek vengeance? Maybe the real truth is I'm using wee Maw's noble advice as an excuse to run away and hide in fear?*' But this mindset is countered by another thought of knowing instinctively, that should the perpetrators of the evil visitations at Glen Afton, Ach na Feàrna and Loudoun hill be stood before him this very moment, he would give up his life easily to destroy their existence. He feels that a great pleasure exacting justice like-for-like would be a hungry welcome companion in attendance. He shakes his head as though trying to break free from a bad dream; then turns his attention to the drove road that leads towards Paisley town, in the vain hope his beloved Marion will appear at any moment. While he sits contemplating, he continues to doubt himself...

*'Maybe I've really accepted what's happened since I've given my word to wee Maw and Marion, but maybe that's just another feeble excuse to hide behind, not to be caught and tortured like the others before me? Maybe I don't have what's expected or even what I would have expected of myself to seek revenge'*

But once again, these inner questions are countered by other feelings of the purest conviction, accompanied by a powerful emotional release when imagining taking a long time to exact revenge upon those who committed the atrocities that relentlessly claw at his heart and soul, haunting his every waking moment. He mumbles. *'Fuck it...'*

Just as he stands up, another unexpected yet beautiful scene catches his attention, the late autumnal woodlands surrounding Paisley and the hills beyond is festooned with a myriad of beautiful pastel colours as nature itself creates its own portrait, where clouds of golden leaves fall gracefully from trees in dancing swirls, a scene that gently soothes his heart pains. He has always been amazed and feels eternal peace when late autumn-fall dramatically changes the colours of the vista.

The scenery around Ach na Feàrna warms his heart, as the many species of differing trees emblazon the countryside with a rich tapestry of green's, brown's, ochre's, reds, gold's with the burnished bronze brackens and purple heather tails shrouding the hills, all of this brings him momentary peace. He watches low-lying morning mists creep gently up from the banks of the river Clyde, then he senses the faint aromatic scents of peat and wet-wood fires. Even the heavy scent of damp decaying vegetation adds to the sensual autumnal atmosphere. He closes his eyes and savours these gifts from nature, instilling in him a feeling of invigoration. *'This is the essence of life that I want....'*

The disarming and satisfying enchantment continues to grow as he gazes at the woodlands and late fall scenery. In the distance he sees little tiny grey figures appearing who commence scuttling throughout the forest floor, he smiles seeing the townsfolk of Paisley and surrounding countryside go about their daily morning chores, completely oblivious to the greater scheme of things. He watches intently as some of the little people tend to the woodlands for the benefit of the wildlife, while others collect an abundance of autumnal deadwood for their home fires. He also notices the good women and their children collecting the over-abundance of bush-fruits, while others crop the woodland saprophytes for their healing and medicinal potions.

These magical moments free William from his constant anguish and torment, his thoughts are interrupted high above by the sharp cackle coming from flocks of wild geese flying gracefully overhead, heralding the first frosts of winter are nigh and adding to the tranquility that now surrounds him.

Stretching his tired frame, William decides to tack-up Warrior and leave Ach na Feàrna for a long relaxing ride out, suddenly, something flashing in the distance catches his attention, he peers curiously to see what it is... *'There it is again...'* Intense glints of silvery lightning bolts glimmer occasionally through gaps in the trees. After a few moments, he sees through a long gap between the trees, a group of armoured riders are travelling towards Ach na Feàrna at speed. The flashes he sees intermittently is coming from a crisp morning sun reflecting periodically off armour pieces. He calmly reaches inside the gatehouse door and pulls out his longbow and a quiver full of heavily barbed hunt arrows. He checks to make sure his grandfather's claymore and broadsword are to hand should he need them, then turns to face the closing riders. He thumps an open hand down on the pummel of his grandfather's dirk, the security of knowing he is well armed as a matter of course pleases him. He laughs and mutters… '*A good day for killing… Or dying.*'

He picks up his longbow, notches an arrow, grips and hangs three arrows between the fingers in his draw hand and stands at attention, patiently waiting to greet the coming group of riders. He lightly brushes his thumb down the outside edge of the goose-wing feather on the shaft of his notched arrow, while keenly observing the closing riders.

Eventually, as the riders approach, he can identify perhaps a dozen armoured riders coming hard and fast, he glances round to see where wee Maw is and thinks to warn her, but he lets her be in her own world, knowing she will say defiantly… "We're Wallace…" and stand her ground beside him, no matter who it is approaching. He laughs at the thought of her grit and laughs again when he considers… '*Well, if I'm of no account for courage and these visitors wish us harm, I'll show them how a coward o' a Wallace can fight when cornered.*'

Pulling high tension on his bow, preparing to loose at close quarters on the leading riders, knowing they are now within range to accurately strike a deadly tracer arrow into each target. He coldly calculates the different ways he will take them out, be it with arrow flights, his grandfather's claymore… or simply to hack through the soft front legs of the horses to bring the riders to earth for swift justice. It matters not, for they will offer little resistance to a sweeping and determined sword-strike to bring each rider closer to his deliverance. William stretches the sinews of the longbow string to maximum while he focuses calmly on the lead rider, visualizing the geometry from loose to target, then he notices familiar colours on the pennants as the lead rider raises his hand and waves to him… it's his uncle Ranald, and riding on a large black Frisian stallion beside him and bouncing about inside his oversized armour is true Tam.

William smiles then he turns and places the bow and quiver back inside the gatehouse, shoulders the great claymore of his grandfather and turns to greet his kinfolks with a wave. The horse troop soon close on the gatehouse and thunder past him into the safety of the main yard, he notices the flash of a white horse between two dun stallions ridden by burly Gallóglaigh men-at-arms.

"Lady Marjorie…" he exclaims. "Co'nas a' tha thu Wallace?" calls out Marjorie, she turns her horse and pulls to a halt beside him. As she dismounts, William enquires, "Marjorie, why are you up here?" Marjorie smiles as she hands her reigns to her bodyguard. "I've come to fetch you for the maid Marion." William desperately looks around for her… "Is she here?" Marjorie replies, "No, she's still at Comunnach Castle with Brannah and Brian." William queries, "I don't understand?" Marjorie replies, "She needs you now Wallace." Perplexed, William exclaims, "What, is she, has she…?" Marjory laughs, "No, no, its nothing to be worrying yourself about, for she's in the capable hands of good Mary Burris." Marjorie continues, "Marion is having woman troubles and not in a condition to be travelling here to see you." Marjorie looks at William and smiles with a compassionate heart born from a bitter experience shared. She says, "You come here big fella…" William grins and throws his arms around Marjorie in a warm embrace. Ranald quips humorously as he walks over to greet William. "Auld Blackbeard Cospatrick would surely no' be appreciating to be seeing that." A delighted William laughs, then he says, "Ranald… it's good to see you here… and there's the Bishop Wishart with yie too… but why are you all coming here, what's going on?"

Wishart walks forward while throwing his great religious mantle over his shoulder, "Co'nas to you young Wallace. I have come here to offer to you my sincerest condolences on your loss… and may God bring you peace my son, for both Sir Malcolm and your father Alain were loyal and very good friends to me." William nods his head in response, and also in gratitude to Wishart's heart-felt gesture. Wishart enquires, "Is your grandmother Bheitris hereabouts?"

A voice from behind them calls out, "You ya auld rascal… And what brings you to ach na Feàrna and takes yie away from your high and mighty pious duties?"

"Bheitris…" exclaims Wishart.

Ignoring formality, wee Maw reaches up and throws her arms around the ample waist of the Bishop. She leans back and looks up into his face with a wonderous smile, "Come on with me now young Robert Wishart and I'll be getting some fine hot scran ready for you and the guests. Then you're to be telling me what you've been doing since I saw yie last."

"Bheitris…" stammers Wishart. "Ach come away with yie now Robert," retorts wee Maw, "I have mind of wiping your bonnie wee bare arse with dock leaves when you were but a wain." Uncharacteristically, Wishart goes red in the face; then he burst out laughing, as does everyone else gathered at the gatehouse. Wee Maw clasps Wishart by the hand and leads him towards her famous kitchens. Wishart laughs as he's dragged away chatting with wee Maw. Marjorie joins arms with Wishart and wee Maw as the group walk over to the main house. True Tam approaches William with another of the visitors, "Wallace, this fella here is chancellor Lambertoun MacLamroch of Glasgow Cathedral, Kilmaurs and Cunningham." William grins when he sees true Tam's visitor, "Lambertoun, how are you doin' old friend?" Lambertoun replies, "Ach ahm fine Wallace, how are you doing yourself since you left the vocation of the truly learned?" True Tam appears surprised, "You two know each other?" Lambertoun replies, "Aye that we sure do."

Both young men laugh and embrace. William stands back in admiration upon seeing the fine clerical apparel worn by his old friend. "Feck… look at you in all your religious finery, that's some progress you've made since you, me, Blair and wee John were getting belted by Wishart for distracting the novice nuns."

Lambertoun grins as he opens up his arms to show off his clerical apparel, he grins and says, "It goes with my new position… I'm now chancellor Lambertoun of Glasgow cathedral." William exclaims, "Feck, you've done really well for yourself right enough." Lambertoun replies, "Aye Wallace, yer right, ah suppose that I have, but the reason ah'v come here is to pay ma respects and express ma deepest condolences to yie for what's happened. Wishart was a' visitin' our Cluniac brethren over there in Paisley abbey, and with him knowing wee Maw so fine and well he said he was coming over here to pay his respects and sit in prayer with her, so I took the opportunity to come over and see yie too…"

William and Lambertoun sit down at the old oak table outside the kitchens to talk while everyone else makes their way into the main house. "So Lambertoun…" says William, "what else brings you here this day ma auld friend?"

Lambertoun sighs, "Ach Wallace, this might sound a wee bitty odd to yie, but I really need to be speaking with yie about a some grave concerns I have." William is curious, "And what are these concerns?" Lambertoun continues, "I spoke with Malcolm just the day before his death..." William looks at Lambertoun then he brusquely stands up and venomously spits out his words, "It wasn't his death Lambertoun... it was his fuckin' murder, he was fuckin' butchered like a wild hog, as was everyone else in Glen Afton." Lambertoun is shaken by his old friends chilling statement and aggression. Nervously he says, "I am sorry Wallace, I didn't know what words to use that would be appropriate..." William sits down again while running his fingers through his long hair.

"Naw Lambertoun... it's I who owes you an apology." William continues, "All I can think about since returning here is what happened in glen Afton and Loudon. I wrack in my mind for who it was that could have done such murderous deeds? I go over it constantly in my head as to what I should do or how I can get justice, even in my feckn sleep. When I returned here to Ach na Feàrna and found the English had played their evil game upon the innocents here too..." he pauses, agitated and obviously still distressed.

Lambertoun enquires, "And no one yet knows who perpetrated this evil?" William replies while shaking his head, "I don't know, no one does. I've only heard rumours that it was the English. Auld Tam had sent messages up here saying English soldiers were camped in the glen under the command of two fella's called lord Cressingham and de Percy, but nobody knows any other names but those two. What I do know in my heart is that these murders were no' carried out by anyone we would know, our Clan doesn't have any enemies in Scotland who would seek to commit such atrocities. They would need..." Suddenly William stops and looks intensely at Lambertoun, "Have you heard anything?" Lambertoun replies, "I have heard it was English troops who committed the killings of your family, but I have also heard that it may have been Gallóbhet brigands, while others say it was Irish pirates on a deep land raid."

William sits back in utter disbelief, "Irish pirates or the Gallóbhet you say? Lambertoun, are you fucking witless? I cannae believe those folk you mentioned are in any way connected to these murders. I'm a Gallóbhet myself man; more than half o' the Wallace clan from Galloway are Gallóbhet too. That's just plain fuckin' madness to even think it so... Naw Lamberton, you're wildly misinformed. I'll personally seek out these Cressingham and de Percy fella's and question them myself..." William pauses, then he enquires, "Lambertoun... who the Fuck told you that shite about Gallóbhet being involved?" Shrugging his shoulders, Lambertoun replies, "It's what I have heard in the markets and what other reliable sources have told me."

"Reliable fuckin' sources?" exclaims William, "Then you must be speaking to fools or mischief-makers, for your reliable sources don't know shit of what they speak o'. Tell me the names of who these folk are? Let them say to my face these words, for I'll find out the truth, or those fucks will never say another wrong word again. The Gallóbhet are all kin to me and there are no Irish that I know who would ever tolerate such a grievous shame placed upon their names." Lambertoun replies, "We cannot rule out anyone till we find out for sure who the perpetrators are, and with iron-clad proof and witness."

Chillingly William replies, "I'll find out for certain who did this Lambertoun, believe that of me if nothing else, I will make it my life's work, for there is nothing left for me now but to seek these murdering bastards... and when I do find them,

I'll take a great pleasure in slowly ripping their miserable fuckin' lives apart." Lambertoun speaks quietly, "Wallace, you must keep a calm head, there is too much at stake for you to lose by your impetuous need for justice." Before William can reply, Lambertoun chooses this moment to get back on subject. "I must tell you Wallace, when Malcolm came to see me at Glasgow Cathedral he spoke of his deep concerns regarding the nobility and the church signing Scotland's rights away to the English. He was greatly disturbed about the English king's arbitration."

Looking intently at Lambertoun, William replies, "Everyone knows my uncle and me Dá were firmly against such a base treaty, but no one of merit would ever listen to them. All the signs were there, but still the nobles and clergy went to the King of England like lambs to a shepherd." William looks over to the ancient sweet grounds, obviously frustrated. "No Wallace," says Lambertoun, "Malcolm told me of a gathering that has since been held in the sanctuary of Beith, hosted by abbot Bernard. All leaders of the Garda Bahn Rígh, Céile Aicé, Breitheamh Rígh and prominent lords were in attendance. Malcolm told me that this gathering of the Garda are proposing an alternative choice for our new King of Scotland and a new legal constitution for the people of our realm, should it be our nobles have truly betrayed us all at Norham for their own avarice."

Staring curiously at Lamberton, William says, "Explain yourself?" Lambertoun leans in closer, "Wallace, Scotland's sovereignty is being held hostage to interests that do not have our well-being at heart; we can see that as plain as day. But this body of Garda, nobles and clergy gathered in Beith, they are prepared to overthrow any decision made by Longshanks,should Scotland truly become a vassal state and mere province to serve the wants of the English crown."

William sneers, "Ha, they will be the Olígos Archos..." Lamberton is puzzled, "The what...?" William replies, "The Olígos Archos, the privileged few who would rule the many by despotism and oppression, something true Tam told me about, when the ruling families of Christendom and religious hierarchy believe themselves to be the true inheritors of this earth, and that we the common folk, we are here with but a single purpose... to serve them as base slaves."

Lambertoun looks at William, "No Wallace, these are all loyal men and women of the ancient Garda Bahn Rígh and Céile Aicé with a cause determined, all of them dedicated by blood oath to Scotland remaining as a sovereign and independent realm. They're prepared to do all that is necessary to resist our own treacherous nobles who now kiss that English Kings arse. You are aware that de Brix is still bitter about being passed over for the crown and that he continues to cause much disaffection abroad, by laying claim to the throne of Scotland as his right."

"Ah'm I Aware?" William snaps, "the murderous fighting in Galloway caused by that fine and privileged noble? Fuck Lambertoun, I'm aware all right. When de Brix and his Pact began seizing castles and territory, his lust for power cost the lives of many of my good friends, thousands of innocents and now I reckon, my own family... and for what reason? You tell me?" Lambertoun sits back then he replies, "Wallace, I wish I could give you a learned reply, but I fear the answer is of a much greater magnitude than you and I may ever consider, but your Father and Malcolm knew something more."

"What do yie mean, what is this yie speak about?" demands William. Lambertoun continues, "Malcolm said that if we don't hold solely to our own ancient laws and traditions, the decision to invite Longshanks will be a disaster for Scotland we may never recover from. Malcolm knew this treaty would be giving the King of England the perfect opportunity he needs to drag the Scots into England's imperial wars and rape Scotland of all our resources in the process, as he now commits upon the Irish and the Welsh."

"Lambertoun, I don't have a fuckin' clue what you're talking about, what would King Edward need with Scotland?" Pulling his chair closer, Lambertoun replies, "Longshanks was but a claimant himself, but when the Bishops and Norman magnates invited him to adjudicate, it was an opportunity to be seized by him. The Scots nobles in seeking his arbitration, immediately elevated Longshanks to a position where he wanted to be… as Overlord of Scotland. Now he has chosen Baliol to become King, but it's obvious Baliol's caught in servitude to Longshanks, and in reality, Baliol only holds limited power as a much as a lowly provincial governor." William enquires curiously, "Is that a good thing or a bad thing?" Lambertoun raises his head to the sky then he answers his puzzled friend, "It is a bad thing Wallace, Longshanks holds Scotland tightly by the bollocks and he will squeeze firmly with an iron grip. He did not choose a king, he chose a mere puppet that now sits on the empty throne of Scotland, and that is John Baliol." William exclaims, "But what matters the decision of this Longshanks to me?"

Pausing to think a moment, William then continues, "Perhaps before everything that has passed I may have had a care, but now, now it is only my family that concerns me. Whoever rules us… why should I care who that may be?" He pauses then continues as an after thought, "Lambertoun, a question for yie… Baliol also takes the throne through the blood of his mother Devorguilla, is this then not the right choice as King?" Lamberton replies, "Aye, but do you ask this question to be in favour of Baliol?" William replies, "Isn't Devorguilla one of the three daughters and heiresses of Alan, the last Gàidhealtachd (Gaelic speaking) King of Galloway? You know the royal lineage too Lambertoun, with Devorguilla being the closest living Aicé relative to King William the lion himself, therefore it is lawful and right that the throne of Scotland should pass to her son John, is this not in accordance by the Aicé Breitheamh law and traditions you painstakingly point out yourself?" Lambertoun replies, "Aye, you're right, that is so, but the problem is, the nobles have gifted our crowns power to rule over us to Longshanks." William says, "I'm curious as to who you favour Lambertoun, tell me?"

Thinking a moment on an answer, Lambertoun then replies, "I don't favour Baliol as such, but what I do favour and abide by is the hereditary progenitory laws of our land remaining sacrosanct, and also the Breitheamh laws of the hereditary Céile Aicé. That being said… I suppose it means my favour must be for Baliol, as he is obviously Devorguilla's first son." William laughs, "So you still adhere to the Aicé Breitheamh prescriptive and Senchus Mòr?" Lambertoun smiles, "I suppose I do." William states proudly, "As did my father and Malcolm, as do many others who now dwell within the sanctum of your good Christian church, the faith followers of the honoured Céile Aicé still exists below the surface in there Lamberton…"

"I know Wallace, for I am Céile Aicé too…" William sits back, surprised to be hearing Lamberton's revelation, but before he can make a comment, Lambertoun continues, "Wallace, it appears as though that of all the claimants, it had looked likely to be de Brix from the house of Brus that Longshanks would have chosen, as de Brix is the King of England's loyal man first and foremost. Old Brix was his first Lord Chief Justice of the Royal Bench in England and he must have been almost kin-close to Longshanks to be awarded such a sanctified position. Though others do think that Longshanks favoured Baliol knowing that he would simply bow and scrape to the English King, when it's commonly known that de Brix would never yield once he gained the power of the throne. But the English King has now chosen his man, yet he still retains absolute control of Scotland's throne and governance, and the consequences are now upon us. I'm sorry, but what has happened to your family, I fear is a mere example of what is yet to come."

"Explain yourself?" says William gruffly.

Lambertoun replies, "Wallace, don't you yet get what's happening in your thick head? Longshanks is now Overlord of Scotland… he is actually here in our realm now as we speak, lavishing gifts upon his chosen lords, declaring martial law and placing his army everywhere to suppress any potential dissention, and all of this against the wishes of Baliol, much to his eternal shame. Baliol is a good man but he is hamstrung by English loving Scots nobles who take every opportunity to shame and besmirch our King." William enquires, "How can a foreign fuckin' King place an army in another's sovereign realm without winning it as a trophy of war?"

Lamberton looks at William. He says, "Longshanks has achieved all of this by first claiming it's his right to be Scotland's Overlord, he tactically employed and applied the highest legal principles of English law upon us, then he sought advice from many of the most imminent legal minds in Christendom for confirmation, and with all the Scots nobles who signed the Ragemanus having agreed to his demands, they accepted his crumbs like starving beggars with all that entails, including accepting him as our Feudal Superior for evermore." William is puzzled, "You mean Scotland no longer exists as a Kingdom, even though we have a King? Is this why there are so many English soldiers here in Scotland now?"

"Aye…" replies Lambertoun, "basically that is the situation. Longshanks is placing his English constables and sheriffs in every key Castle, town, trade route and seaport of substance in our realm." William enquires, "Why would he want to do that?" Lambertoun shakes his head and tries to explain, "The English King and his paid-for Scots nobles say to us that the English army is here merely as peacekeepers, to quell dissent or any potential uprisings should there be any disgruntled claimants, those like Norman nobles de Brix and de Pinkeny, who say they would return to the sword to settle all their disputes. Aye, but that is what the English wants us to believe, the truth appears to be in reality is that the English King really wants is all of Scotland's valuable trade, resources and to use our men as cheap and expendable soldiers for his English imperial wars. English sheriffs are already taking control of all our forests and landed estates, then we as the common people, we will be forever subjects and servile to the English whether we like it or not."

Lambertoun sighs, "Wallace, you only have to look what happened to the unfortunate Cymrans and the house of Llewellyn, look you to the murderous bloody campaigns against the Jews in England then to the absolute tyranny applied abroad in Ireland to see what will happen to Scotland should Longshanks ultimately gain total power over us. Longshanks now has sole power and authority to remove Baliol and place any he chooses upon our throne."

Immediately William thinks of his kinsman Bailey, who had told him about the great slaughter of the Cymrans by the English armies and what he himself had witnessed when in Ireland with his own eyes, the barbaric cruelty employed by England's Imperial warmongers upon the Irish chiefs, their families and followers. Perhaps Lambertoun has a point, that this situation is much greater than he could ever have imagined. He thinks, *'If only Bailey were here with me now, he would know what to do.'* His thoughts are interrupted when a voice from behind them speaks, "It really doesn't matter any more who gains the English King's blessing, be it Baliol, the house of Brus or anyone else for that matter." William and Lamberton look around to see Marjorie standing nearby who has brought them tankards of Ale.

"Marjorie…" exclaims William "What makes you say that?" Marjorie places the ale on the table and sits down beside them, then she replies, "The competitors as Longshanks likes to call them, they must all now go on bended knee to him, there is no longer any choice, and knowing the military strengths of Brix, Baliol, the Stewarts, Comyns Grahams and others, this is going to be a disaster for Scotland. It's nigh impossible to imagine that the losing competitors will long accept Longshanks authority, as they will see rejection as a grievous insult to their blood."

"It's not just that Marjorie." says Lambertoun "It is the price we will all have to pay, I strongly believe we shall all suffer dearly. The power Longshanks grants our new King is non-existent. I fear it is all of us that will ultimately pay for our nobles bloody indiscretions and wanton greed…"

Lambertoun suddenly flushes, "I beg forgiveness m'lady, I meant no disrespect to you or to lord Cospatrick…" Marjorie says, "I understand, I too share your fears Lambertoun, although Cospatrick be my husband of many years, there is very little we share and find agreement upon in regard to Scotland's destiny, in fact, it serves only to further keep us apart, and this too is what is going to happen in all of Scotland. Families will divide and a bloody civil war will be our payment, with Longshanks waiting contentedly to gather what little is left with us having done his job for him ourselves." William and Lambertoun are extremely surprised at Marjorie's remarks, both political and personal. She continues, "I have no love for Longshanks with his ruthless cunning… I am also aware that his clerics have been steadfast in undermining Scotland's sovereignty since before the death of Alexander." William enquires, "How can you know of such matters…" Marjory smiles half-heartedly,

"The old fool… I read for him."

William enquires curiously, "What? You read for who…" Marjorie laughs, "Och Wallace, although Cospatrick is a man of great poise and self-importance, his strength and belief in his noble dignity in his own boots are fine, but his sight so close is blind, he cannot read the charters and dispatches that are sent to him from Longshanks or any of his cronies, so I read them for him. I have seen the lies and deceit used in those communiqué that make reference to the replacement of our ancient charters and writs. The minutia is changed for reasons I cannot yet understand. Little tiny lies and deceptions that on their own are almost worthless of notice or a mention, but I believe there is sinister purpose in their collective creation."

They all sit silent for a moment, thinking of what this all might mean; then Marjorie continues, "I have gleaned much information from my husband over the years, as is his want to boast of his friendship with Longshanks to any group of fools who would sit and listen in awe of his royal connections." Lambertoun says, "I too am aware of such writings being changed Marjorie, and this is a subject that Malcolm and I spoke about in great detail. It's the same with the prominent libraries of Paisley, Dunipace, Dunfermline, St. Andrews and many other religious establishments, where our old books and charters are being affected." Marjorie and William look at Lambertoun, it appears that he is also in harmony with her account, he continues, "It is well known amongst the lower orders of the priesthood that many of the English bishop's and their literary scribes now dwell meticulously upon our history, holy scriptures and ancient laws. We noted too that they have been busily re-writing that same history of our people into archaic Norman script, but the translation is entirely different or simply wrong in literal interpretation. The English scribes lay claim that it is to modernise our libraries and records of family into historical account, but they do not sing in the harmonies of our old songs. I've observed that so much that has been changed, there is no longer any resemblance to the original text and truth as was first written. Now, in its place, it is their false accounts that I believe future generations will deem to be the truth and our true account as mere fantasies."

Marjorie nods in sympathy with Lamberton's angst, she says, "Then the true purpose though it not yet entirely apparent, appears to be widespread in the action, it would seem as though our history is being deliberately altered, which may legally and historically affect our rights to claim our sovereign independence as a Kingdom at some time in the future."

Curious, William enquires, "I thought that Longshanks had pledged his son to marry the maid, therefore Scotland would retain her independence completely separate from England, it's laws, and in accordance with our rightful boundaries and borders, free and without subjugation to him? This is what my father told to me?" Lambertoun says, "Aye Wallace, But that was before the maid's untimely death." William enquires, "Isn't there doubt still afoot as to the manner of her death? I have heard that Longshanks may have had a hand in it." Lambertoun laughs out loud, "We may not wish for Longshanks to govern over us… but regicide? I do not think it so Wallace, for it was Longshanks at his own expense who sent his personal royal ships to Norway for the maid, all of them laden with luxuries and sweet-meals to care for her well-being happiness. Also it was at a time when the Scots nobles refused to bring her home because of the factious disputes riven within the Scotland. King Erik initially refused Edwards ships too, but after King Edward laid a chest full of gold at the Norse King's feet did King Eric promise to send the maid across the sea to England. Edward in turn agreed that only when all disputes between Brix and Baliol were finally settled and the Scots had subjected the realm to a time of peace and tranquillity, would she be sent to Scotland. So it would not appear so by his actions that King Edward would wish the maid dead."

Marjorie agrees, "I cannot see why Longshanks would have a part in such wilful and sinful wickedness, and it was King Erik's ships who finally brought her across the great sea Lambertoun, not Longshanks."

Sitting back, William then speaks, "Whoa… can yie both back up a wee bit just before that… I thought that the Pact was formed before the death of the maid because they were so desperate to claim the throne, could not some of them be culpable?" Marjorie glances at Lamberton, "William," says Marjorie, "Many of the great Norman houses refuse to accept any female on the throne, even more so a female child to be ruling over them, they made it so that they would take to the sword before accepting her, and you're correct, the original Turnberry Pact that was lead by old Brix came into existence only days after the death of king Alexander, but even they would not dare to plot to kill a queen… no, they wouldn't… would they? No, we cannot even begin to think it possible." Lambertoun says, "The rulers the western Isle fleets also joined with the Pact, for they still smart from King Alexander's victory over Norse ambition to rule Scotland from the Innes Gall at the battle of Largs. Should the maid have reached Scotland and taken to the throne they would have had no choice but to yield… or return to war against the Scottish crown, to which they would ultimately lose. If they had been party to such a heinous plot then they would have been crushed between both the crown estates of Scotland and Norway."

"Or join with the English…" smarts William, "I remember the skirmish at Invergarvane where I lost many friends fighting against Norse and English troops of the Pact, led by the treasonous Aslikkør Ranald in particular." Marjorie speaks, "The treacherous chiefs of the isles would rather rule the seaboard of the Innes Gall under Longshanks and be contented to see the line of good King Alexander Canmore extinguished rather than share power with Scotland, or even with their own former Norse King, Erik."

William sighs, "I don't know?" Lambertoun speaks, "The house of Brus pledge loyalty to their Norse and Norman ancestors but show nothing but contempt and disrespect to the house of Canmòre. To murder a child of remote kinship is of little consequence to their hawkish ambitions." William looks away to the sweet grounds and sees the ancient grave mounds of his family; he turns back to the table and enquires, "Marjorie, did you hear of any news that may identify the murderers of my family? Lamberton and I were talking about it earlier and he heard that it might have been Irish brigands? And that I cannot believe, not with my knowing them so well, and I have to many friends in Ireland that would have let it be known to me if that truly was the case."

Marjorie and Lambertoun glance at each other, William instantly sees the hesitation in their eyes, almost in disbelief he perceives that they may know something, but they have not yet said anything to him; this moment leaves William without words. He calms his inner rage during the acute silence; then he enquires with conviction and great restraint, "What is it that you two are keeping to yourselves? Have you heard anything at all that may identify who's responsible?" Again William notices the delay in response, which irks him. He demands an answer. "You know don't you?"

Marjorie looks at William, almost shamefaced that she has not said anything before now about what she has heard. Moments pass as they look at each other intensely; suddenly William crashes his fists down on the table… Marjorie jumps back in fright. She blurts out, "Wallace, I cannot know for sure, as it's only rumours, but everyone in the hills and glens around glen Afton is certain it was English troops under the command of a knight called Cressingham that murdered your family… and there were local hunters who witnessed what happened to Malcolm…"

"What?" exclaims William, he stands up, pushes over the table, knocking Lambertoun to the ground, he turns quickly, grabs Marjorie by the shoulders and shakes her violently, he shouts at her, spitting out his words. "Tell me…" William is nose-to-nose with Marjorie, his eyes blood red with rage in his mistaken sense of her betrayal, then as suddenly as he has risen, he looks into the eyes of Marjorie and sees in her a fear that shocks him to his senses. Lambertoun quickly rises from the ground and forcefully pulls William away from Marjorie shouting, "Leave her be Wallace…" Marjorie is in shock and totally distressed, William drops to his knees and sits on the ground, tears fill his eyes as he looks at her. He raises his hands then slaps them down on his thighs as though all strength has left his body; he looks at Marjorie and tries to utter words that fail him.

"I… I…" Marjorie rushes over to him and cradles his head in her bosom. "Oh William, I feared to tell you of what I had heard, I know how you protected your young friend Coinach likewise when he suffered from such a tragedy as you do now, but please… you must understand, I have no proof of what I have heard, but there are hunters that I trust that you must speak with. I could not tell you before this William, for fear that you would act in vengeance and bring more sorrow upon even more innocents."

Standing up, William puts his arms around Marjorie and pulls her close, they embrace with both shedding tears of pain and anguish, "I am so sorry Marjorie, it was not you I saw, only someone who may hold information that is blocking light from my torn soul, I did not mean…" Marjorie says, "William, I understand, I'm sorry too that I made you feel that I was holding something back from you. It's just that I don't know anything with certainty, I only know what I've heard and that's based on the rumours of tittle-tattles. I considered that it would only cause you more grief and heartache. But the hunters that spoke to me about Malcolm… meet with them when you come back down to Comunnach, I do trust them, they said they observed from afar the murder, but they are certain it was orchestrated by an English knight named Lord Fenwick." William is perplexed, "Fenwick you say?" William ponders, "Fenwick, Cressingham… de Percy?"

They all sit back down at the table, Marjorie holds on to William's hand. She says, "I'll tell you of what I've heard and what I know, but you must hold your temper William, you must gather all information with a cool head of all you need to know and more, and only then you must give me your word that you will share your findings with us in council before you act… And I mean with Ranald, Lambertoun, true Tam, Leckie Mòr, Wishart and I. William, you must promise me you will seek council from us before you act, believe me, time will surely answer all of your questions, and if we ally our heads and wit together, you will gain justice as reward and no more innocents will suffer another great wrong."

William appears devastated; he stares at the table with his head hanging low as though he is in great shame at the manner of his uncontrolled outburst. Marjorie squeezes his hand then she gently places a finger under his chin, lifts his head and smiles, "Right...?" William looks back into the kind sparkling eyes of lady Marjorie; he weakly smiles back at her, then he replies, "I am so sorry Marjorie, please forgive me." Marjorie looks lovingly as a mother into the eyes of her young friend and squeezes his hand again, giving him comfort. "I'll tell you of what I've heard William, but you must promise me to control your rage, for many will surely die should you act impetuously upon my words, and you must remember too that what I say is yet unfounded."

There's a moments pause, then Marjorie says, "For Marion and the little one..." she smiles again. William sheepishly nods in agreement. "Marjorie, I give you my word; I just hope you can forgive me..."

The experience and kindness in Marjorie's demeanour shines in her eyes as she looks at William. She says with maternal comfort in her voice, "We will hear no more about it then." She continues... "The day before you came down to Glen Afton, a large troop of English soldiers came out of the northern mouth of the glen and stopped at Comunnach castle awhile, they wanted to shoe their horses at the smithy and stock up on vittals. There I met with a lord Cressingham, he said they were on their way towards the Loudoun hill to meet a baggage train led by lord Fenwick; then they were going on to Ayr Castle to meet with a Lord de Percy. After they had left Comunnach, our smithy told me he had been talking with one of the English soldiers who said they had came through Glen Afton from down south, the smithy also told me he noticed dried blood on the legs of many of the horses, but he saw no wounds. It wasn't till after they were gone that two of the hunters from the Wolf and wildcat hills came rushing in to tell us of what they had seen in glen Afton. A while later two more hunters came and told us of their witness at Loudon hill."

William puts his hands to his eyes. Marjorie reaches out once more as Lambertoun speaks, "So the first two hunters witnessed the Afton murders, or at least the aftermath, yet the English said nothing to you about this?" Marjorie replies, "Aye, the timing of their arrival and then the hunters following in behind makes me believe that the English troops were the perpetrators." Marjory continues, "Immediately we called everyone together and went into the Glen, that's when we discovered the awful truth. It was later that day when Stephen of Ireland arrived, then you came to us later still, that's when we met you at the bridge of Comunnach."

William paces around the table, he stops and concludes, "Then it could have been no others … If those English troops who called at Comunnach came from the Glen mouth, then they must have travelled through Glen Afton from the southern gateway, there is no other road they could have used or taken. If indeed they were truly travelling towards Ayr Castle, there is no other road there within thirty miles of the Glen that they could have travelled and then arrive at the Comunnach confluence." Lamberton says, "Maybe they travelled over the Carrick hills from Am Magh Baoghail or maybe the Bethoc coastal trail in the west?" Marjorie replies, "They could have, but I don't think so, you're forgetting the English soldiers told my smithy they had came directly from the south, so why would they take such a long detour and not go directly to Ayr from Magh Baoghail, unless Loudoun was their detour, but still...?" William nods, "Then it must have been Fenwick or Cressingham who murdered everyone in the glen."

"Cressingham lead the English from glen Afton," says Marjorie, "But Fenwick was not in attendance at Comunnach William, for he would be arriving at Loudoun hill coming east from Berwick or Newcastle, and if there are no witness to the murders in glen Afton, you cannot yet make public your accusations without foundation." William exclaims, "Loudoun, then it must have been Fenwick who killed Malcolm and Sandy. I must speak with those hunters who were a witness to the murders, they will know for sure if it was Fenwick or not. And if this Cressingham came through the Afton Glen, then it was surely only he who lorded over the murders there, there's no one else could be responsible..."

"It must have been Cressingham," says Marjorie, she shudders, "and he had a very undesirable and arrogant young squire with him called de Percy."

"De Percy..." William exclaims, "I tell yiez, that name de Percy is the common factor in all of this. I saw enough of this English squires atrocities against the Gallóbhet and people of Galloway during the Pact rising to recognise his evil work, for it was the same style barbarity meted out on our kinfolks... De Percy, Cressingham and Fenwick... by the Aicé, they will all answer for this. When I meet with these Englishmen I'll..." Marjory says, "Wallace, you gave me your word, you gave wee Maw and Marion your word too, how may anyone pass you vital information if you are bent thoughtlessly on revenge, it must be justice you seek nothing else, or you put all of those you care about in the gravest of danger." Lambertoun says, "If it truly is those that you say Wallace, and it does seem more likely now, then they will be brought to justice. I say again and plead with you, do not take the law into your own hands, I would be cautious in naming any English lord till you have the evidence."

With a sullen glance, William glares at Marjorie and Lambertoun, then he says, "I have given you both my word… I will wait and I will bide my time, but justice will be done, believe me this."

Reaching out, William takes hold of Marjorie's hand, "I have given you my word Marjorie, I will not break oath with you, Lambertoun, nor wee Maw and Marion. I remember that Coinach's rashness cost the lives of many dear friends, though now I fully understand his will, but his death and the death of my friends is a bitter lesson, and as you say, I have time on my side, I'll use it wisely to search for these perpetrators and I'll seek council with you before I act. On my life I swear this to be my truth before yie both." Lamberton says, "God bless you William for your fortitude. I'll pray that your questions are answered and justice is done in the name of your family." Marjorie agrees, "And I." William enquires. "Marjorie, do you remember the night I left Comunnach Castle for Ach na Feàrna?"

"Aye William, that I do."

William continues, "When I was approaching Loudon hill, I rode blindly into the middle of a large English patrol, they led me into their camp to be questioned by their knight, he was a fella called Seagrave, and I'll tell yie this, I thought I was done for when they captured me." Marjorie exclaims, "They captured you?" William retorts, "Well naw, not really captured… but they took me into their camp against my will, near to the place where I found the body of uncle Malcolm days before." Lambertoun enquires, "So what happened, I mean, obviously they let you leave?" William replies, "They held me to be questioned, they said they were looking to find the folk that had killed some English soldiers a few days before, near to where they were camped, and ah tell yie both, at that moment it wasn't looking se' good for me at all, I reckon they were mightily convinced that I was the perpetrator. It wasn't until some prior called Abernethy who was with them said that he knew my father well and also the family, he is the sole reason ah reckon the English let me go."

"Abernethy?" enquires Lambertoun curiously, "Do you know from which priory he was from?"

"Balin… Balin something or other. He said it was a priory not far from Edinburgh, that's what I think he said. He also asked me to pass on his condolences to wee Maw, but I completely forgot about him till now, though it did seem as though he really knew the family pretty well."

Lambertoun enquires, "Was it Ballentradoch the prior said he was from?" William exclaims, "That's it, do you know him or know of him?" Marjorie says, "I have heard of him, he's the prior for the order of the knights Templar's over near Edinburgh, but I thought he was in the Holy Land… William, does Wishart know of your meeting with Abernethy?"

"Naw, I've no' spoken with hardly anyone since my return from Glen Afton."

Standing up from the table, Marjorie says, "Boy's, I must go back inside and have words with Wishart about this, for if it surely is Abernethy the Prior of Ballentradoch, I'm almost certain that Wishart doesn't know that he is back in Scotland. I must tell him of what you told us William." Marjorie immediately leaves to go and tell Wishart of what she has heard. "Knights Templar…" sighs William, "I didn't know there are Scottish Templar's?"

"None here in Scotland," replies Lamberton, "the ones who are here are all Norman or English and not very many at that. The few Scots Templar's there are all live abroad, but they're really few in numbers." William enquires, "So what are English Templar's doing here with priories that do not serve Scotland's needs, we're not at war with any unbelievers of the Christian faith?" Lamberton replies, "The Templar's are expanding to kingdoms all over Christendom Wallace, they're an extremely powerful sword of God and independent of all kings and princes of Rome. The more secure castles, preceptories and priories they have as they grow, the greater the army of God they will have to fight the Saracens and all non-believers."

Laughing out loud, William says, "Then they may be have to be fighting me soon enough Lambertoun, for I have little or no faith in a God who would inflict such cruelty upon our family and kinfolks. Fuck those religious fanatics, fuck them all…." Lambertoun snaps angrily, "WALLACE… God hears your blasphemy, his wrath will strike you down at his pleasure." William's humour quickly changes as he glares at Lambertoun, "I cannot, nor will I ever understand why a God that we have dutifully served as a family would visit upon us and others such a cruelty as I have witnessed in his name, or in the name of Christ… And if what you say becomes so by this so-called one true God of yours, striking me down for his pleasure, then tell me, what kind of caring God does such a thing?" Lambertoun drinks some more ale then replies…

"You must never lose your faith Wallace, there are many good men in the church who…" William interrupts abruptly, "I know many good men in the church Lambertoun, but I also know of many more who are nought but foul murderers and ne'r-do-wells. They only don the cloth of your God to commit the most heinous and gravest of sins upon others, yet they go unpunished for these sins, claiming to be doing these deeds in the name of that same God, yet free from the laws that all others must abide by. I saw the simplest of souls suffer the most terrible punishments and tortures by the hands of these Holy men, and for no reason other than offending the opinion of a priest. I have seen this too often with my own eyes… these so-called men of God rewarded by their masters for this evil. Naw Lambertoun, this is not a God that I could have ever have any faith in…"

"Wallace," says Lambertoun, "God does his work in mysterious ways, ultimately his purpose will become clear to you one day, have faith." William exclaims in exasperation, "What the fuck ae yie talkin' about Lambertoun… If you were not my friend I would knock you off your fuckin' seat, how can you say such pious pish to me when the blood and brains of my kinfolk still wet-stain my boots, fuck you and fuck your sanctimonious shit."

Lambertoun glares at his irate friend, "Wallace what's happened to you? There was a time when it was you we all thought would be the one to rise in greatness within the church… do you not think it's because you disregard God that it is you who is the cause of his wrath that now visits your kin?"

Suddenly William lunges at Lambertoun, grips him roughly by the throat, pulls him up from his seat then throws him to the ground, contemptuous of his words.

"You Lambertoun, you test me sorely, how the fuck can my faith or lack of it be the cause… I mean, what are you thinking? For a man of faith you show little feeling or sympathies by your reckless words towards my kinfolks, my own family who suffered such cruel murder by mans hands in the name of your fuckin' God. Then you have the gall to say to me that because I have too many questions about a faith that I understand less and less, then my punishment by your almighty God is what has happened to me and mine? Fuck you, fuck your God and fuck his pleasures…"

Picking himself up from the ground, Lambertoun sits back down at the table, he says, "Wallace, I know that your loved ones now sit at Gods side free from such earthly pains and challenges. It is because of my faith I understand Gods ways and the tests that he places upon us."

William shakes his head despairingly, then he says, "Ah don't believe this? If you believe this shit, then you are a fool Lambertoun, you do not question, but I do, that's why I lost my faith, too many questions that still remain unanswered. Every time I would ask a question, I was either beaten or referred to the same scriptures of no reply. When I posed the same question to different priests, their vastly differing interpretations is all I got back by that reply, then beaten or punished again for being persistent in simply needing an answer to truly satisfy me."

"You do not question God," replies Lambertoun, "you serve him."

"That's the problem Lambertoun, I do question, for that is who I am. Fuck, am I the only one who sees the hypocrisy and greed of the church?"

Lambertoun remains calm as he says, "I think you may be possessed by an evil spirit Wallace, your mind is weak and vulnerable to grief. Do not forget Gods teaching; *Cast away all filth and extreme wickedness of thought and receive the blessed lord into your heart with meekness, only then you will save your soul for eternity, for it says as much in the scriptures...*"

William retorts, "Fucking scriptures Lamberton? This is really what your Lord of peace and love has to say... *Believe, or I will fill your mountains with your dead. Your hills, your valleys and your streams will be filled with the blood of your people, slaughtered by the sword of God. I will make you desolate forever then you will know that I am the Lord. Cursed is he who holds back his sword from the blood of heathens."* William glares at Lamberton, then he continues, "Well I am a man of the heather Lambertoun, a heathen and I'll tell you the one single scripture that fits around my heart, I am now quenched by the violence of fire and I have escaped the edge of the sword, now I swear to you, that out of my weakness I have been made strong, I will be waxed valiant in war then I and my host will turn to flight the armies of the foreign King and completely destroy them..."

Lamberton and William glare at each other as an impasse has been struck, both stand their ground in silent loggerhead then William thinks to enquire about the strength of Lamberton's faith. "I thought you said a little while ago you were still a Céile Aicé Lambertoun?"

Another moment passes in stony silence between them, then Lamberton smiles confidently, "I am..." William exclaims, "What the fuck then? How can you revere the Aicé o' Magda mòr yet you hold contempt for all the women who serve your church, disrespecting those who cannot achieve acquiescent virginal motherhood by the age of fourteen years? How can you serve a deity where Christian women are treated less than the basest of slaves to clean the floors of your places of worship on scabby knees, yet they provide strong sons to serve the priesthood? Why do women in your church not have a voice unless it's raised in support of wealth grabbing or for the hysterical condemnation of innocents? And you still think to call yourself Céile Aicé?"

Lambertoun tries to bluster an answer, but he cannot reply coherently, "Well, eh, uhm... I do what I do Wallace." William laughs, "Lambertoun, me old friend... eh uhm is not an answer." Lambertoun pauses a moment, then he too laughs as both friends sit back down at the table. "I'm so sorry Wallace, of course I have my doubts, many doubts actually, but by working hard within the church, I may be able to change the many things I see to be wrong." William enquires, "Then why not live your life openly as a learned freeman of the Breitheamh Rígh?" Lambertoun laughs, "Now you speak to me in the tongue of the bérla Féine, (Language of the free people) so what is your point?"

"My point is Lambertoun, the faith in the Féine na' Céile Aicé has been our belief in Scotland and Ireland much longer than Christianity. And by the will of the free people upon which it governs is by consent not fear, the free people of the Céile Aicé live peacefully by the communal expression of an agreed moral code of honour, between us our faith is reflected honestly and fairly through our ancient laws, upheld by the wisdom and judgment of the Breitheamh Rígh and honouring each individual through respecting faithfully your word as your bond, therefore your faith, so what real need we of Christianity here?"

Lambertoun looks at William in astonishment; then he replies, "Are you fucking mad Wallace? I would be cast out by the Catholic church as a heretic and serve in eternal hell and damnation in the company of your Féinians (Freeborn land Warriors) if it be known openly that I have returned to the faith of the Céile Aicé Fénechas... those days are past us Wallace." William laughs, "You feckn swore at me..." Lamberton laughs too, then he says, "Aye, but you would make a fuckin' saint swear Wallace, you with your stubborn antiquated moral code of Fénechas righteousness." William grins, "Me... righteous...?"

The two friends shake hands and smile as they settle back down to talk. William says, "Maybe there is truth in what you say about change from within the church Lambertoun, if you and wee Blair are the future of the church, then there's maybe hope after all, maybe..." Lambertoun explains, "I only meant you to consider not to be going off and killing every Englishman in Scotland, and subsequently bring death to many innocents from English retribution and reprisals, or by them using legal warrant and some misguided vengeance by friends of those you have dispatched."

"Why would I want to kill every Englishman Lambertoun? Only the murderers of my family do I seek out."

Lambertoun shakes his head again in frustration, "Ach Wallace don't be such an idiot, of course I didn't mean every Englishman..." Lambertoun pauses, then he says, "I'm sorry, I didn't mean to rage at you, I only saw in you a friend who would pay the ultimate price, caused by your enflamed passion to seek out and deliver well founded revenge without a care." They are interrupted when they hear slow hand clapping behind them, they look round to see true Tam and Wishart applauding them.

Wishart turns to true Tam, "Hardly the most enlightening ecumenical debate we have ever witnessed Tam, but very interesting nevertheless." True Tam laughs, "Aye Wishart, it was interesting right enough, just like the two us were when we were younger. Aye, very much younger..." Wishart commands, "Wallace... I want you and Lambertoun to go to Saint Johns Toun right away and meet with your old tutor Mydford." William exclaims, "Mydford, what do I want..." Wishart interrupts, "Shut up and listen Wallace... When you meet with Mydford, you must then go to Dùn Dèagh (Dundee) I need you to meet with sir Andrew Moray the elder, if he is not there, find him. I want you to deliver to him in person these sealed documents, then you must await his reply. I will give you both personal clerical passports as emissary pilgrims to get you past the English garrisons. Take Warrior and leave now. And you Lamberton, I want you to go on up to Spynie and deliver this dispatch to Bishop David de Moray at Elgin Cathedral, then you too must await his reply before you return." William exclaims, "Yie mean today, now...?"

"Aye now Wallace," replies Wishart, "you say you met with prior Abernethy at Loudon hill didn't you?" William replies, "He said that's who he was." Wishart continues, "Then it is now you must leave, there's no time to dally about here, both you and Lambertoun must leave immediately. I want you by return to go to Kilspindie where your brother Alan is with your aunt Margret, you are to meet with them and bring them all back to Carr's Castle near Dalrymple. I have enclosed passes for them to travel as pilgrims too." William enquires, "Are you taking them all to auld Angus at Crauford Castle?" Wishart replies tersely, "Aye Wallace, now get yourselves ready to leave and I'll complete all the paperwork necessary for your journey." William feels elated that he is escaping the confines of Ach na Feàrna, he thinks, 'What about wee Maw?' True Tam smiles, "Don't worry Wallace, I will care for wee Maw, you just get yourself ready to go to Dun Dèagh."

A surprised William thinks to himself, 'That was so like Bailey, how does true Tam know what I am thinking?' True Tam laughs, "I know what you're thinkin' Wallace because of your youth, you are yet so predictable, but I will reveal the knowledge to you another time, for there will sure be another time for you and I." Wishart and true Tam turn to go back into the house, when Wishart stops and looks back at William who is still amazed at the mindreading of true Tam. Wishart calls out, "NOW Wallace..." William and Lambertoun immediately rush over to the stockade.

"Thank feck for that," sighs William, "I need to get out of here Lambertoun, a run to Dun Dèagh will blow away ma cares, and you're coming with me too?" Lambertoun looks sternly at William, "Naw, it's you coming with me..." there is a tense pause, then the two friends laugh out loud. Lambertoun says, "I wish I was staying here though, Wishart has a meeting tomorrow in Paisley priory with the Franciscan John Duns Scotus and Bernard the abbot of Kilwinning." William exclaims, "Feck, a Cluniac a Franciscan and a Tironensian having a meeting in the same place? That's either the making of a good inn jest or there is something very serious in the planning with those three getting together." Lambertoun replies, "Then we shall find out by our return Wallace, won't we." William says, "Maybe you were right earlier Lambertoun, with one of us in the church, you, and the other out... me, this may be a situation of use for both of us some day." Lambertoun laughs, "I never ever doubted that Wallace." true Tam calls out to them from the big house. "Wallace, Lambertoun...?"

"What's up Tam?" enquires William. True Tam replies, "Feckin' hurry up..." Lambertoun and William laugh, Lambertoun then says, "We had better get a hurry up then." True Tam calls out once more, "Tack Warrior and use Fleetfoot as a packer too." Lambertoun helps William tack up the horses then they make their way back over to the big house as wee Maw and true Tam come out the door.

Wee Maw says, "William, walk with me to the sweet grounds, I want to be talking with you and your grandfather Billy before you go away up to Dun Dèagh." William mumbles, "Grandfather?" but he knows what wee Maw means, or he hopes he does. Lambertoun says, "I'll final tack the packer for us Wallace, away yie go with wee Maw, I'll give you a shout when Wishart has all our documents ready." True Tam says, "Aye, Wishart is still writing up the passes you'll need and lady Marjorie is affixing her ring-seal too as the wife of Lord Cospatrick, between them their seals will ensure you that will have no problems with the English soldiers on your journey." Wee Maw tugs at his léine sleeve,

"C'mon son," she insists, "lets walk over to your grandfathers sweet ground, for I have somethin' very special for yie." Wee Maw hooks her arm around William's then the two of them make their way slowly over to the great oaks and yew trees that stand sentinel over generations of the Wallace clan of Ach na Feàrna. Wee Maw is comforting William along the way with talk of his father Alain, Malcolm, Mharaidh and little Caoilfhinn, till eventually, they arrive at the side of his grandfathers sweet ground.

Wee Maw sits down on the old oak bench that overviews the graves, she says, "Sit here with me William, for the other night I had meant to give you these wee somethings but you must have fallen asleep, for the next day I noticed I still had them in my wee box." William replies "Aye, ah remember, you mentioned something to me Granny, but you're right, I must have fallen asleep." Wee Maw fumbles about in her pinnie and pulls a small bundle of cloth from a deep pocket in her apron; she looks at it for a moment then she hands it to him. "This is for you and Marion."

She looks up at him and her nose wrinkles as she smiles and gazes at him. Still clasping his arm, she says, "Go on son, unwrap it." William slowly unwraps the small cloth bundle to reveal two little amulets. Wee Maw grins then she says, "These are the amulets of the Aicé and the Guardian of the Aicé William, they were passed to me by my grandmother as they were to her and hers and all of the family directly till yie reach the blood o' Morríaghan, Aicé of Alt Cluid, aye, the mother of our bonnie Clan." Wee Maw smiles, "They're yours and Marion's now son, and when yie are very old like me and happy to be getting yerself ready for flying with the Wild Geese, you're to pass them on to your eldest daughter, whenever Marion begins to bear you both your bonnie offspring that is. The amulets of the Aicé will always remind you of who you are, why you are and the very reason for your being, and if you only have sons, mores the pity, but then you tell them the stories we have told you, offer them a reason to be proud of who they are son, and remember this, may the amulets of the Aicé always remind you of that and bring you both the blessed life that I have had."

Holding the precious amulets tightly, William says, "Granny, I want to thank you, I do thank yie, but words of gratitude could never come close to how you've really made me feel… I don't really know what to say?" Raising her frail old body to stand before him, Wee Maw holds his face with her tiny hands, she says, "Ach no words are necessary son, I see the love for life you have in your eyes, you're a good and fine young man William, and you'll be a good father too one day, just like your grandfather was to me, mine and ours. But now you must be taking me away back over to the big house, for I am awfy tired."

Looking directly into his grandmother's eyes William smiles, her wrinkly grin and steely blue eyes are so amusing, he's seated leaning forward and she is standing full upright, making them almost eye to eye with each other. "William son, I have passed you the amulets of the Aicé, though I know your heart screams out for vengeance… and if I were ten years younger I would join you…" William laughs, "I know yie would granny." Wee Maw continues, "Aye, ah would, but please, you heed my words son, I have given the amulets of the Aicé over to you for many reasons, and unless you pass them on to the next generation, then there will be no more of our line of the Wallace left on this earth." William thinks as he holds the amulets in his closed hand, 'She's right…'

Wee Maw takes the amulets from William for a moment, then she says, "Lean forward son," she hangs both the amulets around his neck, held by a leather lace, then she stands back and smiles as he rubs both talisman between his fingers, feeling the warm almost sensual glow of the purest white and sunburst gold. "C'mon son, lets be going." They begin walking towards the big house chatting along the way, then wee Maw looks into his eyes as they reach the main door, "William, when your life is defined by one single action, your life changes forever, thereafter time no longer has relevance, so you be making that single defining action your love commitment to Marion…"

William is surprised and thinks about the clarity of wee Maw's words, when the door opens behind them. Wishart and Marjorie come out the door with Lambertoun and true Tam who says, "That's Fleetfoot packed and loaded up for yie Wallace."

Wishart hands William two full saddlebags, "Now listen to me Wallace and listen well, you'll find Mydford at saint Mary's church in Saint Johns Toun; give him this dispatch. I also have papers for you to deliver for Lord Moray of Petty, the Justiciar of Scotia. I want you to give him this particular dispatch, True Tam here has sent up some pigeons a wee while ago to let them all know you're coming, so Mydford will be waiting to take you to the Blackfriar's Chorister house in Dun Dèagh. We've buried our information in code amongst legal writs and ecclesiastical papers, should you be stopped and the contents of your bags examined. Now, when yie get there and speak with Lord Moray, tell him you need nothing other than a verbal reply, then you must return home as soon as possible and seek us out to deliver his words as a matter of the greatest importance and urgency, I'll leave someone here that you may trust to await you by your return."

True Tam says, "Mind this too son, as Wishart here already said, I've sent a couple o' messenger doo's away up for Lord Moray's son young Andrew too, he should be waiting in Saint John's Toun to meet with you. As his father is the most senior Mormaer in Scotland, its unlikely you will find any trouble from the English travelling with young Moray in your company as an escort."

"How long will I wait in Saint John's for Andrew?"

"Don't wait." replies Wishart, "It's imperative you meet with Lord Moray as soon as possible. You should find young Andrew waiting in the nave of Saint Johns Kirk, but if he is not there, take a brief rest then just keep going on up to Dun Dèagh with Mydford." William nods in understanding.

As he prepares to leave, wee Maw approaches him, reaches up and gently clasps his face, "You travel safely now son… be wary of all those yie meet and don't be picking any fights now, do yie hear me?" Wee Maw continues, "And when you see your aunt Margret, tell her to come home son, for I miss her so." William replies, "I will do Granny." He then turns to Marjorie, "Will yie tell Marion when my duties are complete, I'll be coming down to Comunnach to take her away over to Lammington; then we can make our arrangements to visit saint Kentigerns." Marjorie smiles, "She will be so happy to see you William, now then, you take extra care as wee Maw says." Wee Maw looks at Marjorie and laughs, then she exclaims. "Who are yie callin' wee Maw?"

Everyone laughs at the lighthearted moment.

Wee Maw and William embrace then say a tearful farewell. William dawns his brat and mounts Warrior. Lambertoun mounts his horse too. As both prepare to leave, William pulls Warrior and Fleetfoot around then looks up at the grey clouded skies. True Tam calls out, "Mind you two, travel in plain sight." William smiles as he replies, "That we will Tam, that we will." He pulls his brat close for warmth then looks back at Marjorie, "Will yie tell Marion I love her…" Marjory smiles then she replies, "William, I will give to her all of your love." William clicks his tongue and Warrior walks on towards the fortalice gates. Without looking back, both he and Lambertoun leave the lands of ach na Feàrna, set firmly on their mission…

# Christina's Ale

Sinister Black and darkening skies loom ominously overhead as William and Lambertoun finally approach the outskirts of Saint Johns Toun. Both are feeling sorely tired and extremely cold after almost three long early winter days travelling along the old drove roads from ach na Feàrna; a journey that had taken much longer than expected, caused by having to avoid the many English patrols on the roads and intermittent guard pass-points.

Eventually, they wearily pull their horses to a halt and sit in silence awhile on the crest of the Dens of Brox hill, that overlooks the busy sea-barge port on the great River Tay.

William reflects and laughs to himself when thinking about the ridiculous and almost farcical encounters he had experienced on his last visit when he had been erroneously branded as a notorious ale thief, with a band of English soldiers as his contraband confederates and supposed gang. He laughs at the memory of the strange encounter with the English soldier who wanted to arrest him for murder, but after a hard fought and brutal street brawl, the Englishman then helped him to escape almost certain capture from an English patrol. Then there was Affric, she had walked up to him absolutely stark naked in the bargee square, punched him on the jaw for refusing to bed her, then she threw a bucket of stale piss all over him in front of a large baying but very appreciative mob. But then he thinks of Coinach, her brother, the massacre of their family at the Corserine Gap and how he himself now fights to control his own chaotic thoughts in sharing the same grief and need for vengeance as Coinach once did. He thought he had understood Coinach's manic drive for vengeance at the time, but he never have imagined to own such thoughts as he does in his reality now, suddenly his memories are broken by a loud command from nearby…

"Who goes there…?" William curses at his lapse in concentration. He looks around in the darkening evening but he sees no-one. "What's your business here?" commands the voice. William looks around again, this time he sees the glint of a helmet coming towards him and instantly recognises the outline of an English soldier. More soldiers with halberds pointing at both him and Lambertoun begin to appear and begin to surround the two weary travellers.

The first soldier approaches William and taps the blade-tip of his sword on the horn of the saddle, another grabs Warrior's reigns near the bit, while others secure Lambertoun's reigns. The first soldier enquires, "What's your business here?" William is angered being caught off guard through fatigue and tiredness. He thinks fast to try and talk his way out of trouble, "I have legal communiqué from Lord Cospatrick the Earl of Dunbar; it is to be delivered personally to Lord Moray, the Justiciar of Scotland." Lambertoun says, "I am the diplomatic emissary from the Bishop and Lords council of Glasgow, I have in my possession on behalf of Rome, important dispatches and vital ecclesiastical papers to be delivering to master Mydford, the vicar of Dundee, and for his imminence, Bishop Moray of Elgin cathedral, this fellow here, he is also my manservant." The soldiers scrutinise William when another gruff English voice from the doorway of a makeshift shelter calls out, "Hurry up, it's freezing out there."

The two English soldiers at the head of Warrior look at each other as William carefully watches their body language. The soldier holding Warriors reigns simply shrugs his shoulders and glares at William, then the soldier holding the blade close to William's groin enquires, "Where are your passes?" William replies, "I have them in my saddlebags sir, here, ah'll get them for yie." As he turns in his saddle to retrieve the passes, the soldier calls out, "Hold Scotchman…" William glances round and looks at the soldier.

A cold freezing sleet is beginning to fall as the two stare at each other, the English soldier says, "Be on your way… and you had better be seeking a residence here quickly, as darkfall and storm are almost upon us and its not safe to be out here, there are many bandits and outlaws hereabouts, they would kill you just for your boots." William is surprised, but doesn't need told twice to leave. Lambertoun replies to the English soldier "I thank you good sir."

They nudge their horses and walk-on calmly towards Perth Saint John's Toun, Lambertoun says, "That was rather unpleasant." William replies, "Aye, changed days since we could roam freely in our own land Lambertoun." They can hardly believe their luck; then the English soldier calls out to them, "EMISSARY…"

William curses and pulls Warrior to a halt, he turns and looks over his right shoulder while he slowly and discreetly crosses his right hand over to his left side to firmly grip the handle of his sword, ready to pull. Lambertoun enquires, "Aye, what is it you require of me good sir?" The soldier calls out, "You two Scotchmen, you should seek warm shelter in the town this night, for there's a martial curfew now employed in the country hereabouts, the whole of this shire is militarily governed and under severe martial law. Any wastrels that are caught outside the town walls of this dung heap are to be imprisoned… or hung." The soldier then points towards something not far away in the distance to the front of them, both William and Lambertoun turn to look where the soldier is indicating, through the gloomy darkness, they see a tree with many bodies hanging by the neck, all swaying gently in the light breeze. Lambertoun freezes as he stares at the lifeless bodies. William just shakes his head forlorn. It's apparent even in the darkness, that many of the bodies have been mutilated. Some had been terribly beaten, their faces bloodied and all with long stretched pinched necks, their heads bizarrely lopsided with thick blackened purple tongues protruding grotesquely from the mouth of every man, woman… and child.

Dropping his head, William turns and glares at the soldiers, his thoughts are to turn back and kill them all while they carelessly warm themselves in their makeshift bivouacs, but then he thinks of the importance of his mission. Lambertoun waves to the soldier, "I thank you once again good sir for your thoughtfulness; and for your kindness. May God bless you." William scowls then simply clicks his tongue; Warrior immediately breaks into a canter, Lambertoun quickly follows him. They ride on in silence past the impromptu hanging trees towards the gatehouse entrance to Saint Johns Toun, eventually slowing their horses to a walking pace as they gain on the guard's gatehouse.

Lamberton is still greatly disturbed by his witness to the hanging bodies as they join anxious crowds desperately seeking shelter within Saint John's boundaries before the martial curfew. Unfortunately, as they approach the town gates, they see that there are many more unfortunates in hanging cages, clearly suffering from privations and biting cold of the elements, others have been bound tightly to posts and black-tarred from head to foot, with countless more unfortunates strung up on makeshift gallows all along the perimeters of the town wall, as far as the eye could see.

Small flocks of crow, magpie and jackdaw peck and tug at the unseeing eyeballs of the corpses, while dogs fight amongst themselves, vying to tear at the meat of the victim's lower extremities. William and Lambertoun cautiously approach the portal of gatehouse; there they enter and produce their travel warrants. They are simply waved through by the English guards, who appear to be too cold to be asking questions or searching anyone other than the poor and wretched country souls seeking shelter and the safety of the inner town boundaries. Unexpectedly and with a great sense of relief, the two of them pass easily through the last gatehouse and on into the safety of the town boundaries.

As they meander down the long winding hillside road towards the town, Lambertoun eventually speaks out with concern in his voice, "Wallace, you appear to display no obvious feelings nor any sympathy regarding the wickedness that we've just witnessed, how so?"

"No feelings you say? I am beyond any feelings Lambertoun, for my blood is running cold to hunt down my familie's murderers. If it were not for the importance of our mission, those English guards that we met earlier would now be long gone from this earth."

Lambertoun says, "I don't understand all of this cruelty and what's happening to our realm Wallace, I never thought it could be as we have just witnessed back there, I didn't think…" William shakes his head, "Naw Lambertoun, that's the fuckin' problem with our lordy Nobles and your church hierarchy, the supposed leaders that we common folk trusted in this realm… you lot just didn't think… C'mon, we'd better get goin' for Saint Johns nave and find a crib for the night." It isn't long before they reach the friars houses near the nave of Saint John's, there they stable their horses and meet with Vicar Mydford and deliver to him the dispatches from Bishop Wishart; then they retire to break food with the vicar.

Sitting at the long oak friars table, Mydford speaks, "I heard what happened to your family Wallace... may I offer you my deepest sympathies and condolences." William merely nods in response as Mydford continues, "I knew sir Malcolm very well, he was a good friend and a good man, but I never had the opportunity of meeting with your father."

"He was a good man too vicar." replies William.

Lambertoun interrupts, "Forgive me vicar, but I have no appetite for this food, the poor wretches I have seen on my journey here... I don't understand, I have only ever seen murderers hanged, but never women and children..." Mydford says, "English martial law." Lambertoun exclaims, "But why, why such wanton killing, I don't understand...?" Mydford could offer no other words of explanation. "Because they can." replies a surly William.

They continue to sit and eat in silence at the table of the darkened room, lit only by a few candles. Mydford sighs, "The mood of the country hereabouts is of a great despair that smothers the community and surrounding lands." Lambertoun stands up, his face ashen grey and he is clearly in a state of distress.

"Mydford, may I be excused, for I must seek solace to pray for those poor unfortunates that I have seen."

"Of course Lambertoun, but remember, you must be ready to leave for Elgin by first light, it's a long journey and you will be travelling with many from this order with other pilgrims on route, your passes have already been arranged. I'll be accompanying Wallace up to Dun Dèagh along the coast road." Lambertoun nods as Mydford continues, "There are makeshift cribs made up for you both in the chancellery."

William gets up from the table, "I've no need of sleep this night Mydford, I think I'll go down to the barge square awhile, I was supposed to meet young Andrew Moray here, but I take it he's no' arrived yet?"

"No, I've not seen him, but if he's not here by daybreak, then we cannot wait for him Wallace, we must as a matter of great urgency leave here by first light regardless, then make haste for Dun Dèagh."

Lambertoun washes his hands clean in a stone bowl filled with water, then wipes his hands on a cloth, he says, "I'll see you the morn Wallace, I shall pray for the souls of those departed we saw earlier." William puts his hand on his friends shoulder, "Then you'd better pray for all you're worth Lambertoun, for what you have seen this night is but a mere taste of what is going on outwith the protection and sight of your faith." Lambertoun is still clearly upset, he says, "I shall pray for us all Wallace."

Watching Lambertoun depart, William sits back down at the table and spoons some more lukewarm gruel. For a long time no words are spoken while Mydford scrutinises and decodes the information sent by Wishart.

Eventually Mydford speaks, "These are extremely dangerous times Wallace, Edward crowned John Baliol as king of Scotland, but he will not turn over nor return the keys of the major towns or castles of our realm to our King. It would seem that Longshank's true intention is that the future for the Kingdom of Scotland is to be naught but a mere province of England." William enquires, "So, do yie really think the English intend to be staying here permanently?" Mydford replies, "Aye, I reckon they do, even though twenty five of Scotland's major castles and eight major towns have been partially handed back to Baliol by legal writ, the reality is that these places still retain the same English garrisons, Governors, sheriff's constables and soldiers. Another obvious sign is that Longshanks has his English fleet still blockading all of our ports, supposedly to thwart any invasion during our time of flux, but in reality this only ensures that no trade is allowed to come into Scotland except through English ports, this has been a disaster for us, as the extortionate taxation forced upon our traders now by the English sheriffs is destroying our international trade."

Supping some ale, Mydford thinks a moment; then he continues, "Did you know that when Baliol was crowned as King at Scone, the English King took the Great Seal of Scotland away and had it broken into shards, then he sent the pieces to England with most of our antiquities, relics and all the ancient treasures of Scotland."

"What… why? Exclaims William, This is a grievous insult Mydford, not only to Baliol, but to all Scots, what's Baliol going to do about it? I mean, how can he respond without an army?" Mydford replies, "Wallace, you must remember the information that I am now about to part with you, Baliol has had a secret seal made that clearly identifies with only those that are supporters of his court. You may see it on occasion as a signet, or at other times applied as the affixed seal on writs and charters, perhaps even as a locket or talisman, however way that you do see it, you also see a friend. It's vital that you remember these following details. It's a cast seal in a fixed emerald green glaze, the obverse of the seal has King John's image mounted in chainmail and surcoats with sword in hand. He is riding to the sinister wearing a royal barred crown helmet, to the shoulder left, the mark carries the Scottish lion rampant with double and tressure on both the shield and housings. On the Dexter, our King sits upon a carved throne, with a scepter and a shield charged with a discreet Orle, representing the house of Balliol. The sinister is also accompanied with the Lion Rampant minor of Galloway. Do not forget these details Wallace, for many lives will depend on it, including your own." William replies, "I'll remember them Mydford… but why did Longshanks break the Royal Seal of Scotland in the first place?"

Placing his ale back on the table, Mydford replies, "Longshanks broke the Royal Seal of Scotland in front of our King and his supporters during the ceremony at Scone, it was his way of publicly demonstrating his indubitable superiority and lordship over both Baliol and of Scotland. Now the English King demands that the new Seal of Scotland must be re-framed to carry his image, insignia and the English royal arms." William exclaims, "This is so much worse than I thought…"

"It gets much more worse than that Wallace, much worse. Longshanks has also removed Baliol's sovereign right to hold court justice and ruling supremacy of trial decisions over all of Scotland's Knights, Baron's, Earls and Magnates and all who signed the Ragemanus, this is to apply with immediate effect in any and all cases of dispute in law, even those with minor legal contretemps, like a burgess with a trader or even a simpleton to a trader, they can now all choose to have their cases decided in England by English courts and jurists, who's final conclusion annuls any legal findings declared in a royal or provincial court of Baliol."

"What's happened to our King?" exclaims William.

"I'm afraid that our King has been truly emasculated by Longshanks, now it would seem that any person who swears fealty to the English crown may seek to appeal against any decision made by King John's courts in Scotland, to be favourably overturned and admonished by the judges, jurists and the Justiciary in the Law courts of England."

"I've heard some of these things in the passing," says William, "but only as loose-mouthed rumours, I didn't think it or even consider in such detail that this madness would be possible Mydford. I am starting to feel that maybe I should have a care who rules over us." Mydford replies, "Wallace, we need you prepared to take up arms, we need you both in heart and soul, we also need all of those too who are your kinfolks and friends down in the bandit country of Galloway, we need every man and woman prepared and resist this takeover of our ancient realm, for this is not the end of things for us, you mark my words, it's only the beginning, and I think you're families demise is a part of this takeover the English are making upon our realm. Are you with us now Wallace?"

William is morose upon hearing this information. He looks at Mydford and enquires, "How can you relate what has happened to my family to this English takeover of our realm?" Mydford replies, "All of those who were supporters of King Alexander, in particular, those who served him as his council or commanders, they are being systematically eliminated… and their families too, in that, none shall ever grow old to seek revenge upon the perpetrators at another time. Your uncle Malcolm, he was personal confidante to the late King and also the commander of the Garda Bahn Rígh, a powerful man in a very powerful position to call-out the Garda army to raise arms and fight back, making him an obvious target for English murderers, but you ask why was Alain and everyone in glen Afton was murdered… I can only think it was by his association and family blood tie's like I said earlier being the reason for such a terrible act of barbarity."

William sits awhile pondering over Mydfords words. He says, "Then that would make all of my family a target it would appear." Mydford replies, "Aye, I think it is so, but until we can get our hands on a copy of the death lists, we cannot know for certain, but I strongly advise that you take all necessary precautions to protect your family Wallace."

"So tell me then Mydford, if I do prepare to come to arms as you say, and that too of my blood and kinfolks, is the making of this new seal of Scotland by Baliol a signal act of defiance? Is it a call to arms to defend our realm against this English insurgence?"

"It certainly is a signal of defiance, and this is only the beginning Wallace, Baliol will fight back by the use law... or by the use of arms if it comes to it. Hear me well Wallace, Baliol is not the fool or buffoon he is made out to be, he's a good man of the fold of the late King Alexander. But time and many of our own nobles stand heavily against him. So tell me, what is your will Wallace?"

Sitting back in his chair, William scratches his beard thoughtfully, he says, "I don't know, I don't yet fully grasp or understand truly what's happening Mydford, tell me this then, why do most of our nobles accept this state of affairs, why are they so hungry to be ruled by a foreign King who imposes his brutal will and laws upon our people, as barbarous and cruel as it is?"

Uncharacteristically Mydford spits on the floor then replies; "Arrogance, self-entitlement, greed, wealth, status... all of those things Wallace, but who really knows what goes on in the heads of those who wish to pursue this subservient union with England. All I do know as a proven fact is, the Scots nobility because of their avaricious and rapacious ambitions, are fast losing us our realm to be absorbed without a challenge into the English Crown Estates. The most obvious factor in all of this is Scotland's nobles are unequally divided between those who have possessions in

England and France, which is the majority of the Norman nobility now sworn to serve the English King, against the minority who only look to their own blood and their landed estates here in Scotland, who wish only to serve the King of Scotland, Lord John Baliol. The English are a very clever and astute race of people Wallace, Longshanks will foster and use these divisions to fulfil his need to purchase cheaply our manpower for his foreign wars and take or tax profits from our land and trade resources to fund those wars."

Shaking his head, William says, "I once asked a friend what difference would it make to me who was our King, be he Scots, French, English, for it mattered not to me, but what I have seen, what we have already suffered and what I now hear in your words Mydford, I cannot see why I should give up my freedom cheaply whilst my wits are ravaged by grief and a want for vengeance. It would appear from my experience, it is my freedom that the English want to take from me, and my life. If I truly find that it was the English who murdered my family, then I swear to you, Baliol will have a loyal soldier in me." Mydford says, "I understand you Wallace, there are many of us who will never accept this current state of affairs. Whilst this tyrannical politic is still in its infancy, we must take our throne and realm back into our own hands, by force if necessary... and we the people must do it now, before it's too late, with or without Baliol, with or without you Wallace."

Still curious at Mydford's comments, William enquires, "Baliol is still our King by our ancient laws of tanistry, he's the rightful and just King of Scotland, so who would allow any to take the throne away from him, be it the English King or our own nobles, surely the little people who till and nurture the land are one hundred maybe even one thousand times that of every single noble by numbers? But the little people could not do this on their own Mydford, they need the leadership of a good King, we don't need these treasonous nobles to lead us. Though, I have often thought of this idea of a realm that is nurtured solely by it's own community could be possible, if it were a king elect rather than a throne inherited, especially so after I studied in great detail the rebellion of the peasants during the Sicilian Vespers."

"We would not take it from Baliol Wallace, we will steadfast support him… many of low rank and station of this realm do support him too, for as you say, he is our rightful King. The ordinary peasants who are now being brutalized, the merchants who are severely taxed or have their goods seized, low rank nobles who's trade in wool, hide and fisheries who's wealth, land and title is now being confiscated, and sadly, those who are upon the death lists, such as your own family, there are many who still vigorously support our King. As I said before, it's mainly the Norman nobles who stand with Longshanks and Scots barons who appear to have been bought who thwart and ridicule Baliol's reign. Aye, there are many who would Join Baliol in resistance and we will fight an all out bloody war if needs be."

"What about the church?" enquires William, "where does the religious establishment stand… with Longshanks?"

"No Wallace, absolutely not, the church is fully behind Baliol, but unless we have all the Barons on our side, then I fear a brutal civil war in Scotland or a war with the English is fast looming upon us, no matter what we do, but do something we must, or Wallace I tell you this, not as your old tutor, but as a friend of both yourself and this land of ours that has nurtured us so well, what's happening now within our realm is nothing to what will become of us if we do not fight back. And should the English be allowed to remain in all our castles and continue to have free riding roughshod over our country and our people… we cannot let these murders go unchallenged, not with the native population suffering so greatly under this brutal martial law. If we don't act now, it'll be certain Baliol will be lost before he begins."

Feeling a chill on hearing Mydford's words, William enquires… "Why not just eject the English army and take out all the nobles who refute Baliol… hang the treacherous bastards, they cannot be that many in number. Far less I reckon than those poor commoners who feed the carrion outside your town's ditches. Those same nobles you speak about show no protection nor care for the ordinary folk of this realm." Mydford sighs, "If only it were that simple Wallace, when Baliol and the claimants made their submission to Longshanks at Norham, none thought that the fealty was anything other than a temporary arrangement. When King Alexander previously gave his oath for his holdings in England, as did Longshanks for his lands in France, which is what monarchs do, everything is placed back in good order as it was. But when Baliol made his final oath in Newcastle, Longshanks clerics had already undermined Baliol and the fealty was written in as absolute, leaving Scotland with the same standing as an English shire and bound by the same governance under English law, with Longshanks declared as Lord paramount supreme of Scotland sacrosanct."

William enquires, "Then why didn't Baliol just refuse the crown under those conditions?" Mydford replies, "It was too late by then, he couldn't refuse at that point. Baliol has now been crowned King and he rightly expected that the Lords and Barons of Scotland would see through Edwards mischief by his return from Newcastle, but they have betrayed him and now use English law to maintain their position to keep favour with Longshanks. Those who did not sign the second Ragemanus in good faith with Baliol now appear to be on these death lists."

Shaking his head in frustration, William enquires, "Are we now subject to the laws of England?" Mydford shrugs his shoulders, "Aye, that is the supposition. Longshanks has embedded an Englishman called Thomas Hunsingore from his own exchequer upon Baliol's neck, already he is setting in place new taxation and fiscal rendering of all our trade goods in Scotland, completely foreign to our traditional ways and understanding. Hunsingore is also in the process of establishing a Scots fiscal exchequer under English jurisdiction, in order for us to pay for all English expenses of maintaining a standing army in Scotland. Longshanks has also sent into Scotland a second army commanded by a noble called De Warenne the earl of Surrey and also Bishop Bek of Sunderland as his Lord Lieutenant, both now enforces strict martial law upon us. With the imposition of these new laws and taxation, we're completely subordinate to the English crown now."

Looking at Mydford in dismay, William enquires, "Does this mean we're all English now?"

Mydford, amused by his former students naïve enquiry replies, "No Wallace, we as Scots are not even regarded as that high a station by the English, it means you are nothing but a bonded slave under an English yolk. You don't have nor even merit subject status in their eyes." William glares at Mydford, "Aye, do yie fuckin' think so?" Mydford ignores Williams profanity and continues, "You should also be aware there are legal writs to enforce the subjugation of any native Scot, meaning, all those over twelve years of age are to be enlisted into the service of any Baron or Sherriff who is deemed the Lieutenant of whatever shire as is their warrant. This service is for toiling in the fields, households or for military service of the said Sherriff, or Longshanks, and should any native born Scot refuse this feudal imposition, it will be seen as sedition and those who resist, both they and their families are to be tried and executed immediately for treason."

Slumping back into his chair again, William pulls his hands down his face then shakes his head, "I've lost so many kinfolk and so many good friends already to this madness… and much of my youth and innocence too Mydford. I've already witnessed such grievous torture, cruelty and murder caused by the nobles politic during the Pact rebellion in Galloway a few years back…"

William hesitates then he says, "Then the visitation upon my own kinfolk at glen Afton and Ach na Feàrna… and it was by an English death squad you say?" William puts his hands to his eyes as emotion begins to well up in his heart. Mydford says, "Wallace, it may best serve you and your families future if you were to join the English army…" William is astounded by these words, he exclaims, "What… are you fucking jesting me? What was all that rhetoric you preached to me about moments ago?"

"No, I do not jest with yie Wallace, it would be a great vantage to have our own men placed within their ranks, think about it, we need to know much information about their plans, how they fight, battle orders. We already know the English have death squads afoot in the realm; they are slaughtering or imprisoning Alexander's entire former household that they deem to be no apparent use or who may be a potential threat to the English crown. Important burgesses, merchants and other good men and women of note in this realm have been murdered, tortured or imprisoned, we know from our sources that the English plan to enforce new punitive laws upon us very soon, in that, no Scot may travel without carrying port pass papers under pain of death, and no man or boy will be free to leave the boundaries of his shire without permission of his English master.

Those that do so or attempt such a movement, will be subject to penalties most severe. Wallace, we need to know who all is on these death lists and it may be that this can only be discovered if we have men in place within the English army…"

Aghast at the thought, William replies, "No Mydford, this I cannae do, for if all you say is true, then I must stay with ma family and protect them." Perplexed by this information from Mydford, William continues, "All I wish to do is return to ma home and go back to the hunt. These last few years with my father Alain, learning his trade as a hunter in the Wolf and wildcats o' Carrick and Galloway, has shown to me that I'm of no use to town or church… or an English army. All I want is to be left alone with my family."

Mydford shakes his head, "You cannot even go back to the hunt Wallace; for hunting the forests has now been outlawed by the English… haven't you heard?" William looks at the vicar in complete disbelief, "What the fuck do you mean, I cannot hunt no more?" Mydford replies, "Wallace, haven't you heard or haven't you been listening? The English imposition of martial law is not just for the town's clachan's and balloch's… all of the great and lesser forests of Scotland are now under the jurisdiction of King Edward's Sheriffs for the sole preserve of his nobility. They intend to cut down all our forests for their town and castle building in England. All our forests belong to Longshank's now as a part payments levy for all the expenses the English army incurs by being here to maintain the peace. All known hunters have been declared outlaws and must now deliver themselves up to the new sheriffs for a pardon, under pain of death."

"Fuck off Mydford, they cant do that… the fuckin' English are taking away all our freedoms, we can't hunt, they torture kill and murder as they please and don't expect us to react, then you ask me to join their ranks, have you lost your wits

Mydford?" A sympathetic but frustrated Mydford exclaims, "Wallace, use your brains, the English now control everything, the only use that you may serve is to be in their ranks, at least for the duration. It's the only way that you and yours will survive. The English do not only need our trade tax and resources, our vast woodlands are a vital commodity to them, without wood you cannot build a house, a castle or a boat, you cannot even build a fire or bake bread without wood. England has sorely depleted its own natural woodlands. Don't you see what's happening? The English need Scotland, not as a friend, but as a resource."

Recoiling, William enquires, "What use would I be to my family by dying for a foreign King in some war I don't believe in or to fight and kill a man from another faith for a faith I don't believe in, what's happening to us Mydford, have I gone completely mad or has the whole world gone mad? All I want to do is go home to my family and leave well alone all o' this madness." Mydford replies, "Wallace, I will tell you again, for it appears you do not yet grasp the severity of your situation, you will not survive, nor will your family of Riccartoun, Ellerslie, ach na Feàrna, Craigie, Black Craig, Carrick Rhinns, and Machars if they are all mentioned on the death lists, and it certainly looks like it is."

"What is this you dare say to me?" Exclaims William. Mydford nods, "You really don't know do you, why am I not getting this through to you? Wallace, this is why you have to go to Dun Dèagh and meet with Lord Moray. As the senior Justiciar of Scotland he has been privy to most of the names on the death lists, but not all, it would appear to be a complete annihilation of our race is planned, like the Cathar's before us, you must see that it's vitally important we hear from Moray and then you take his instructions back with you to the west, do you understand me now? It's almost certain that you and yours are all marked by the English for death." William is stunned by this information, his head spins trying to take it all in, suddenly a clarity of understanding comes to him, he now knows in his heart it wasn't brigands or robbers who had visited Glen Afton, it was an English death squad. "De Percy..." exclaims William. "Who?" Enquires Mydford. William springs from his seat, picks up his chair and hurls it with force against the wall; then he begins smashing the pieces over the table in a rage. As he runs amok, Mydford, though old and frail, has no fear as he grabs William and backslaps him hard across the face,

"WALLACE..." William immediately reaches for his dirk while throwing his old tutor against the knave wall, pressing the lethal dirk blade against his throat. Mydford again shows no fear as he looks into the primeval eyes of rage. For a mere second that seems an eternity; Mydford can see the savage lone wolf features deep within Williams animated expression. "Wallace..." says Mydford in a low calm voice.

"Wha... fuck... I'm so sorry Mydford." exclaims William; realising he had lost his wits in a blind rage. Mydford holds on to William's wrists as he pushes the dirk away from his throat, William groans, "De Percy and Cressingham..."

As he is about to put his dirk back in its scabbard, he notices the inscription, he mutter's, "I will not die a slave..." He puts his dirk away and lifts a tipped chair, pulls it to the table, sits down and rests his head in his arms. Mydford speaks, "I don't know of which de Percy you speak Wallace, but Cressingham is one of King Edwards most trusted lieutenants and an advisor to sir John de Warenne the earl of Surrey. Why do you speak of these men?" William lifts his head and gazes at the candle flame as it flickers in the damp cold room. He mutters, "I'm so sorry... I'm so lost..." Sitting across from William, Mydford says abruptly,

"Wallace, why do you mention these names, speak, tell me man?" William replies, "It was those two particular names mentioned when one of my fathers tacksman auld Tam sent a warning up to Ach na Feàrna, that those knights and their troops who were billeted in Glen Afton the day of the murders. It was those same two names that were told to me by Lady Marjorie Comyn who said they visited Comunnach castle the day after the murders… it must have been them." William realises something, "It's also the same name of de Percy that a survivor of brutal massacres in Galloway told to me was responsible many years ago… now I know he was right. Fuck, how could it have taken so long for me to see the truth…" Staring at Mydford remorsefully, William enquires, "And you say my family is on these English death lists, are you sure?" Mydford replies, "I'm not sure…"

The solemn expression confirms to William that his family is likely on a death list. "I don't know Wallace, but I reckon it must be. There are lists for the different shires, I've seen only part of one for Galloway and Carrick… and your families name's upon that list as I mentioned earlier, many others too. That's why it's imperative that you meet with Lord Moray and obtain all the information you need that will give the west coast families and Clans a chance and time to prepare. William looks about the room as though seeking to escape.

"I must get back and warn ma family…" Mydford immediately reacts, "No Wallace, listen to me, we have already dispatched riders and sent carrier doo's with as much information as possible to your uncles and others that we think are on the list, but we need you here now, if you leave, many more will surely perish. Wishart will protect your family till we can find safe sanctuary for them." William enquires brusquely, "What do you mean 'we' need you?" Mydford replies, "We do need you Wallace, the Céile Aicé needs you, Scotland needs you. All of the elder masters and commanders of the Garda Rígh have been murdered, you must take over their positions with the other sons and daughters of the Garda Rígh commanders." William replies in anger and frustration, "It's my family who needs me Mydford not Scotland. I must get back to them now. I'll take them to Ireland, for I cannae sit idly here while they're still in grave peril." William pauses; then in an almost farcical moment he says, "Fuck, we can't go to Ireland..."

Curiously Mydford enquires, "Why not?" William looks at him then replies, "My friend Stephen is no' long back from Ireland, he told me that a law has been recently passed in Ireland that says if any Scot is to be found there and not in indentured service to an English lord, that he or she can be freely put to the sword without prejudice. There's also a reward to be paid for the ears of any Scot delivered to Norman Sheriffs."

Mydford shakes his head as William continues, "I must leave Mydford, I need to get back to my family. I must get them out of Scotland somewhere, somehow." Mydford says, "You will put them all in a much greater danger if you leave before your mission is complete. I have passes for you, your aunt Margret and your brother Alan to be travelling back to Ach na Feàrna as pilgrims on route to saint Ninian's at Taigh Mhàrtainn, there will be no more passes after that, as any Scot caught moving around Scotland without a pass will be imprisoned or executed. This is what I told you earlier, there is no time other than this limited time you have for your mission, that's the only chance your family will have if they are to survive this madness."

Holding his head in his hands, William is near overwhelmed as his living nightmare continues, his mind races with grief, anger and confusion. Whichever way he turns, he cannot see a way out of this situation; he exclaims, "Marion…" As he rises from his seat, Mydford grabs William firmly by the sleeve of his léine, "Wallace listen to me, your family are safe for the moment. Wishart and true Tam look to their protection, but if you do anything other than complete your mission then you may kill them by your own witless arrogance… NOW SIT…"

Meekly William sits back down in the chair and again puts his head in his hands. Mydford continues, "Wallace, on the morrow we will make haste to meet with lord Moray and his men. When he informs us as to how we may get our hands on whatever will identify all names on the death list for Scotland and any other relevant information, you must make for Kilspindie and gather your family, from there you may return to the safety of the west coast. Once you delivered the information to Wishart, gather all your family at Ach na Feàrna and make haste to the safety of the Wolf and wildcat forest, for I know the English will be a long time penetrating that part of the country, if at all. For I also know that they fear it as a place full of unchristian and demonic sorcery."

Mydford half-smiles then continues, "Also because it is their least favourite part of Scotland, no ports, no roads… nothing useful as far as they are concerned, nothing except savage gangs of cannibalistic Gallóbhet… and young Brigand chiefs like you." William glances at Mydford a moment; then smiles at the backhanded compliment. Mydford smiles as he continues… "Do yie think Wallace that I wouldn't hear about your reckless ventures and courage during the Pact rebellion, or your time as a Gallóbhet chieftain with your exploits in Ireland fighting successfully alongside the Irish chiefs over there, or even the fishing incident down in the shire of Ayr? Then there was the timely incident with the Robert Brus and the red Earl of Ulster's men on the shores of Domhnach Daoi…" Surprised that Mydford knows of these things, William says, "There was no courage by me at Invergarvane Mydford, it was there I lost control and then I lost my friends because of my lack of understanding. I was absolutely bereft of any courage there, and that I confirm to you now." Mydford smiles, "Wallace, courage is not necessarily a willingness to be a classical hero, it comes in many forms that many miss but a few does see. And it is so important now for all of us that your grief does not cloud your understanding once more." Mydford continues, "You are marked for great things Wallace, Wishart, Leckie mòr, true Tam… even your grandmother Bheitris, a revered Aicé herself have all said as much to me, do you think that any of us may escape our duty to the Aicé? I see that you have two amulets of the Aicé there around your neck; do you deem those rare amulets to be worthless gestures or simply romantic trinkets given over to you to pander to your own self-esteem? Or do you think that you have been gifted these precious treasures for a reason beyond your ken, and would you not wish to ken?"

Again William is surprised by Mydford's intimate observations, he enquires, "How can you know of these things, you being a Christian?" Mydford laughs, "Only my instinct reacting to your consistent actions." William sighs, "Awe naw, don't you be telling me that you think that I'm predictable too." Mydford laughs then he replies, "Not predictable as such Wallace, maybe you are what all old men like myself would wish to have been when we were your age." William is amused by this answer. Mydford continues sympathetically, "Cool your spurs, if it's vengeance your heart is understandably set upon, then follow our advice and complete your duties, for regardless of how you deal with it, the time will come when you will be faced with the murderers of your family. Learn our calling of the Céile Aicé and Garda Rígh proper Wallace, for that is the only way that your remaining family and Marion may have any hope of surviving these terrible days."

Mydford yawns, "Now, it's time for my crib, follow me and I will show you where you may lay to rest this night." William replies, "Naw… I'm going down to the Bargee Inn tavern Mydford, I want to see if Andrew Moray has maybe arrived there, and there's also one other from the Wolf and wildcat forest who now resides here that I would wish to speak with." Mydford laughs, "Another of your fishwives or milkmaids Wallace?" William smiles at the memory, then he replies, "Naw Mydford, not this time, that was a long time ago, perhaps another lifetime ago. I'm hoping to meet with a Ceàrdannan princess I once knew, for she was the sole survivor of a visitation and suffered terrible injuries when her clan was attacked and slaughtered, I reckon it was by the hands of the same men who carried out the murders of my family… it just might be that she can help me to be sure, that's why I would wish to speak with her." Mydford sighs, "Aye well, you be extremely careful, there are many English patrols about at night and they show no mercy if they doubt you motives." William sighs, "I will." He stands up and pauses as he pulls his brat around his shoulders and looks around the nave that had been his old classroom.

"It's a long time gone since the sun shone upon my days here as a student, but it was good times old friend." Mydford says, "Aye, that it was Wallace, the last time I saw you I reckon was when you were here with the young prince Alexander, your brother wee John, young Blair and Duncan of Lorne… and none of you with whisper of a hair to be seen on your faces in those days boy." William laughs thinking of his childhood moments in Kilspindie. "Aye, I remember that you gave us all tutorage during the summer harvests, when everyone else our age were running free to fish and to hunt as they pleased, but you were good to us Mydford, I thank yie for that. I think that the only time you ever had us belted round the head was when we worked out the words of how to say 'Fuck you ya old bastard…' in archaic Latin… and if ah remember it right, you had hair on your head away back in those day's too." Mydford laughs, "Now Wallace, no need to curse, for I'm still a religious person as yie know… Ach but, you boys were a handful right enough, and aye, your right, I did have hair in those days didn't I?"

Mydford looks kindly at his former pupil, then he says, "Wallace, if you wish to be hanging on to your bonnie locks o' hair and reach my age, then you must trust me now as you trusted me when you were but a boy. We all saw something special in you then, and even more so now. If there's any way that you may save your family, then I ask you to listen to the old ones." William reflects his younger days when Mydford had tutored him in Latin and history during his summer residence with his uncle Alex at nearby Kilspindie, he remembers too how much he had liked Mydford and his peculiar almost eccentric ways of the teaching.

"Aye, Mydford," says William, "I'll listen, I give you my word as a Wallace that I'm listening, and please, forgive me for my thoughtless rage earlier." Smiling at the words of care, Mydford replies as he goes around the small room extinguishing all the candles, "You'll have to find a way to temper your rage Wallace, for you have the gift, the ability to see and the heart to know right from wrong. There's no need to ask forgiveness from me, for my reward is in your friendship young man… and by you following your heart." Turning to face William, Mydford looks at his former pupil, "Be careful going out there this night Wallace, for yie must be back here and ready to leave by the first cock crow's."

William enquires, "Is there martial law or curfew within the boundaries of Saint John's Toun?" Reaching the door Mydford turns and replies, "No, just evil intent… Now I'll bid you a good night and I'll see you in the morn." William bids Mydford a goodnight, "Oidhche math." Mydford mumbles something by way of reply and simply waves his backhand as he disappears into the dark gloomy corridors of the old church.

Standing alone in the darkened room, William is deep in thoughts of all that has passed. He thinks of everything that's happened and where he is now, all he ever wanted to do is live his life as a hunter, now he's being drawn into a hellish dark place he has no wish to be. He ponders over why so many folk he respects keep saying that he is special, gifted and needed. Why so many ask him to keep his word not to react and keep away from trouble?

Shaking himself from these thoughts, he knows he must go to try and seek out Moray, but equally important is to make contact with Affric… for there is much he needs to know from her. He wraps himself tight in his brat, leaves the nave of Sainte John's and makes his way down the old narrow and twisting streets to the inn at the barge landings. It doesn't take long before he approaches the rear of the inn tavern of his last visit. He stops in the shadows and looks across the market square, there he sees a dim light glowing through a small window in a tiny bothy, the abode of his old friend Affric.

While standing in the dark shadows of the inn, William looks around the square, thinking of the chaos that unfolded the last time he was here, now the place is eerily deserted, nobody appears to be about, not even English patrols. With the words of Mydford still nagging at his thoughts, he looks once more across the square towards Affric's Bothy, he is indecisive as to whether he should go see her, especially after the chaos of his last visit, but he desperately needs to talk to her about de Percy, he needs to know from her if that truly was the man responsible for the slaughter of her clan. The cold is beginning to bite and William decides to enter the inn first, then consider what he will do next, for Affrics demeanour and candor towards him the last time they met… he cannot afford another incident that would bring his presence here to the attention of the English. He is considering that the risk in meeting her may be too great, but if Affric is in the tavern, then so be it, if not, he'll wait there for his friend Andrew Moray and make up his mind before he leaves. Cautiously, William moves out of the dark alley and walks below the overhanging thatch of the inn then he enters quietly through the small door.

Upon entering the Inn, he can see the place is very quiet, but for a few old wretches huddled round the inglenook fire trying to keep warm, then he notices in a darkened corner, a stocky drunken character sprawled across a table sleeping. A female voice growls. "Come on inside and shut the fuckin' door, ya big useless lookin' lump o' shit, it's freezin.'" William quickly shuts the door behind him and pulls back the hood of his brat. A thin spindly man comes over and takes his brat then grabs William by the wrist, "Ahm sorry about that welcome big fella, ahm the innkeeper here and that's ma wifey who told yie tae come in, ach she is no' much acquainted wie decorum yet. Anyways, now come you wie me young sur and ah'll fix yie a seat by the big fire."

The innkeeper drags William towards the inglenook while shouting at the wretches huddled round the fire, "Move yer manky bones ya bunch o' shifty-lookin' bastards… we have a payin' customer here." The innkeeper turns to William, smiles and politely bids him to sit. Then he looks at William curiously. "Don't I know you from somewhere young fella?" William replies, "Naw, I wouldn't think it so, ahm no' from these parts." The innkeeper scratches his chin, "Aye, ah know yie from somewhere, for ah never forget a face." William thinks the innkeeper had better forget his face or he will be found in the morning face down in the fire.

"Aye, there is definitely something familiar about yie…" the innkeeper continues, "Anyways young fella, is there anything I can get for yie, maybe some food, ale, whisky… a wumman?" Leaning forward, the innkeeper gleefully rubs his hands together and whispers, "Findin' a decent wumman' about the Toun this night is scarce, and they're no' very handsome at all son, yie know, all poxed up and that… maybe you would like to have some long-sup ale time in the crib wie ma bonnie wifey?" Suddenly the innkeeper straightens himself up and appears indignant, almost sobbing, he continues, "Ma dearest wife, God bless her… she's only for special customers yie understand son, ah wouldnae just offer her to any stranger yie know, that's why she costs a wee bitty more, but ah'm sure yie'll no' ever forget the experience." Before William could refuse the lucrative offer, the innkeeper calls out to a woman sitting at the far end of the inn bar in a doorway…

"CHRISTINA…" William's jaw drops when he sees a woman as wide as she is tall with clotted dirty ginger hair hanging about her sweating pock-marked red face. She's sitting on a bench with her skirts raised to her hair-infested thighs with her feet firmly buried in a deep churn. Christina enquires, "Aye, what th' fuck do yie want now, can yie no' see that ahm busy for fuck's sake?" The innkeeper nervously replies, "This eh, this fine young fella here, he would like some private time with you ma lovely… he's in an awfy desperate need o' a shag ma dearest…" There's a biblical pause, then Christina bellows back at him, "He can fuck off, or he can shag one o' the sucklin' sows oot th' back o' the Inn, ahm far too busy here." she spits in the churn then continues, "It's ma wummin's time anyway… unless the fancy big bastard wants to pay a wee bit extra for the privilege." William can't believe what he is seeing… and what he is hearing. The innkeeper turns and declares with pride, "Isn't she the very vision of wummanly lovelyhood?" William, who is still gawping in disbelief, is quite speechless as the innkeeper continues, "Would you like some fine special ale young sir, before you have a memorable shag with my bonnie Christina?"

Becoming amused by the innkeeper's kind offer, though still feeling threatened by the hospitality, William looks at the wretches who have been moved away from the fire. They're old fishermen by their appearance, who are grinning at him with very few teeth inanely, then they wink and nod in the direction of the glorious Christina. William looks over and stammers out a reply without taking his eyes of the wonderful and buxom Christina, "Eh, ah… eh, can I have a wee weight of some Lübeck ale?" The innkeeper wrings his hands by way of an apology, "Ach am afraid no' young sur… ever since the English blockaded our ports, nuthin' has been able to come ashore." William enquires, "Then what do you have that would quench ma thirst." The innkeeper replies, "I have either sweet-meadow ale, bitter with heather root or bog-myrtle… it's your choice sur…"

Meanwhile, Christina has softened her outlook towards William; charmingly she smiles, obviously warming to the thought of being pleasured. He smiles weakly back at Christina, then replies to the innkeeper, "Eh, maybe ah'll have some o' the sweet-meadow with heather tips tá," The innkeeper calls out to his amiable wife, "Christina my dearest… bring over this fine young sir a weight of sweet meadow an' heather tips." A now jovial Christina replies,

"Fuck aye… Ah thought yie would never ask yie useless auld bastard." The bold brewer of the sweet-meadow ale stands up with her feet still in the churn, she steps out onto a filthy cloth laying on the floor, lifts up the churn, picks up the sodden floor-cloth with her other hand, throws it in the churn; then walks over and crashes herself down beside William on the bench before the fire. She grins and says, "Get this fine handsome big bastard here a jug."

The innkeeper snatches a jug out of one of the wretched fisherman's hands, empties the remaining contents on the floor, wipes the jug with his shirt, then lay's the dirty cloth over the mouth of the vessel and hands it to William, who immediately enquires, "What's the cloth across the top of the jug for?" Christina flutters her eyes at William as she replies, "To keep out beasties, bugs, dirt and the odd toenail… William humerously recoils at the thought, then he realises her intent, before he could politely refuse, she says. "Now, hold it up the jug ma big bonnie boy." Slowly and dutifully, William nervously holds up the cloth-covered jug as Christina pours out the clotted contents of her churn to filter through the cloth until the jug's full.

The innkeeper, Christina and the wretched fishermen stare at William intently, it's a moment before he realises they're waiting for him to drink the contents, William panics, thinking to himself, '*Awe fuck naw… what the fuck have I just walked into, and the buxom Christina has just had her filthy feet in ma ale… and then she spat in it?*' He tentatively sniffs the contents and swiftly recoils. The innkeeper grins, "Good eh? Christina has her own recipe young fella, she's very well known about these parts for her special ale brewing." William is in a quandary when a voice calls out, "WALLACE…" Everyone turns to see who's called out the name and see a petite female form standing in a darkened doorway. William mutters, "Is that you Affric?" For a moment, nothing is said, then, "WALLACE..." came a drunken shout from another part of the inn. William looks across at the drunk who had been sleeping across the bench, he's now standing upright with the physique of a small bear and glaring at William through bloodshot eyes...

Suddenly the drunk throws the table aside and charges at William, knocking one of the unfortunate wretches into the fire on his way past. As the drunken bear tackles William, both of them fall into the corner of the inn fighting viciously, the bear gets on top, pummeling at Williams head, but William quickly heaves the drunken attacker off, then he catches him in a tight headlock, "WALLACE?" shouts the innkeeper as Christina tries to pull the smoldering wretch out of the fire while William tries to hold firm the raging bear. Affric comes running over from the door and grabs the bear too as Christina shouts at William with venom in her voice, "Wallace, Wallace... I know you..."

The innkeeper calls out. "Wallace, now I remember, you're the durty big bastard that stole my fuckin' Lübeck Ale..." Affric pulls a knife from her belt and begins screaming at the innkeeper and Christina, "Help me get this mad bastard off o' ma Wallace, or I swear I'll kill every fuckin' one o' yiez..." Christina points at William, "But that's William Wallace, he's a robber and a murderer." The innkeeper, who is now standing behind Cristina exclaims, "I knew I'd seen him before." Meanwhile, William has his forearm round the bear's throat squeezing hard, slowly knocking him unconscious. William keeps up the pressure till the bear goes limp, then he manages to get out from underneath him and sits with his back to the wall in the corner of the inn, gaining his breath back. A confused and breathless William enquires, "What the fuck was that all about, who the fuck is he?" Affric throws herself at William and begins kissing him profusely about the face; then she looks at him, "Oh Wallace, I knew you would come back for me…" William stands up as the bear groans and begins to regain consciousness. The innkeeper slaps William on the back, "So you're William Wallace big fella, you're the big feckr who stole my Christina's ale a while ago." Christina, who is sitting the smoldering wretch back down on the bench beside his shaking friend, says, "So you're the famous William Wallace our bonnie Affric talks about all the time?" A somber voice calls out from the floor of the inn, "Wallace… help me up…"

William is surprised to hear the strange English accent, but there's something familiar about the bear as he obligingly pulls him to his feet. As he brushes himself down, the Englishman says, "I'm sorry about that Wallace, I just heard your name and thought we were back in the fight." A puzzled William enquires, "What fight?" lifting his head the Englishman smiles, "You know, don't you remember, no, please, don't be insulting me now…" he continues, "Remember that day when you were about to be arrested for murder…" suddenly William recognises him "You, you're that English soldier I was fighting that day… it was you who let me go free?"

The Englishman sits down beside the two wretches and looks curiously at the one still smoldering, "What happened to you?" Before the wretch replies, Affric cries out, "Oh Wallace," she clasps William's face, "I knew you would come back for me and take me back to the Wolf and wildcats." William gently clasps Affric by the wrists and pulls her hands down, he's shocked by what he sees. The once beautiful Affric, the Elvin Ceàrdannan princess of Galloway now looks like an old haggard fisher wife, her complexion is ruddy, her jowls pronounced and cheeks sunk into her face. Her Almond eyes are sallow and aged, her lips are edged with open sores, and an overpowering stench of stale sweat and urine emanate from her clothing. William barely recognises his one-time woodland lover. "Affric," says Christina, "Help me clean up this fuckin' mess."

Gazing lovingly at William, Affric says, "Now don't you be sneaking away again." He replies with a smile, "I won't." He feels a nudge in his side, "William Wallace eh?" It is the bear talking to him, but this time he has a grin. "A good fight as I remember it." William laughs, "Aye, even though it was unexpected and the crowd there thinking that we were Fer fichters."

They both laugh heartily while dabbing at their bruises. William says, "I don't know your name Englishman…" The bear extends his hand in friendship, "My name is Fellows." William shakes his hand and replies, "Well I thank you Fellows, but for you, I reckon I would be pitched or bleached bones by now and hanging on the perimeter ditches o' this place, like so many others I've seen." Fellows smiles as William enquires "I thought you were an English soldier?" Fellows replies, "I was a sergeant-at-arms… one of Longshanks chosen few you might say, but I'm retired now after thirty years service." William enquires, "What are yie doin here?" Fellows replies, "At one time I thought I liked this God-forsaken shit-hole. It was busy and thriving then, so I bought into this inn as a partner with Christina, but then you fucking Scots lost the will to live, and ever since the riots here after martial law was applied, I have lost everything."

William raises his jug to drink some ale, but the pungent smell reminds of how the Brewster Christiana had added some of her special fermentation techniques with her filthy feet. He glances at the two wretches then he laughs, as the one who got shoved into the fire is still smoldering.

"Here" says William "You two can have this… its on me." The two wretched fishermen jump up and take the ale jug and churn from William, then they leave to sit in the corner, jubilant at the thought of more of Christina's fine nectar ale, William says to Fellows, "I couldn't drink that shit…" Fellows laughs, "I've a cask of Lübeck that I've kept back and hidden away for special occasions Wallace, I reckon that this is one such occasion. I'll get you some if you would be so kind to share a hearty drink with me?"

Fellows stands up, he places his mighty broad hand on William's shoulder and laughs. William enquires, "Can you pour some into two bladders for me Fellows, as I've to be leaving soon. I must be leaving here by daybreak." Fellows replies, "I'll do this just for you Wallace." As he gets up to leave, Fellows says, "Affric has told me about that incident with the fish in Ayr… I didn't think that you were a murderer…" Fellows walks away and disappears through a door to fetch some Lübeck Ale as Affric comes back and sits on William's lap. Shockingly, he can smell her pungent body odour and it takes all his willpower not to appear repulsed.

The smell of stale ale on Affric's breath and her mature controlled drunkenness makes him shudder. Affric puts her arms around his neck then she clumsily presses her lips against his, but William doesn't respond, he couldn't, he has to pull away. Affric senses that something's wrong and pulls her arms away, "I knew it Wallace… you're just like every other fuckin' man who has known me. I was fine enough to lay with when you thought me young and fresh, but now with my scars and my condition, you think I am naught but another poxy whore." William looks at Affric and puts his arm around her shoulders and pulls her close in warm embrace, like nurturing a child, "Naw Affric, me bonnie woodland princess," says William, "It's because I am now betrothed to

Marion and I cannot find it in me to be pleasuring another." Affric looks at William and feels a slight sympathy in his reasoning, she takes a drink of Christina's ale then replies with a slight slur in her voice, "I've heard that love does this to a person Wallace, I don't understand it myself, but I have heard it so… Since the English hung my young prince of Galloway, I'm now cursed with only my good looks as a my companion." Affric nudges him in the ribs, "Then why do we not just have a fuck for auld lang syne, that shouldn't affect your sensibilities?" William shakes his head and smiles as he looks at Affric, her demeanour being that of an experienced drinker who now lives in a perpetual state of alcoholic control, but it makes him cautious. Even though she speaks with limited understanding, her underlying aggressive and violent anger is veneer explosive, and he knows it.

"I cant Affric…" replies William, "Love has surely shown me a way to peace and I cannot fuck with you like we used to when we lived our ways in the Wolf and wildcats… that was another lifetime ago, and darlin' we both knew that one day each or one of us would find love. Affric, I have now found that love and I need you to understand this, you are still one of my closest lovin' friends in this life, you always will be." He looks into Affric's almond eyes, there's a hint of understanding; and for a moment, her beauty flashes through the filth and dirt that now cloak her like a skin.

"Fuck you Wallace and fuck your whore," growls Affric. William stands up in anger, raging inside. He's being honest with her, yet she speaks to him in this manner, Affric immediately jumps up and throws her arms around him, she pleads, "I'm so sorry Wallace, I am so sorry, please, will yie forgive me?" William, still angered, tries to push Affric away, but she clings on to him, "No Wallace, please… don't push me away, I'm so sorry, please forgive me…" Her pleading and the fragile tone in her voice softens Williams resolve. Then he reflects on everything she has been through. He stops pushing her away, instead, he holds her close in warm embrace once more, "Oh Affric, I'm so sorry too. Sometimes I wish that we were back in the Wolf and wildcats, just you and I as we lived that life so many years ago, when all we had to worry about was the seasons catch, a time when everything was simple and everyone seemed so happy, but now, now we are older and many of those that we have loved are long torn from our hearts…" Clinging to the affection she shares momentarily with William, she says, "Aye, between us we made some very fine catches indeed Wallace. Do yie remember your father that night in the Lanark tavern when he red-faced you about his experiences with the leathers and the whips?"

Suddenly Affric senses something changing in William's body, she leans back and looks up into his face… "What's happened to your father Wallace, something's happened hasn't it?" Affric frowns and a part of her old self takes over, "Tell me Wallace… for you know you cannot hide from me what you are watching in your mind, wait, what? I, I see your father in the otherworld don't I…" Affric hesitates then she exclaims, "Oh no, he's not alone…" William stares at the small flames in the inglenook fireplace, "Tell me Wallace, there's something terrible amiss, I sense it, I see it, I see them…"

Sitting back a little, Affric drops onto he bench then shakes her head, tears well up in her eyes and begin to flow, she looks into Williams eyes, almost in disbelief, "Wallace, what's wrong with Alain, and Mharaidh, Malcolm… awe naw…" she cries, "And the wee one Caoilfhinn too…?" Affric appears shocked at what she senses; and then what she sees… tears again come to her eyes, "Wallace you must tell me, what's happened? I see many of your kinfolks spirits from the Glen all around you with my own kinfolk from the

Corserine too… am I drunk, cursed, witless? Ahm ah gone mad… or is what I see the truth?" Affric looks at William intently, then she continues, "I see it all in your minds eye Wallace, yie cannae hide these things from me, the wraiths have been set upon you too, I sense their glee all around you, they are crushing your spirit too, tell me… It's the name de Percy you want to hear isn't it?"

William slumps back down on the bench as Affric cradles his head. He gazes at the fire with thoughts of the funeral pyres of Glen Afton before him as he begins to tell Affric everything about what has happened at Ach na Feàrna and Glen Afton. He also tells her in detail of the cruelty that had been inflicted upon the bodies of his family and kinfolks. He loses all sense of time sitting with Affric when he feels a sob beside him, he looks at Affric and sees she's in tears, then he feels a gentle arm lay across his shoulders as Christina smothers him in a caring embrace, she stands back, wiping tears from her eyes. "We are so sorry Wallace," says Fellows. William turns round and sees Fellows and the innkeeper standing with two full bladders of Lübeck ale… also red eyed. "We brought you our best of our ale Wallace, but when we heard you telling Affric of your families awful demise, we couldn't walk away, we overheard everything." William looks to the fire once more; he hadn't meant to ever tell anyone…

Greatly saddened by talking of his recollections, he puts his head in his arms on the table as Affric puts her arms across his shoulders, "I truly understand you now Wallace," says Affric, "I understand your love for Marion and why you want it so pure and untarnished." Affric sobs again, then she continues, "I'm so sorry for my thoughtlessness, I truly would no' have wished to have heard all o' this. Oh Wallace, will you please forgive me?" William sits up and embraces Affric, for they are kin bonded in a shared grief. Christina sits on the other side of Affric and embraces both of them. The two wretches raise their jugs to William and smile with compassion in their hearts. Fellows and the innkeeper both sit inside the inglenook, looking totally at a loss upon hearing this story, Fellows speaks, "Wallace, I know now from Affric that English hands were at play in this, I say to you now that I am truly ashamed, I can only say that all English are not the same." William looks at Fellows, he's a bull of a man, strong and thick set. His eyes are like Affric, almond and deep. He thinks a moment then reaches out to Fellows and they shake hands, "I know…" sighs William. Everyone sits awhile saying nothing and drinking in moderation the Lübeck ale, even the two wretches share in the beautiful nectar.

Eventually William stands up, "I must be leavin' yie now ma friends, for I travel at first light to Dun Dèagh with vicar Mydford and a company of pilgrims." Affric stands up too, "Will you be coming back for me Wallace, take me home…? And I promise I will make my own way in life, I just want to get back home to my people the Gallóbhan Ceàrdannan." Affric's words strike a chord of understanding in William; perhaps this impromptu meeting and sorrowful sharing of grief has finally expelled her own demons. Putting his arms around her, William says, "I reckon it's time we all go home and live in peace Affric, for now I know that de Percy was responsible for all that we have suffered…. perhaps it is the right time for us to go back to our woodland home."

Affric clings to William while jumping with joy, "Oh thank you Wallace, thank you, thank you… I'll even bathe and ready myself for your return, oh, and Wallace…" suddenly she pauses apprehensively. Curious, William enquires, "Aye, what ails yie Affric…?" She looks at Fellows then she reaches out and holds his hand, gazing at him with affection. Realising Affric and Fellows have a hearts comfort with each other, William exclaims, "Mind…" he grins, "I would be honoured, for I owe this man so much more than I could ever repay." Affric turns and grabs Fellow's by the cheeks and shakes them, she says, "I am going home… we are going home… and Christina and Inny can come visit us too."

Christina and the Innkeeper pull Affric close in a warm tearful embrace. William jokes, "If the English don't arrest me, then I'll be back the morrow eve… Eh, no offence intended Fellows." The burly Englishman appears slightly shamefaced, he stands up and clasps William by the arm and takes him by the hand, "If there's anything I can do to help Wallace, you just have to ask." William looks at the Englishman and believes his sincerity. He says, "Look after Affric and I should be back for you both late the morrow night." Fellows replies, "I'll care of her Wallace, for she has all of my heart."

Looking at Fellows, William realises that the big Englishman is deeply in love with Affric, he can see there is a genuine bond of friendship growing between the Englishman and himself too, he says, "I'll come here and meet yie both, then we have to go to Kilspindie to meet with my aunt Margret and ma brother Alan, we can all travel back to Ach na Feàrna together, then we'll go on to the Wolf and wildcat forests after that." Affric exclaims, "You will take us back with you Wallace, wont you… take us home?" William looks at Fellows who nods back in approval after hearing Affrics heart felt plea. "Aye, that ah will bonnie darlin."

"Meet me here about midnight the morrow night."

Affric gazes at William, overjoyed. He sees her youthful beauty when they played and hunted the Galloway forests together as teenagers… "Wallace," says Fellows, "I've a brother soldier we may trust to help us move through to the west, Mathew of York, he too is an Egyptian, we can trust him. He'll get port passes for both Affric and I." Affric nods in agreement, "Aye, he's a good man too Wallace, we can sure trust him." William is heartily warmed by the bond that is forming with this Englishman, he knows now that not all English have such a hatred and contempt for his people.

Smiling at Fellow's, William replies, "The word of a Ceàrdannan is good enough for me." William sees Affric shaking with anticipation and joy, he says, "My word I'll be back the morrow night Affric, just you all be ready to leave." She immediately throws her arms around him. Years of pent up anger and grief being released near overwhelms her, William also feels the emotional release of all that has beset him since Affric confirmed the name de Percy. Affric sets her head back. Looks up at him and smiles innocently, "Thank yie Wallace, I thank yie for everything. Now I'm free to live and love once more." She reaches out to hold Fellows hand… "And Wallace, I promise I will never ask you to lay with me again… unless Marion and Fellows here are feelin the heat of the Ceàrdannan Fèis, then it should be fine and dandy for all four of us?"

Everyone laughs, then William embraces Affric, knowing his heart has a settled place for his friend… and just as importantly, Affric knows it too. William bids a warm farewell to all and makes his way back to the safety of the nave of Saint Johns. As he lay in his crib later that night, he reluctantly reflects on the brutal changing world he now finds himself in…

# Youɴg Selby

A ground frost glistens in the early morn as William, Lambertoun and Mydford stand shivering in the nave doorway of Saint Johns Kirk. Mydford speaks, "It's time to leave for Dun Dèagh… and you Lambertoun, God speed and we'll meet again soon at the great Council of Glasgow gathering next month." Lambertoun mounts his horse as William approaches him, "Go in safety Lambertoun, for ah'v enjoyed meeting with you again after all these years, and our friends from our past are fast disappearing… so I sure don't want to be grieving you next." Lambertoun smiles, "Wallace, you watch out too for we still have much to talk about." William smiles "Aye, and remember I have to continue with your religious education too yie know."

"MY religious education…" exclaims Lambertoun, "I think it otherwise Wallace." Both young friends laugh then Lambertoun continues, "You go safely my friend, for you're more at risk than anyone else that I know. God speed yie Wallace." Lambertoun waves, turns his horse and canters onto the north road on his long journey to Elgin. Meanwhile, the last of the Applecross pilgrims of Saint Máelrubai have gathered outside the nave and begin their slow processional journey towards Dun Dèagh, before their long sojourn to the northwest. Mydford calls out to William, "C'mon Wallace, the pilgrims are leaving and we cannot be tarrying here."

"I hope Moray is all right," says William, "it's not like him not be where he said he would be." Mydford nods his head, "Pray that he will be fine Wallace, for none are safe from the English should we displease our new masters." They mount their horses and amble slowly down through Saint Johns Toun and out the east gate in front of the pilgrims on their journey towards Dun Dèagh. As they clear the town perimeter defences, William speaks, "There are no' se' many English soldiers about this morning, what do you think the reason is for that?" Mydford replies, "I don't know, I can't be sure… but I heard some conflicting news after you left last night."

"Good news I hope?"

Mydford shakes his head and appears very somber, "I received dispatches informing me that Longshanks has seized the Kings treasury in Rosbroch and has withheld all our annuities due to King Eric of Norway for the Innes a' Gall and Sealtainn. (Shetland isles) Now King Eric is threatening to send a great fleet to take the Western isles back into the Norse dominion, which could mean a war between Scotland and Norway." William exclaims, "A war with Norway, how the fuck can Scotland go to war with Norway, Baliol's no' got an army and Longshanks has our necks under the boot of the English?" Mydford replies, "Precisely, But that would seem to be part of the plan by Longshanks, we Scots are a soft tongue caught between an anvil and a blacksmiths hammer." William enquires, "How long is Baliol going to appear as a complete incompetent fool? How can he defend the Innes a' Gall and the Sealtainn when he cannot raise an army on the mainland." Mydford replies, "Baliol is no fool Wallace, do not make that mistake, he has been trapped by the Scots nobles who woo Longshanks with his astute knowledge of internationally agreed laws of Kingship, but if it hadn't been

Baliol, then whoever took the Scottish crown would have been sold back an empty throne anyway. King John is a good man Wallace, I trust in him, as do many, as should you, for he is the only hope we have of pulling Scotland away from the abyss we now precariously hang over."

"Fuck," exclaims William, "It would seem that very few of our precious nobles show King John the same respect they showed to the Canmòre." Mydford nods in agreement, "Alexander Canmòre was a strong but fair ruler, though the dynasty he sprang from were extremely ruthless and very powerfull. Baliol by contrast is but the first of his line to be seated on the throne of Scotland, maybe the last of his line too, for many nobles including the houses of Comyn and the Brus believe that it should be them that is ruling this realm and do not support Baliol as they should." William exclaims, "The Comyns abuse him too?" Mydford replies, "Aye, though they and others should take their mark of honour and example of loyalty from lord Moray, for if anyone had a claim to bitterly resent a royal house of Scotland, it is the Moray."

"How so?"

Mydford replies, "The house of Moray suffered terrible injustice and much cruelty when the house of Canmòre quashed their power base in the North only a few generations ago, but the personalities of Alexander and Lord Andrew brokered a strong friendship and mutual loyalty for each other, all to Scotland's benefit I may add, a loyalty that has since served all who dwell here in this realm so well. That's why Alexander granted Lord Moray the title as lord chief Justiciar of Scotia, and by his good grace lord Moray is now passionately supportive of Baliol."

William looks past the majestic Kinfauns hills towards Kilspindie and sighs, "Do you ever get the feeling that you are being sucked into something really bad, and the harder you try to get away from it, the more you feel you are being pulled into it?" Mydford says, "Wallace, when this mission is accomplished, you must look to your own people and get them to safety in the heart of the Wolf and Wildcats until the English are driven out of our land. Once you have completed your duties for the Guardians, don't you get involved in anything that will jeopardise your family, we'll help look after your needs and wants while you prepare your kinfolks and the Gallóbhet, for someday we will call upon you and others like you when the time is right, and that can only be done when we are sure all our families are safe from retribution."

Listening intently, William nods in agreement, then he begins to observe the pilgrims walking over the freezing ground with only skin thin sandal's on their feet, he can't understand their belief and faith, not when so much has already happened abroad in the whole of the realm, leaving no family untouched by the troubles.

Mydford says, "There appears to be little sign or interest shown in us by the few English soldiers and guards we've seen this morning, I think we can safely leave the pilgrims behind and ride on to Dun Dèagh. I'm thinking it's safe enough now to do so alone." William smiles, "Lead on then Mydford, the sooner I get this information to Lord Moray, the sooner I get back to gather ma family and get into the Wolf and wildcats for safety, I'll also be taking a wee Gallóbhan Aicé back to Galloway with us too." Mydford glares at him.

William enquires, "What's wrong?"

Mydford reaches behind him and pulls forward a heavy black brat and cowl. "Put this over your léine Wallace, for you're dressed like a murderous Galloway Gallóglaigh. The least attention we bring to ourselves the better." Dutifully, William pulls on the black monks brat and cowl then smiles at Mydford, he enquires with a cheeky grin, "Any confessions?"

Mydford glares humorously at William, "I confess that you most certainly made the right decision to leave the calling of the faithful Wallace."

They both laugh and move their horses into a canter towards Dun Dèagh, crown of the ancient kingdom of Circeànn. After a few hours of uneventful riding, they reach the wooden outer defence pickets of the Dun Dèagh seaport. On their approach, there appears to be many English squadrons of cavalry and soldiers milling about with purpose, William enquires, "What do you think is going on?" Mydford looks around then points, "I don't know, but look over yonder to the port beaches, there are many English ships coming ashore on the high tide… and they are sitting high in the water-line, which means they cannot be here to deliver any cargo." William says, "That must mean they're here to take something away." Mydford nods, "This is very strange, very strange indeed."

They wander unchallenged past Dun Dèagh castle and notice that the English are leading many carts laden with tremendous amounts of meat, dried fish and wool-packs towards the boat landings on the foreshore. The town of Dun Dèagh is bustling and thronging with many traders gathered for the winters fair on the Mayfields. Unusually, William and Mydford notice many lowly Scottish knights and their entourage are mixing freely with their English counterparts, but what the companions notice most is the atmosphere of an extremely tense township. "What's happening?" enquires William. Mydford observes the unusual stream of Scots knight's, English soldiers and variety of tradesmen thronging the narrow streets of the seaport.

"I really don't know Wallace, this is a most unusual sight." They ride on through the centre of the ancient town, passing the busy the Marketgate and on towards the Seagate, till they feel a great sense of relief upon reaching the safety of the Blackfriars College, a place familiar to William, where he had spent many summers as a pupil and where he had first met his old tutor Mydford. As they pass under the first arch into the courtyard, William looks up at the carved stone lockstone and sees the words 'Prestante Domino' he remembers those words so well, 'Under the Leadership of God' he thinks, But who does God really lead?

On entering the main courtyard, William sees a few horses tied in the courtyard of the old church college and some surly looking Scot's soldiers, all well armed and looking extremely agitated. William studies their dress of chainmail haubergeon and sealskin brats, they also wear Norse style helmets with long nasal pieces, similar to his own Gallóglaigh brethren. "Wallace…" A voice calls out. William looks around to see who calls out his name, when he sees a stocky Grey-friar standing looking at him from below the shelter of a broad cowl. "Who…" The stocky Grey-friar pulls back his cowl. "Dáibh." exclaims William. Dáibh grins then calls out, "How are yie doin' there brother Wallace?"

Jumping from his horse William embraces Dáibh then stands back and looks at his strange religious apparel. "Friar Dáibh…" laughs William, "What are yie doin' dressed up as a feckn Grey-friar?" Dáibh laughs, "Ah was going to ask you the same question Wallace, with you dressed up as a Black-friar." William looks down at his own black bell-sleeves and remembers he's wearing Mydfords brat and cowl.

"C'mon Wallace," says Dáibh, "Lord Moray and Bishop Nicholas of Brechin are anxiously waiting to see yie, they don't have much time here as Longshanks is travelling throughout Scotland and everyone of note must pay homage to him. Lord Moray must be travelling back to the lands of Petty and Avoch directly after this council." William looks

at Dáibh curiously, "So Longshanks is still here in Scotland?"
Dáibh sighs, "Aye… So much for us having a new King, well
we do, but it's Longshanks who struts his bones as he pleases
all about our realm now, not Baliol." William sighs, "Though
Baliol be king in name, I fear that his tabard will remain an
empty one that rules nothing but a poisoned chalice."

Dáibh stops and faces William, "I've heard what happened
to the family Wallace, if there's anything that I can do, you
just ask, and I mean anything…" William looks keenly at
Dáibh, though they only ever met on rare occasions in their
lives, they are kindred spirits and strongly bonded by honour
as brothers. William replies, "I thank yie for yer thoughts
Dáibh, but I want to get this duty over with and get back to
the Wolf and wildcats and then get lost as far away from this
madness as ah can, for the bonnie Marion is now with child
and all we would now wish is to be left alone and in peace."
Dáibh puts his hand on William's shoulder, "Ah understand."

Suddenly Mydford calls out, "WALLACE… Come with me,
we have no time to be wastin' with idle chatter." Dáibh smiles,
"I see that Mydford has no' changed much." William smiles
as Dáibh continues, "And you're going to be a father, Lady
Daun will be pleased to be hearing o' this Wallace, hmm…
dyie think the wain will have ginger hair?" William laughs,
"Fuck off." Then he enquires, "Is young Andrew Moray here?"
Dáibh looks back at William with concern, "Naw, I thought
he went to Saint John's to meet you, I assumed he was behind
you or nearby when you and Mydford rode into the college
quarters." William says, "I didn't see him in Saint John's Toun,
he was not at the Kirk or Bargee Inn, I wonder where he
is then?" Dáibh looks at William, "Ach he'll be fine enough,
he and big Robyn MacGilchrist rode away 'Officially' with
a troop of fifty of Lord Moray's retinue on state business…
something to do with Longshanks visit, so no harm will be

his from the English soldiery this day." William and Dáibh continue talking as they follow Mydford into the religious college. They walk along the cloisters till they come to the east door of the chapter house.

As they enter a large octagonal room, William sees a group of men dressed in a variety of lavish clothing, noticing that four are from the religious hierarchy, then he sees what he thinks to be the lord Moray, a tall man with his long black hair tied back and wearing very fine chainmail cloaked in surcoats emblazoned with the Moray coat of arms. He also wears a fine wolverine brat and golden chains of office, he turns on hearing them enter; William senses he is in the presence of one who carries great authority. "Ah Mydford," says Lord Moray, "At last, your here…"

The two men shake hands warmly upon greeting, then Mydford speaks, "My Lord, this is William Wallace, son of Alain." Lord Moray looks deeply into William's eyes. "I offer you my hand in your time of grief Wallace, your uncle Malcolm was a very close and loyal friend, as was your father, I was greatly distressed when I heard of what had happened to them, and that of your family." William replies, "Thank you ma Lord, my father always spoke with a fondness when he talked of you and the house o' Moray."

Lord Moray smiles briefly, "I thank you Wallace. Now, to the business in hand, may I introduce to you Bishop Nicholas of Brechin; he's drafting appeals to Rome that urgently requires the signature and seal of Wishart." William and Nicholas warmly acknowledge each others presence, then Nicholas says, "It's good to meet you Wallace, you do understand the importance of making delivery of this appeal to Wishart, Scotland's very future as a sovereign realm is contained within these documents." William replies, "I do." Nicholas continues, "Good, we will have them all prepared and sealed for you by the mid-day bells." William enquires, "I thought it was to be a verbal message my lord." Lord Moray replies, "Too much has transpired in such a short period Wallace, everything in the dispatches is coded in the event you are stopped and these writs are read, none shall know the truth of the content, not even you should you be pressed." Nicholas says, "All the dispatches will carry the diplomatic seals of His Holiness apostolic legate, even Longshanks himself would dare not stop you if you carry those."

Nicholas and some of his scribes move over to a bench in the charterhouse to continue with their deliberations and to provide William coded tang scrieve. Mydford speaks, "My Lord, why are there so many English ships berthing in the sand ports, what's going on?" Lord Moray replies while William and Dáibh listen nearby, "Longshanks is cutting short his imposition of homage and returns to England in great haste, he is raping our country and taking all our winter stocks of meat, meal corn and all taxations raised to London, and anything else the English can carry away with them as part payment for their garrison expenses."

Mydford is perplexed, "Are the English garrison troops leaving Scotland for good?" Lord Moray replies, "If only it were so Mydford, I have it on good authority that they leave so quickly because of the trade denied them by a French naval blockade, many of our friends from Bayonne and Flanders are running blockades in the absence of the main English fleet being up here, they're even attacking Longshanks ships in Yarmouth and Portsmouth. The Flemings, Genoese and also the French fleet of King Philip is driving the English navy away from their French coastal berths too. Now Longshanks gathers a large seafaring force at Tilbury docks near London, with the aid of the Gascons and low country fleets from count Floris of Holland who are now sending their combined fleets across from Ireland to help repulse these attacks." Mydford replies, "This is surely good news my lord and it must bode well for Scotland. So this is why Longshanks ships are on the longshore, he must now release his blockade upon us to send his navy and soldiers back to England against any possible French attack, perhaps Baliol can now gather an army to protect us from this English King and his evil yolk... is this not possible, for we see this English Kings weakness, his ambition is greater than his resources?"

"It's a disaster either way we see it Mydford," replies Lord Moray, "The English have already stripped the north of all grain and cattle, they've impoverished the country by penal taxations, now they intend to impose the harshest of martial law upon us. I know of many treacherous Scots nobles who have broken bread with Longshanks who now plan to bring the north to heel and under feudal servitude and into his service, already many of our young men are in the holds of those ships, bound against their will to serve in his coming war with the French. I tried to intervene, but Longshanks said that I must swear fealty to him or resign into exile."

Mydford exclaims, "They would remove you as lord chief Judiciary of Scotia?" Lord Moray says, "The Scots lords of the North who are in the pocket of Longshanks are to raise their retinues and march into my lands with an army under the command of the new English governor of Scotland, Lord John de Warenne, a prominent English nobleman and military commander of high rank. He is to contain the whole of the north at his Kings peace and maintain English authority. Amongst these Scots nobles in receipt of the English king's good grace who will march with de Warenne into my lands are Sir Gartnait MacDomhnaill the Mormaer of Mar, and John Comyn, thane of Buchan, they've been instructed to remain in the lands of Moray under the orders of De Warenne until all dissent and disturbance has been crushed or eliminated."

"Eliminated?" gasps Mydford, he shakes his head, "we all know that this simply means murdered my lord, we should be rallying all of the west coast and border clans who are kin to us, Gartnait is married to the sister of Robert Brus so he is in Longshanks camp for sure, MacDomhnaill is also in league with Longshanks and King Eric of Norway, for he has no love of Scotland, but Comyn?" Lord Moray replies "Comyn has no great love for the house of Moray, didn't his ancestors dash the brains of our children on great stones for the cause of the house of Canmòre, all within living memory, and all that slaughter so the Canmòre house may rule unchallenged on the throne of Scotland." Mydford sighs, "Then all is lost in this forsaken land Lord Moray, if Baliol cannot unite all Scots against English tyranny, then who is there to free Scotland from this impending catastrophe?"

"Wallace," whispers Dáibh "This is a serious feckn situation…" They continue to listen as Lord Moray replies, "I fear it is only a matter of time before I am imprisoned or executed, that is why we must move now with extreme prejudice for our cause, and you Wallace, we must waste no more time on politics. I have the completed death lists for you to take back to sir Ranald. The Bishop of Brechin will soon have the papal communiqué ready for Wishart and your writ of pass. Now come with me and I will tell you all you need to know about the death lists."

Suddenly a guard comes barging in through the door and calls out, "A large group of armed riders approach my lord, they are riding fast and hard towards the College." Lord Moray calls out, "Quickly, prepare yourselves." William turns to Dáibh, "What will we do?" Dáibh replies, "Follow lord Moray, if this is the English come for him, we must protect him at all costs, even with our own lives if needs be." Dáibh sees the uncertainty in William's face, "Just stick by my side Wallace."

Everyone pulls their swords from their scabbards and make ready to exit through the doors of the chapterhouse, when another guard calls out, "It's young Andrew and his men…" Lord Moray turns to William; "This has become our daily life now Wallace, we do not fear the English, but we certainly fear their intention. You should prepare your horses to make speed back to the west coast as soon as possible." The doors to the chapterhouse open and young Andrew comes rushing through, accompanied by his loyal bodyguard Robyn MacGilchrist and a group of his loyal men. As Andrew approaches his father, William could see an expression of extreme concern on his face. Lord Moray enquires. "What ails yie boy?" Andrew looks at William as Andrew replies, "Wallace I don't know…"

William is puzzled by Andrew's hesitation. Lord Moray glances at William; then he looks at his son and enquires, "What news boy?" Andrew hesitates, still looking at William, then he says, "Wallace, the English were combing the country around Saint Johns Toun looking for cattle, corn and gathering taxes… they showed no mercy upon those who resisted…" William is still puzzled then it hits him like a lightning bolt, "Affric…" Andrew shakes his head, "No… there is no other way to say this Wallace; it's your foster mother, Margret, your uncle Alex, his wife and sons too…" William immediately reacts, "What about them?" Andrew puts his hand on Williams shoulder, "They are all dead Wallace. I'm so sorry…" William is stunned to hear this news. He staggers back and stammers, "What… How? I mean how can they be dead…" his head spins with such nausea he almost passes out. He turns and grips a handrail to steady himself. Lord Moray and Mydford reach out, but he pushes them away, "Leave me..." The room falls silent. Many in attendance who have already experienced what William is going through say nothing, nobody knows what to do or say to their young friend. Lord Moray approaches him. "Wallace, whatever you may wish to do, these next words will not bring you comfort and may not make any sense right now, but you must get back to your kinfolk in Ach na Feàrna, we will find alternative measures for our needs." William retorts in anger, "I have no family needs at ach na Feàrna, wee Maw is protected, as are my sisters, oh lord, but how do I tell them..."

William bows his head... no one knows what he is thinking or what he may do. For the next few moments the silence in the room becomes almost unbearable; then he speaks, "I will fulfil my duty to yie Moray, but after that it would be best that you all leave me well alone, for I fear for anyone who would call me a friend when I react to this..."

There is heartfelt sympathy and understanding for William, as he looks at young Andrew Moray and enquires, "Moray, how did it happen?" Andrew replies, "We were travelling at speed to meet with you last night, but we got held up by English troops coming out of the Glendale's of Kilspindie. One of the English soldiers told us of their mission there, and that's where we went instead of our meet with you, to see if we could find and help any survivors. But when we reached Kilspindie, we found that the English had swept through and slaughtered everyone..." Andrew falters, then he continues, "We found Margret hanging from the gatehouse walls with other members of your family and all of the cotters and villagers. Apparently when the English heard that they were Wallace and originated from the west coast, they executed them immediately and everyone else they found in the Balloch of Kilspindie." William pleads, "There were no survivors?" Andrew replies, "There was a survivor who told us everything, we found him hanging, but he wasn't dead." William grabs Andrew, "Where is he, is he with you, I must speak with him?" Andrew replies, "He is being tended in the college hospital Wallace, I'll take you to him now." William stares manically at Andrew.

"What, where is Margret, what's happened to her body, I must take her back to Ach na Feàrna…"

Andrew replies, "We've shrouded her and all the family Wallace, then we buried them all in an unmarked grave for fear the English would cause further desecration upon them. I'll take you there and show you where they rest." William enquires desperately, "What of my brother Alan, where is he, is he dead too?" Andrew appears confused, "We never saw your brother; I didn't know he was there. It is likely he may have been meeting with the Applecross pilgrims, for we heard they were gathering for religious blessings for their journey." William exclaims, "We must leave now…"

"NO," says lord Moray. He continues, "I am truly sorry for your loss Wallace, but if you intend to fulfil your mission, you must not go near Kilspindie, your duty is now to the living. You must get back to Wishart as quickly as you can, for there is none other that I can spare that Wishart could trust but yourself." William rages and punches the door, splitting the thick wood panel, Dáibh puts his hand on his shoulder, "Wallace, Lord Moray is right, I'll come with you and then we may consider what is best for your kinfolk when you've delivered lord Moray's message to Wishart."

Andrew speaks, "I'll come with you too Wallace, and my men." Lord Moray says "No, you cannot go with him Andrew, it's paramount that you do not fall into English hands without a warrant of protection, Wallace must risk all on his own, for on first light the morrow, the English will employ a new martial law here that no Scot may move freely or travel about any shire without a port pass from an English sheriff or Constable, even a messenger of a Papal Legate. Also, none may leave this shire's borders under pain of death. I dare not risk your life my son."

Looking at Andrew and Dáibh, William says, "Your father is right Moray, I would travel faster and be safer on my own." Andrew looks back at his father in reluctant resignation, William enquires, "Moray, will you take me to see the survivor from Kilspindie?" Lord Moray nods to his son in approval. Andrew replies, "I will Wallace, come with me now." William enquires, "Who is this survivor, what's his name, do you know him?" Moray throws back his mantle over his shoulders then replies, "He said his name is Short Jock of Kilspindie." William thinks a moment, "strange, I've not heard of that name before around Kilspindie... but I must speak with him, take me there now Moray, for I must know everything that has happened and who was responsible."

Raising his hand, Lord Moray says, "I offer you my sympathies once more Wallace, but I urge you to linger only a little time with this man, for come the midnight hour, and though you carry the warrant writ and seals as a messenger on behalf of the Papal Legate, none may travel freely or safely in Scotland by morn. When you hear the mid-day bells, return here and be prepared to leave at once." Andrew, Dáibh and William acknowledge Lord Moray then leave immediately to go to the college hospital to meet with short Jock. As they exit through the door, Lord Moray nods to Robyn MacGilchrist.

"Follow them Rob, and make sure they do not leave the College, for I saw that Wallace shed no tears for his dearest kin's demise, only inflamed anger... and that's a dangerous sign, for it fuels the burning hatred he has raging within him. I fear he may be reckless and could be dangling from an English gibbet soon, I don't want my son with him when his rage erupts, and it will." Rob replies, "Aye my Lord."

Rob exits the chapterhouse just as the three friends reach the hospital doors. William pauses, "Wait here, I'm wanting to talk to Jock alone." Dáibh and Moray look at each other, they too had noticed William had not shown any sympathy or grief upon hearing the terrible news, quite the opposite of what any could have expected, they also know that makes him a danger and a great risk to those near him. William's demeanour is stone cold emotionless as he talks to Moray and Dáibh, "I must speak with Jock alone, for I need to know everything, who, why… I want to know every piece of information that this man remembers, so I ask of you, will yie please wait outside ma friends, I need your understanding to favour me?"

The two friends nod in agreement.

Andrew says, "We'll wait here for you Wallace." Dáibh says, "I'll tack up Warrior and harness Fleetfoot, but yie cannae be long abiding about here, as soon as you have gleaned all from this Jock fella, you must be going back to Wishart and then on to protect Marion."

William looks at his friends as though his mind is now in another place; then he speaks with a fondness in his heart, "Aye, my Marion…" He turns and enters the hospital and closes the door behind him. Dáibh says, "I've no' seen the Wallace look like that before." Andrew replies, "I thought I knew him too Dáibh, but that look in his eyes, and the feeling that emanates from him, I wouldn't want to be the one who tries and stop him venting the murderous conviction he has in is his heart, especially if he meets with the opportunity for release, and who could blame him?"

Rob silently catches up with them, he says, "I have seen

that look before, young Wallace in there is soon for the hangman or the headsman's sword… and before the next full moon ah reckon. Your father's right Moray; keep away from Wallace, for death stalks his kind."

Andrew and Rob wait by the small hospital door as Dáibh goes to tack up Warrior and Fleetfoot, preparing them for William and a fast move out of Dun Dèagh, then homeward with his vital information for Bishop Wishart. Almost an hour passes then the mid-day bells can be heard. Dáibh comes back with Warrior and Fleetfoot, he enquires, "Is he no' out yet?" He continues, "Lord Moray is growing impatient and needs Wallace to be leaving Dun Dèagh soon." Moray and Rob look at each other in sudden realisation, they burst open the doors of the hospital and rush in to see Jock laying fast asleep on a crib, but no William to be seen. Moray shakes Jock violently, waking him, Rob grabs Jock, "Where's Wallace?"

Jock, still sleepy and in great pain as he wakes, tries to answer… Rob shakes Jock and demands with a thunderous voice, "Where's Wallace?" Jock sits up holding his throat, still pained from the rope burn blisters on his neck, he speaks with a broke and croaky voice; "Isn't he with you?" A young friar approaches and enquires about the disturbance, "Good sirs, are you looking for the big Gallóglaigh who was speaking with master Jock?" Rob replies, "Aye…Where is he?" The young friar points to the back door, "He left by the east gate a while ago." Andrew exclaims, "Fuck… Go quickly Rob, tell my father that Wallace has disappeared, Dáibh and I will go up into the town and try to find him." Rob says, "No Moray, you go and report this to your father that Wallace has disappeared, Dáibh and I will search for him, we cannot take any chances with the English over your safety." Andrew feels frustration and anger, but before he can object, Rob commands, "Go Moray." Andrew replies, "Aye fine, ahm goin' but if your not back with Wallace within the hour; then I'll bring my men and we'll tear this town apart till we find him, and the English too if they try and stop us… be warned."

"C'mon Dáibh," says Rob, "We'd better be finding Wallace before he finds the English, for ma bones are telling me that no good will come of this. Wallace has the madness in his head so bring your bow and a full quiver too, we'll need them if Wallace entangles himself with the English before we can get a hold of him, then it's up to us to kill him."

Andrew is aghast upon hearing these words, he stammers in disbelief, "Kill him? You can't kill Wallace…" Rob replies resolutely, "Aye we can, and we will, for he knows too much. If he's confronted and caught by the English and they question him, then for sure all will be undone if he talks, and we cannae take that risk Moray." Dáibh nods in approval, "Aye Moray, though he be like a brother to us all, any who does not pull a forelock to the English when they meet with them on the streets, they will surely be beaten or even killed for sedition, and by the look on Wallace's face and his dwelling on the thoughts of Margret and his kinfolk of Kilspindie, he'll not be thinking what the consequences would be from any confrontation." Andrew stammers, "But yie cannae kill Wallace, he's our friend, our brother…" Dáibh replies, "Aye, a good friend and the finest brother a man could have in this life, I vouch for him on my own life, but even though he be my brother in spirit, for the sake of our realm I agree with Rob here, if we cannae find him in safe countenance, then we must surely make his death clean and make it swift."

Not far away from this life or death debate, William wanders aimlessly through the old streets and markets of Dun Dèagh, his mind lost in another place, thinking of Margret, his uncle Alex, the family… he tries to rationalise why the English are singling his family out for murder. '*Why?*' he mumbles. That little word has returned to his thoughts to haunt him, a small word that holds in its own peculiarly passive way, the future of his world. '*Why*' He keeps repeating in his head, if he knew "why" then he could be decisive, he could be better disposed, he could be free of a heavy burden and free to choose his future without the pain of grieving and the unknown, but as much as he tries to rationalise the cause or purpose of English intent, there is no answer that comes to him as to "Why."

His sense of surroundings briefly returns and he finds himself outside a busy Inn near the Westport of the Castle. Resting on a bench, he tasks the innkeeper to bring him a flagon of whisky, which is duly delivered. He sups the nectar copiously while brooding and watching the life of Dun Dèagh pass by. He studies the miserable downtrodden faces of the Scots, so strained and etched with a fear of the English as the local population shuffle past. He watches curiously as those who pass near English soldiers immediately look down to the ground and pull their forelock. He observes as rowdy and drunken English soldiers abuse, misuse, push and bully their way through the frightened population. William laughs, thinking that he could just rise up and defend them all right now, for he feels no fear, no fear at all, then he's lost again in his thoughts once more, ignoring all the trepidations and tribulations suffered by everyone else around him, for he sullenly believes he hadn't defended those who needed him most, his family.

The day is getting late, with Rob, Dáibh and the men of Moray searching the streets and markets of Dun Dèagh for William, but to no avail. He sits alone on a bench outside the inn, oblivious to the angst of his friends. He drinks his last drop of whisky from the large flagon, which has no apparent nor obvious effect on him, then he stands up and wanders across the Mayfield's and closer to Dun Dèagh Castle, where many English troops are busily travelling to and fro. He slumps down against a far corner of the castle wall to watch the English soldiers and their knights go about their business of bringing peace to Scotland. Suddenly he's disturbed by a hefty kick in the legs, he stirs with the impact, he lazily sits up thinking, '*Fuck, where ahm I? Ah must have fallen asleep...*'

Again he is kicked hard on the thigh, he raises his hand to shield his eyes from the bright daylight as he looks up to see who's kicking him.

An English voice commands, "Raise yourself you drunken Scotchman... and bow low before your betters." William slowly pulls his legs close as he squints up and tries to focus on who it is that has disturbed his respite.

The whisky hasn't made William drunk, it has only served to make him sleep and give his torment momentary peace. The voice again commands curtly, "I said, raise yourself up you great Scotch clod." William is still trying to gain a focus when he hears the voices laughing, then feels warm water pouring on his head, then suddenly he realises... '*Ach naw, fuck, what the fuck... not again, not this time.*'"

He pushes his back hard against the castle wall and woozily stands up, wiping his léine sleeves and pulling his fingers through his hair, he sniffs his fingers, recoils and spits on the ground. His demeanour immediately changes as he growls, "Ya dirty English Bastards." he moves sluggishly forward, but before he can make contact... "Hold him fast." commands the voice. William is gripped firmly from behind by both arms and held securely by two English soldiers. He tries to focus on his antagonists and sees two English squires in fine tabards and chainmail with dropped coifs staring at him, they are obviously from families of great importance. He looks at them with their peculiar styled haircuts. Unexpectedly, William laughs out loud… "Fuck, this is the first time I've seen Englishmen dressed as women, fuck me, aren't you two a pair o' right ugly bitches, go on, fuck off and gie' me peace." Then he spits on the ground at the feet of the Englishmen, much to the chagrin of the two squires.

One of the squire's says, "What shall we do with this ignorant Scotch clod who robes in these party coloured rags that Scotchmen appear to be so fond of wearing?" The other squire laughs, "This befuddled Scotch simple thinks something is so very funny… then let us make the clod laugh some more by providing sport for our men?" the first squire is curious, "How so?" the second squire replies, "May I suggest perhaps, a public flaying?" The first squire exclaims, "A flaying?" The second squire replies, "Yes Selby, I believe your father would enjoy a spectacle such as a flaying, I have seen it applied with great delicacy once before only recently." Selby replies, "My dearest Percy, what a wonderful idea, and by the size of this creature, it may take some time though." William overhears the name of Percy and thinks quickly as his befuddled brain begins to clear. *'Too many times have I been carefree and unsuspecting of my circumstance in the company of the English, and I've suffered for their version of peace, but this time I'm brought to front a Percy?'*

Selby sneers, "Look at you Scotchman, what devil hath dressed you in a mantle of green rags and shit coloured plaid, don't you know that green is a colour your station may never wear? What say you dressed in the garb of rebels… are you a spy?" William drops to his knees, freeing himself from the surprised soldiers. He covers his head with his hands and begins sobbing and pleading, "Please my lord, I am but a simple hunter who is lost, I seek only to return to my native lands to be with ma family." De Percy speaks, "Don't you know hunting has been outlawed in the name of King Edward, we may now hang you as an outlaw by your own confession." Selby and de Percy laugh out loud; then Selby nods at the two soldiers who are holding William loosely by the shoulders to let him go. The two soldiers look at each other then cautiously release their grip. William drops his arms by his sides and begins rocking back and forth on his knees pleading, while looking at the feet of Selby, much to the amusement of the English squires. Selby then notices something peculiar and interesting, he enquires, "What is that you have in your belt there Scotchman, is that a noble's dagger?" Selby has noticed the pure polar-white hilt of Williams dirk... the honour of William's grandfather. De Percy sees the head and handle of the dirk, thinking it looks very familiar... Selby commands, "Give me that dagger..."

Without warning, de Percy kicks William hard in the face, his head strikes the castle wall with a sickening crack, but still he reverts to rocking on his knees, pleading to go home. Selby laughs as William slowly pulls out his dirk, "This Scotch brute makes great humour Percy, what a coward, I ask you once more Scotchman, give me your..." Seeing William's dirk, De Percy suddenly remembers... immediately he shouts aloud in a great panic, "SELBY..." But it's too late, William thrusts his dirk forward at speed and stabs upwards driving the fifteen inches of keen blade deep into the groin of the first English soldier, as he falls William rises up pulling his blade out of the man; then he sweeps backwards, cutting deep through the jaw and down the side of the second soldiers throat, slicing through a major artery, causing blood to spray out and hitting Selby in the face. As both soldiers drop to the ground dying, de Percy pulls out his sword and backs away. Selby wipes the blood from his eyes and looks up at William who is now towering over him. Stepping back in fear, Selby pulls his sword from its scabbard and shouts at William, "Drop your weapon Scotchman, or I shall run you through…" De Percy shouts from a distance, "Selby, wait for assistance, I think I know this man and his cowardly breed…"

Selby enquires desperately as he trains his sword on William. "What say you Percy?" William glares at de Percy while keeping Selby securely in his peripheral vision. De Percy momentarily can't speak because of the intense glare from William, in that instant both men know in a primeval sense who each other actually is. De Percy calls out, "He's from a house of seditioners Selby, they are all traitors, bandits and murderers, this man is a brigand chief, I know this from the markings on his dagger, he's a Wallace…"

Suddenly William roars at the top of his voice and lunges directly at de Percy, Selby raises his sword to smite him down but William quickly sidesteps the downward strike and slashes Selby across the face with his blade, cutting deep through Selby's ear, cheek and down through his jaw to his top lip. Selby screams in pain as a large crowd begins to gather around them, hemming them both inside a human cock-fighting pit trapped against the castle wall.

Selby is in shock and in total disbelief as he tries to stem the blood pouring from his face. Meanwhile, de Percy uses the shelter of the gathering crowd to start running at a fast pace towards the gatehouse of Dun Dèagh castle gates, screaming for help. William and Selby are now locked in a human arena as more gather to witness the spectacle of a lowly Scotsman standing up to the slight and aggression of an English lord. Selby regains his composure as he And William begin to circle each other. Selby senses the very real danger that he is now in from the giant stealthily stalking him like a rabid hungry wolf. Panicking, Selby blurts out nervously, "I… I am the son of Lord Selby, the honourable constable of

Dundee… a brother knight to sir Alan Fitz-Alan of Beedale, governor of this province. So I order you immediately Scotchman, put down your weapon and I give you my word, your death will be swift and I shall be there to make sure it is merciful." William's face carries a thunderous expression as they begin to weigh each other up, he watches the body language of the Englishman closely, then says, "Your courage doesn't back up the vinegar and vim of your false-based words Selby. So I say to you now Englishman, I'll relinquish my weapon to none other than my maker."

Selby becomes extremely nervous at this momentary impasse as he studies William; perhaps he has been sorely mistaken in thinking this "Scotchman" to be a coward. His dilemma is interrupted as William speaks to him calmly, "Listen to me Selby, I will leave you in peace, for I've no quarrel with you, even though you mistreat and dishonour me in front of my fellow countrymen, but I implore you, let me walk away… and you may live…"

Selby hears the words, everything in his mind is telling him to heed the warning and just let William go, but his pride is too great, misguided honour and saving face is uppermost in the mind of this proud young Englishman, even though his heart is telling him, Don't do it. Squire Selby tries desperately to summon up his courage in front of the mob of Scots, nervously he replies, "Wallace, de Percy says that you are seditious and from a family of vermin that must now be extinguished, so I order you for the last time, lay down your weapon."

Dáibh and Rob are drawn to the large gathering in the Mayfield, then Dáibh sees William standing near the centre of the crowd, but he is not aware of the fraught situation as he can't see Selby. Dáibh calls out to Rob, "There he is over there…" Rob looks across the Mayfield towards the gathering crowd and sees him too, he says, "It looks like trouble brewing over there, quick, we'd better get him out o' there before he gets involved and any English are drawn to notice him." Dáibh and Rob move into the large noisy crowd, but they struggle to push their way through.

The hum of mumbling and whispering voices in the crowd sounds like the collective from a large honeybee hive. Rob pushes the stocky Dáibh through the crowd in front of him, and Rob, being of similar stature to William, gets close enough to look over the head of Dáibh and the crowd, he immediately realises the severity of the situation.

"Fucks sake," exclaims Rob, "he's facing off an English fuckin' squire." Dáibh exclaims, "Awe fuck naw… that there's young Selby, he's the son of the English Constable up here in Dun Dèagh." Rob pushes Dáibh forward aggressively, "Hurry Dáibh, shout out to Wallace, tell him to get th' fuck out o' there…"

Lowering the point of his blade, Selby has second thoughts, he utters, "Perhaps I have been mistaken Wallace… if you sheath your weapon, I will do likewise, then we shall go our separate ways, then perhaps we may settle this matter at another time as men of honour…" William looks intensely at Selby; he can see in the squire's eyes his desperate need to bring this to a bloodless conclusion without losing face. Tentatively they agree to part ways as Rob looks over the heads of the crowd, "Quick Dáibh, let him know we're here." Dáibh cups his hands and shouts at the top of his voice, "WALLACE…" Suddenly the crowd standing next to Rob and Dáibh look round; startled by the volume of Dáibh's call.

For a moment there is absolute silence… then a few of the crowd grin, turn and raise their fists in the air and begin to chant… "WALLACE…" Suddenly all of the grey looking inhabitants of Dun Dèagh start chanting, "WALLACE…

WALLACE... WALLACE..." Rob glares at Dáibh in utter frustration, "What the fuck have yie done Dáibh?" Looking back at Rob curiously, Dáibh shakes his head in dismay... "What the fuck do yie mean, what have 'I' done? It was you who told me to shout his fuckin' name."

As the roar of the crowd relentlessly chant 'WALLACE,' they both curse and begin to push their way aggressively forward and through the ecstatic chanting crowd of Dun Dèaghachan's. William and Selby hear the growing murmuring turn in to a chant, then riotous cheering... Selby desperately looks around, he realises he is surrounded by 'Filthy Scotchmen' now baying for his blood. He turns and looks at William, who speaks quietly to him, "Selby I appeal to you, let me go, for I only have one thought and that is to be home with my family, I have no wish to cause you harm." Selby laughs nervously, "It's too late Wallace... I cannot let you leave, for you have murdered two English Yeomen right before my very eyes... I cannot let you go, even if I wanted to... and I have my honour to think about, you understand."

Sensing the fear and reluctance in Selby's heart, William makes to move away, but Selby trains his sword and blocks his escape, he tries again to sidestep the Englishman, but he is blocked once more from leaving by the blade of Selby. Dáibh and Rob reach the inner circle that forms this human arena.

Dáibh calls out, "Quickly Wallace, get out o' there now, for English troops are coming fast from the castle and they'll be here in a few moments." William tries to duck away from Selby who has been momentarily distracted by Dáibh. Selby sees his opportunity when he understands Dáibh's words, he grips his sword with both hands, pulls back the blade for an overhead strike at William's head, but it's too late, with lightning speed, William steps in towards the impending blow and stabs Selby deep into the sidewall of his chest, piercing his heart. Appearing momentarily stunned, Selby freezes where he stands, holding his sword with both hands high above his head, William pulls the blade out and roars in anger as he drives the dirk blade deep under Selby's chin and pushes up with all his might, raising the shuddering body of Selby high into the air, for a moment Selby grips Williams wrists as his legs kick and flail about, then William heaves the body of Selby against the wall of the castle. Upon seeing the Englishman's body slump to the ground, the crowds erupt wildly, cheering "WALLACE… WALLACE… WALLACE…"

William stares at the bloody shaking body of Selby, again all he can think of is *Why?* He stands transfixed, completely oblivious to the noise and rapturous celebration now spreading throughout the Mayfield's of Dun Dèagh. Many start slapping him on the back as though he is their blessed saviour returned, then he hears Robs voice, "Wallace, for fucks sake; let's get out o' here." Catching William by each arm, Dáibh and Rob drag him through the crowds to make their escape with their young charge while the entire populace rapturously chant his name.

The massing crowd quickly degenerates into a riotous mob baying for English blood. As English soldiers arrive on the scene, they are pelted with rocks, eggs, shit… anything the mob could get their hands on. Ominously, the mood of the mob begins to change when they see the English soldiers hesitate. Years of repression and brutality now release and turn the mob into a rebellious assembly. The English, being heavily outnumbered, begin to back off and retreat towards the castle. At this sign of momentary weakness by the English, the mob gains courage and charge directly at the English soldiers, bludgeoning many to the ground, pulling others from their horses, beating them severely and taking their weapons. Dáibh, Rob and William stop for a moment under a sheltered walkway of a tavern observing the chaos. They witness English soldiers fleeing in all directions, trying desperately to get away from the murderous rioters. Rob looks at William, he says sternly, "What the fuck have yie done Wallace?" William shrugs his shoulders, "What have I done? I've done nothing other than grieve for my kinfolks. Me and that Englishman settled our differences and had agreed to part ways when you two started this riot." He looks at Rob, then his demeanour changes as he spits out words, "What the fuck is your problem MacGilchrist… would you rather I was dead?"

Rob is slightly taken aback at the anger and venom in William's voice, William continues "What do you mean what the fuck have I done? Do you want me to lay down where the English may piss on me and murder me? You can fuck off MacGilchrist, and ah'll warn yiez both here and now… I'm going home, and if you, Lord Moray or anyone else here tries to stop me…" Dáibh looks at Rob, "He's right Rob, what would you have done if these evil visitations had been brought upon you and yours, I would do no different if I were Wallace."

Rob looks at both his friends and knows that despite the greater scheme of things, he's relieved that William has survived. He shrugs a smile that's shared by all, then he grips his sword, "Come on then, we've go to get back to the College charterhouse before the English get consolidated and put this fuckin' riot down by extreme force, for it'll sure no' take them long to retaliate." Dáibh shakes his head, "Wallace, you've just killed the Constable of Dun Dèagh's son, there will be a fuckin' hell to pay for this now. Lord Selby will take revenge on the people of this land." Looking at his bloody hands, William whispers, "What choice did I…" Rob cries out, "LOOK OUT…" William turns and pulls away as a sword blade flashes across his face, he instinctively catches the wrist of the assailant and with his other hand still clutching the dirk, he stabs viciously into the neck of an English soldier, then he reverses the strength and direction of his grip, causing the soldier to flip onto his back, dropping his sword at William's feet. Another English soldier thrusts at him with his sword, William turns on the spot, stoops low and picks up the fallen Englishman's sword, spins on his heels and brings the sword down with such torque force, he cuts deep into the English soldiers neck, as he falls forward, William quickly plunges his dirk deep into the Englishman's head through his eye, killing him instantly. Immediately, William glances across the footpath to see Dáibh and Rob cleaving their way through four English soldiers…

Suddenly a red hot pain sears through Williams skull as large clump of hair on the side of his head is ripped out by the roots, he winces away as the sharp edge of a halberd axe pushes past his face, with clumps of his hair attached. He instantly grabs the passing halberd staff, raises the point high into the air then he spins low, catching the Englishman completely by surprise and bringing the keen edge of his sword with brute force across the legs of the English soldier, slicing cleanly through the kneecaps. As the soldier collapses to the ground, William swings the sword in an arc to bring it crashing down on the neck and collar bone of the hapless soldier, cutting deep, he pulls his dirk back then sinks it hard into the soldier's face. He turns to seek out Rob and Dáibh and sees that they too have felled another four assailants who now lay bloodied dead or dying at their feet. William laughs as he shouts to Rob and Dáibh "Now what the fuck have you two done?" Taking advantage of the momentary break, Rob and Dáibh rush over to William. Dáibh grins, "Fuck you Wallace, you've really started something now, but

I tell yie, this day has been long awaited and badly needed. Though I don't know how the fuck you will explain this to Lord Moray and the rest o' the council, for I don't think this is what they really had planned for the day." William looks at them, "What dyie mean, I should have to explain this, I had everything under control till you two butted in and started the riot up at the Mayfields." Rob and Dáibh are speechless at William's rational assessment, he continues, "I didn't fuckin' start this, you two did, I'd convinced the Englishman to let me pass, I could see it in his eyes. Naw, It was you Dáibh, you started it by chanting out ma name and getting the crowd to join in." Dáibh can't believe what William has said.

"I started it…?" exclaims Dáibh "Yie can fuck off Wallace, It was Rob here that started it, he told me to shout out to yie, so it was him who fuckin' started it, no' us…" William and Dáibh look at a surprised Rob as Dáibh continues, "You had better have a good explanation for Lord Moray Rob, not me or Wallace here." Rob looks at them both totally perplexed, William and Dáibh smile and wink at each other. They quickly regroup and begin to make their way back to the college charterhouse, as Dun Dèagh is now being set to flame and sword amid complete riotous chaos caused by the local populace uprising. English forces rush from the castle as more arrive from the harbour fleet. Now outnumbering the rioting population, the English soldiers beat them back by superior numbers and skill of war and weaponry.

"Look…" exclaims Rob, pointing towards the castle gates, Dáibh curses, "Fuck." as Squadrons of knights on heavy horses pour out the Castle gates, followed by light cavalry and more armed soldiers. Immediately they launch into the population of Dun Dèagh without mercy. Many fight back, but the English force is overwhelming and push the crowds back towards where the three of them now stand. Rob nudges

William, "Lets get back to the charterhouse and see what lord Moray wishes us to do."

The three companions make their way back to the College charterhouse, where a very agitated group of church hierarchy and nobles wait impatiently. After a short period of explanations, lord Moray slams his fists down on the alter, "You bloody fools, the whole of the north may see this as a signal to rise up against the English, and it's all because you idiots couldn't control yourselves…" Lord Moray glares at William, "And you Wallace, you were tasked with a simple duty, be discreet don't attract attention… and what do you do, you kill the Constable of Dundee's only son and many of his soldiers, then between you Dáibh and Rob here, Dun Dèagh now burns to the ground and there are riots in the streets, with maybe hundreds dying because of your reckless stupidity…"

Everyone remains silent, but William is infuriated, he cannot take any more chastisement.

"Fuck you lord Moray…"

The charterhouse council is stunned into silence once more, for none has ever spoken to Lord Moray this way… William continues, "I was sleeping, I awoke to find Englishmen pissing on me and kicking me about the legs, then they were going to flay and hang me just to satisfy their humour, and all because they could. I had to fight for my life, the fuckin' English, they kill and murder as they please. My kinfolk are still warm in their shrouds, and those of my family that are still alive, are either in fear for their lives or sorely wounded. It was not I that drove the folk of Dun Dèagh to rebel against this tyranny; it was the English themselves. You and your nobles Lord Moray, it's all caused by your fuckin' indecision over losing land, title and privilege while the rest of our people are being murdered, all because yiez cant make your fuckin' minds up, that's not putting Scotland first, that's putting your own self-interest first. Whilst I have respect for you as a man, how can I have respect for any Scottish noble who now feasts and sups with the English simply to save a privileged way of life, and all of this while the rest of us low-born Scots must bow our heads, or we face death every waking moment when we're met by any base English soldier on our own land, fuck you and fuck all our noble bastards, for they leave us commoners to our fate to save their own skins…"

Mydford attempts to intervene, "Don't Mydford…" growls William, "I will do my duty by delivering your deal with the devil, but don't expect me to fight your nobles war, not when you are all so keen to desert us common folk at the first sign your own life of luxurious living is threatened. I'll return to Marion; then you'll never see me again. Now give me what you need me to deliver and then I'll be gone from this warren of fuckin' white rabbits." The entire gathering of the charterhouse remains in stunned silence, no-one has ever heard Lord Moray spoken to this way; nor any noble.

"My lords," says lord Moray calmly, "If you would please give me a few moments here with young Wallace?" Everyone hastily leaves the Charterhouse to stand in the cloisters, all discussing the turn of events and waiting anxiously the outcome of the private meeting between lord Moray and William. Suddenly the door opens and a guard rushes in, "The English are coming here and fast…" Rob enquires urgently, "Are they troops or knights…" The Guard replies, "Both, it's Lord Alan Fitz-Alan with Lord Selby. They're approaching with a large contingent of soldiers." Rob opens the door to the charterhouse and shouts with great urgency to Lord Moray, warning him the English are gaining closer. Lord Moray waves everyone back inside, "Mydford, Wallace… Dáibh has your horses ready at the west port gate of the college, go now, we'll meet again, soon." Mydford and William make to leave when Lord Moray calls out, "Take care Wallace, and remember what I said…" Lord Moray grasps William by the hand and shakes it firmly when a voice calls out, "English soldiers are coming through the nave now…" Lord Moray puts his hand on Williams shoulder, "Go in safety Wallace… leave us, for if the English catch you here, all is undone." Acknowledging his companions, William and Mydford quickly depart through the south door of the Charterhouse, barely exiting when Fitz-Alan and Selby barge in through the front door of the charterhouse, "Lord Moray…" says a grim faced Fitz-Alan, "A word if you please…"

A little while later, William and Mydford reach the Dens of Brox hill. They look back at Dun Dèagh, glowing hellishly in the falling dusk sky from the fires set by the rioters. They turn their horses westwards and ride on towards Saint Johns toun. A few miles into their journey, they soon meet up with the pilgrims who had left with them earlier that morning. Mydford explains to the pilgrims about the draconian curfew that will be in effect by the morn, he also explains that it would be best for them all to return to Saint Johns Toun with them in relative safety, as it would most certainly not be safe to go on any farther, particularly the revenge the English will surely be meting out to any Scot due to the death of the Constable's son Selby. And so, the pilgrims of Saint Máelrubai turn and make their way back from where they had came from, escorted by Vicar Mydford, and William, safely disguised once more as a Black friar pilgrim of Saint John. Mydford looks at William and smiles… "God surely does move in mysterious ways Wallace…" William laughs, "Don't you mean the Goddess…?"

# Four Silver Pennies

itter driving sleet closes around the pilgrims as they struggle on their journey west on a darkening moonless night. The freezing sleet and rain soaks everyone to the skin, their misery compounded by the constant harassment from English night patrols ranging out from Dun Dèagh, desperately searching for the Brigand Chief William Wallace and his band of cut-throats, making the pilgrims arduous journey almost intolerable.

As time wears on, many are beginning to suffer from the intense biting sub-zero wind and incessant sleet driving hard into their faces. William turns to Mydford, "I can't do this anymore…" Mydford replies, "You cant do what anymore?" William replies, "This, I mean this madness that has engulfed us all, I can't get into my head what's happened, where everything we do to maintain our own peace only leads to cruelty, harsh reprisals or senseless killings from the English… Fuck, all I want is just to live in peace with Marion and get away from all o' this, though I will tell you this Mydford, the killings of my family haunts me each waking moment and I want to have my revenge so much… I need revenge… I need to do something. But when all thoughts of revenge are exhausted; then most of all, I just want left alone with Marion and live my life as it once was." Thinking awhile, Mydford replies, "I wish I had an answer for you Wallace, I truly do, but I don't, and you may take my word on what I say to you now, none of us may escape the changing world that is now falling upon us. Look you to your own experience and your own grief. Your family posed no threat in the greater scheme of things, yet they were touched brutally by forces greater than we could ever imagine and believe you me, it will come to pass that you will have to choose on which side you stand, or death will surely take you and all of yours, no matter where you run or try to hide."

Shaking his head in dismay upon hearing these words, William says, "I need to find the grave of Margret, I didn't have the time to question Moray as to where she is buried." Mydford replies, "I have already spoken with Lord Moray about this Wallace. It's been agreed that we will wait till we know what the English are planning next. When we deem it safe, Andrew, Lambertoun and I will travel to Kilspindie and take Margret's mortal remains to be interred in the holy ground of Dunfermline Abbey. When we have finally got rid of the English from our realm, we'll return all your uncle Alex's families mortal remains back to ach na Feàrna for a proper holy internment."

"I can't believe it." William takes a deep breath, "Mydford, it's so difficult, the loss of Margret, Alex, my family down in glen Afton and Ach na Feàrna, what harm had any of them done to warrant such cruelty. I tell you this, my mind is but a keen edge from madness, the visions, it's getting to me every waking moment and I feel it's tearing at my gut that I should strike every Englishman down as my sworn enemy rather than to meet him as another fellow traveller with an open hand of welcome, Mydford… I need help." Mydford replies, "I wish it were different for you Wallace, I wish it were different for us all, for I too have lost many of my own family under similar circumstances." William is surprised,

"I didn't know…" Mydford continues, "It's not just your family Wallace, we've all learned a very bitter lesson at the hands of these supposed English peacemakers."

Nodding his head by way of understanding, William says, "I've learned my final lesson in regards to the English." Mydford enquires, "And what is this lesson Wallace?" William replies solemnly, "I have learned that the English cannot be approached with an open hand of friendship, it would seem their holy men must be sanctifying them to lie and betray any who is not of their race; though I truly believe we are no different as a people. I have learnt to my cost that I can never trust them, nor will I have any dealings with them till we are free of their shackles to be our own people once again, just to be… all I want is the freedom for us to choose our own destiny, not to be told what to do from some usurper from some foreign city called London or Rome. Fuck, how could the world we knew change so much?" William pauses a moment, but the angst of seeking an answer burns his waking moments with raw torment.

"Why Mydford why…?" But there is no reply from Mydford as William continues, "They treat us like rebels, outlaws, less than vermin in our own land, yet our realm is full of enlightened Universities, schools and hospitals of learning, great cathedrals, prosperous towns and seaports. We have produced many great men and women of learning, yet the English say we are ignorant stinking savages. I just don't understand Mydford, we must gather our forces and fight back before it is too late." Mydford nods in agreement, "I understand and agree with you Wallace, many do, the English treat us as a conquered race, yet we have never shown them malice nor aggression, and though the Holy Church of Scotland is autonomous and seems to be separate from their imperial agenda, I see how their imported English clerics are now seated in all our places of learning. Many of those English had gained my respect, but now I find that they merely act for their paymaster Bishop Bek and not God almighty."

"And you Mydford, where are you in all of this?"

Mydford replies "I'm with Wishart, Bernard of Kilwinning, John Duns Scotus and many other great imminent faith leaders of Scotland who all feel as I do. We will defend our blessed right to be an independent realm and be free to worship as a citizens of this realm not subjects." William says, "I never knew nor thought for a moment what freedom could mean till now, though I am fast gaining an understanding of the freedom that's been taken from me in such a fashion. I think I'm beginning to understand what freedom is and why people would die to let their children live as a free thinking people, not to be merely existing under the crushing weight of English slave masters."

"Wallace." says Mydford thoughtfully, "Freedom for the individual is dependant on a society that collectively consents by a majority, to be governed by Royal ascent and agreed legislation. The empowerment of our law is the rule by which the legislators enforce the just will of those same people; therefore the enforcement of our law is applied on behalf of those governed and only by their common consent. So by definition, if we do not consent to the imposition of English statutes, their laws should not legally affect us in any way whatsoever, therefore English law is an imposition that does not apply to our community here in Scotland. That's the importance of the documents that you now carry for Wishart that will then go to Rome."

Puzzled, William enquires, "Then by your reckoning, I cannot be charged or penalised as a brigand or an outlaw, as I have broke no laws of Scotland?" Mydford replies,

"That's true, but as we have no legislators left other than those appointed by English governance, we must tolerate them till we find a way to drive the English out of Scotland, or we gain his Holiness support to get the English King to withdraw his army from our soil." William sighs, "Then as long as we wait for this fella from Rome to be making up his mind, the nobles will play a double face at saving their own skins, leaving none to protect our freedoms in the land of our birth against English law, nor is there any other jurisdiction to which I may seek justice for the murder of my family… in other words, I'm still to be hunted down by the English as a Brigand chief and a fuckin' outlaw." Mydford looks at William, but he chooses not to reply and leaves him pondering with his thoughts of freedom.

"Mydford, I'm thinking… if that Holy fella in Rome does either not support us, or he takes his time about giving us that support, there will be none of us left alive in Scotland to benefit. It would seem that the only law that will drive the English out will be by the bladelaw, and if that be so, many thousand will surely die on both sides. But then, if it's the only choice we have, that is also the only way we may save many more thousands of Scots lives, and those that do survive, they will live free and not be subjected to a brutal foreign power." William ponders, "Then it would seem the die is cast." Mydford knows that by leaving William to analyse everything with the minimum of input, his young friend will come to realise there is only one way left for them to act, and that will be to take up arms against this foreign invasion of imperial murderers.

The pilgrim's cortège continues on their hazardous journey as the weather worsens. The freezing temperature is dropping and now a thick Hoare sub-zero mist begins to envelop them. It's becoming apparent to Mydford that if they do not find shelter quickly, many of the pilgrims will not see the morning sun rise, for it's the wind-chill that's severely weakening and exhausting all the pilgrims. Mydford senses this and knows he must make a risky decision if any of the pilgrims are to survive this night, "We must find shelter Wallace, or we will never make it to Saint Johns this night without many of the older pilgrims open to perish under our watch." William replies, "I'm unfamiliar with this road and we cannae see more than a few feet in front of us, this is near impossible… where can we find any shelter this night, do you know?" Looking behind him, Mydford can see the lamps of the pilgrims are stretching out farther and farther apart into the distance.

Away at the rear of the pilgrim's procession, he sees stragglers are falling even further behind. He turns and looks in the direction of the high hills north of the road, then speaks to William, "I know of a weaver's Balloch not far from here, he has low-hung barns that may serve as shelter for us all till the morn, I reckon we should go up there." William enquires; "What dyie want me to do?" Mydford replies, "I want you to turn your horse and go back to the last of the pilgrims and push them on, by the time you catch up, we should be close to my friend Smith the weaver at his Balloch up at Longforgan."

Immediately turning Warrior and dragging Fleetfoot, William rides down the long strung out line of pilgrims to the back of the motley procession and catches up with the last of them, there he sees two frail old characters and four very young children sitting exhausted, wet and obviously freezing near to death at the side of the drove road. He pulls Warrior and Fleetfoot to a halt beside them and dismounts. When he looks into the wretched faces of the old man the woman and the children, he can see the old man is suffering badly and turning deathly blue in the extreme cold, causing him to lose control and the functions of his limbs, all the while being cared for by his tearful wife. William watches the tenderness and desperate nurture the old woman gives to the old man by simple loving comfort, her care and concern reminds him of his wee Maw. The old woman and children look at him, showing a great fear in their eyes. The old woman pitifully raises her hand towards William then points at the old man, the health of the old man is beyond any concern she has for her own wretched condition and well-being. The scene touches William's heart, suddenly he becomes aware of how emotional he feels for these strangers, yet he had locked away any emotional tears of his own grief when told of the deaths of Margret, Alex and his family at Kilspindie. Holding back his own tears now, he searches for any whisky, oat bannocks and poddynox he has left in his saddlebags.

"Here," says William, "Let me help you, for you will surely all die out here if we don't get yiez movin." He reaches into the saddle bags of Fleetfoot and hands the old woman and children the last of his food, then he gently cradles and lifts the old man and places him into the saddle of Warrior, next, he lifts up the children and places them on the pack-bags of Fleetfoot. Finally, he helps the frail old woman to her feet; then he lifts her up and places her behind her husband on the rump of the saddle. He unties his own brat from his back and takes the Wolverine brats from behind the saddle then throws both of them around the old couple and the children, pulling and tying them tight to keep in the warmth.

As he walks to the front of Warrior and grips the reigns to lead them on, the elderly couple thank him profusely while eagerly biting into the morsels, William catches food the old man drops from his frozen fingers and holds the old mans hands a moment to pass him some warmth. The old man grips the food with both hands then gazes into Williams eyes, the look in the old mans face says more than words ever could. William takes hold of Warriors reigns and begins to walk on through the bitter wind and sleet, following the last of the pilgrims walking towards the sheltered barns of Longforgan.

"Wallace," enquires the old man. William replies "Aye what is it yie want?" The old man shivers and stammers in the biting cold, then he continues, "That is your name is it not, William Wallace?" William replies, "Aye, so why do yie ask?" The old man smiles as he wipes his runny nose on his sleeve, he looks back at his wife and wipes tears away from her sparkling eyes, then he gazes at William with ecstasy in his heart, but says nothing by way of a reply. William enquires, "Why do yie query ma name?" The old man finally replies, "William Wallace, I have never sat on a horse before…" William laughs; surprised at something so simple bringing happiness in the midst of such a perilous situation. He looks up at the old couple and can see in the dull lantern light, the absolute joy in the old mans face, despite his watery eyes and sniffing runny nose in the freezing wind. Then the old woman pops her head out and looks down on William, she grins in a way that carries a message of love, comfort and absolute gratitude to him for helping strangers in distress, William grins too as they trudge onwards through the mire and freezing sleet.

By the time William and his new-found companions reach the Balloch, Mydford has gained them all shelter, food and warmth in the barns of Longforgan, from his friend Smith the cottar and his wife. William settles the two old pilgrims and their children then repeats the same journey time and time again till all the pilgrims are sheltered and warm. William finally stables the horses then he sits exhausted on a stone grinding-wheel near the central fire beside Mydford, who hands him a bowl of much-needed hot stew broth and fine medicinal craitur. William finishes his vittals and looks around the barn as some of the pilgrims settle in to dry their meagre cloths and then huddle near the centre fire, while others get some much needed sleep. Turning to Mydford, William says, "I'll continue with my journey homeward, I couldn't sleep this night anyway as there's too much in my head after the killings of Selby and his men in Dun Dèagh, I think it might be best that I travel at night and free you all from my company, and most likely harm by association."

Mydford replies, "Perhaps you're right, there will sure be a sore price to pay for what's happened this day, by the morn the whole country will be swarming with English set upon your capture." Mydford pauses a moment, then he says, "Do yie still have your port pass from the bishop of Brechin and the coded writs for Wishart and Ranald?" William reaches into his side-pouch and pulls out the pass, "I do." Mydford continues, "And you've memorised the list?" William replies, "I have, and I wont forget any of them, for it is all who did not sign the Ragemanus." Mydford nods his head as William continues, "I'll go on to the Bargee inn, for there I must meet up with Affric, I promised to her take back down to Galloway with me." Mydford interrupts abruptly, "No Wallace, you cannot do that. There is too much at stake, you must travel fast and alone, if you travel with others then the risk of your capture will be so much the greater, leave her be."

Thinking on Mydfords words, William doesn't want to argue, but he couldn't leave Affric again. He knows that if he abandons her to the short violent and diseased life of a drunken whore, he could never forgive himself. He feels a duty to one of his few remaining friends, knowing he can do something rather than nothing, why would he leave her, for what? Or what was all his talk of freedom all about. He knows to take Affric home to Galloway could bring back to her the life of the woodland princess she deserves, as the warm and joyous human being she once was, and likely hasten the return of the gorgeous Elvin-like smile he so loved and that brought joy to everyone, she was worth at least that. He thinks a moment then says… "You are right Mydford, It will not take me long to ride to saint Johns Kirk on my own, then it's a quick ride to Ceanncardine where I can get a barge across the forth, or if the tide is out maybe I can wade across between the Ceanncardine skinflat lagoons and into the Airth forest without being seen." Mydford nods in approval, then he enquires, "When will you be leaving us then?" William replies, "I'll leave now Mydford, then I hope that we meet soon at the great council of Glasgow." Mydford looks at William curiously, "You're going to the council?"

"Aye," replies William, "That's what Lord Moray asked of me when he took me aside, he said the sons and daughters of the Garda Rígh, Garda chiefs and commanders of the Céile Aicé are to gather and prepare for defence of the realm in the name of King John. He also asked me if I would consider taking my uncle Malcolm's place as Ceannard of the Southwest Garda Bhàn Rìoghail." Mydford enquires, "What did you say by reply to Lord Moray? William smiles, "I said no… But I also said I would think about it. He said that his son Andrew and MacGilchrist will be the Ceannard of the Northeast. Red Comyn and Duncan of Lorne the Northwest, MacDuff and Stewart will command the Southeast and Borders, with myself and the Graham to the Southwest." Mydford and William talk quietly together as they walk to the stable where the horses are tacked ready for the journey. As William mounts, Mydford looks up, "God speed you William Wallace." He smiles, for Mydford has never called him William before, not even when he had tutored him all those years ago in the auld Kirk and up in Dun Dèagh, William replies, "And may your God look after you too William Mydford…" They both laugh as William nudges the horses then they canter onto the main drove road towards Saint Johns Toun. As he disappears into the stormy night, Mydford closes the barn doors behind him, saying to himself; "God speed you Wallace… may the Angels of the divine sisters protect you."

* * *

Less than twenty miles away, Affric is sitting in the busy Inn of Christina with the innkeeper and Fellows. She has everything packed ready to leave and has waited all night for William, who apparently has failed to arrive on time as he had promised. Affric is slouched across an empty wine barrel, extremely drunk and belligerent from her excess drinking of Ale and whisky, "He's not coming." groans Affric. Fellows looks at his young friend, he is so much in love with her, but only coin will buy her affection, though he could see below her hard-bitten exterior a heart and soul that he is smitten by.

"Don't give up on him Affric," says Fellows, "He'll be here soon, it's likely something simple has delayed his return, have some patience woman." The inn is unusually busy with locals, and English soldiers taking a well-earned rest, many who had earlier been searching for the Brigand chief, William Wallace and his gang. The soldiers are stripped of armour and warming themselves by the inn fire while gaining the dubious benefits from Christina's special Ale. As the evening passes, Affric makes good her presence by serving the lusty needs of the English soldiers in the grain store at the back of the Inn. Even Affric has succumbed to the lethal alcoholic strength of Christina's special Ale. She finishes pleasuring another English soldier and wanders bare breasted back into the main Inn, pushing her way towards the Inglenook. She slumps herself down between two English soldiers busily warming their cold bones. Affric calls out in a slurred voice, "Ale Christina, for I have some silver pennies here to spend, thanks to my new English friends over here." Affric puts her arms round the shoulders of the English soldiers, who are more than delighted to accept her liberal hospitality. Fellows, Christina and the innkeeper look at each other with concern, for Affric is getting very drunk and extremely vitriolic. Christina hesitates, which is noticed instantly by Affric, she calls out, "What are you waiting for bitch… If you're still waiting for that big cunt William Wallace to come here before yie serve me, I fear I may never drink your stinkin' fuckin' Ale ever again."

The English soldiers who hear Affric's outburst go silent and glance at each other. Affric mistakes their attention and glares at them. "What the fuck are you all looking at, have you never seen Gallóbhan breasts before. Here… have a good look at these." Affric stands up, sways her breasts then gyrates her hips for everyone to see, she laughs then grips her breasts firmly and shouts out loudly, "Suck on these ya dirty man bastards." Christina rushes forward to cover Affric and take her away, for both she and Fellow's noticed the change in the demeanour of the soldiers when Affric called out William's name. A burly English soldier stands up and blocks Christina, then he gives her a glance that causes the usually stoic and fearless Brewster to consider her own safety.

The English soldier puts his arm around Affric and insists that she drinks some ale from his flagon; then he enquires, "Who is this Wallace that you speak about?" Affric drinks from the soldier's flagon, spilling much of it down her face and breasts. Wiping her mouth, she sneers as she replies… "William fuckin' Wallace, you know… the famous fuckin' brigand chief and notorious outlaw who steals ale from inns. Aye right, he was supposed to meet me here this eve and take me back to Galloway in the morn, but he's likely putting his prick in some whore right now up in Dun Dèagh." The soldier looks furtively at his companions, "Dun Dèagh you say… this Wallace friend of yours, is he still in Dun Dèagh?"

Affric slurs her reply, "Aye, Dun Dèagh… are you fucking deaf, he was here last night, then he left and went up there early this morn on some special mission as he called it, the durty lyin' bastard, he told me faithfully that he would come back for me this night, but he hasn't returned, nor will he, the selfish loved up cunt… He said he would return for me, but as he did once before he's run out on me again and left me behind… fuck him, fuck all you men."

The soldier stands up and calls over two of his subordinates and speaks with them quietly; then they quickly leave the Inn. The soldier sits down and plies Affric with more Ale… and more questions. Fellows walks over and speaks to Affric, "I think that you should come with me and help me bitter some more Ale." The English soldier says abruptly, "She's staying with us," the soldier places his hand on the handle of his sword, as do his companions who now surround Affric. Fellows backs off and wanders back over to the serving barrels and talks with Christina and the Innkeeper, it's becoming noticeable that the inn is beginning to empty quickly, till the only clients left are seven English soldiers and Affric. Fellows turns to Christina, "I think our young friend Wallace will be in serious trouble if he comes back here this night, we must think of a way to warn him without raising any suspicion from these soldiers." Christina replies… "I don't know how we can do that, those dirty fucking Englishmen are keeping a keen eye on us now." Christina suddenly remembers Fellows is English, "Oh, no offence intended."

Fellows smiles and puts his arm across Christina's ample shoulders, "Even though I be English, I have a fondness for Wallace too, as I'm sure not all Scots have young Wallace's welfare foremost to their mind this night Christina. And I've no doubt that there are many Scots here would also have no qualms about claiming the few silver merks they may gain as a reward for his capture." An English soldier overhears the last part of the conversation, and hearing Fellows speak in an English accent and being so forthright in his comments, he offers Fellows information, "More than a few silver merks sirrah, a reward enough to retire on from Edwards army methinks for bringing in this Wallace back alive... or dead." Fellows enquires; "Why do you say that?"

The English soldier leans forward and whispers, "That Brigand chief Wallace you talk about; he slew young Selby, the son of the English Constable of Dundee and several Soldiers in the young lord's retinue yesterday. Then this Wallace dog and his gang of brigands set an affray in the town close to the castle, many good Englishmen are now dead because of him. Lord Selby is beside himself with grief, he wants Wallace's head served up to him on a platter and he will pay handsomely too." The English soldier smirks as he continues, "Lord Alan Fitz Alan, Commander of the English forces of the north, has declared Wallace a Brigand chief, outlaw and murderer, anyone is now free to capture or kill him and receive a substantial reward for his head, enough silver that will match the weight of his laden skull I've heard. If Wallace comes in here this night and you help us, we may share the bounty with you." The soldier winks, tips the end of his nose with his finger and wanders off. Fellows and Christina look at each other, shocked at this news. "Fuck, this is far more serious than we could of thought," says Fellows, "If we help Wallace and we're caught, then we'll surely feel the hot irons and blunt end of the headsman's axe on our necks." Christina says, "But if we don't warn him, he may walk directly into this and be caught in a trap." The innkeeper comes over with empty flagons and speaks quietly, "Did you hear about that young Wallace who was in here last night… he's raised an army and defeated an English army in Dundee, killing hundreds I hear." Christina slaps him across the head with a wet cloth; "Oh, come here you old fool with your tittle-tattle… we need to think of a plan or Wallace will walk into a trap."

Meanwhile, Affric still sits brooding with her new friends when the English soldier speaks to her… "This William Wallace, would you like us to catch him for you?" She looks warily at the soldier, searching his face for any sign of lies or deceit. She throws her hair back then enquires, "What do you mean Englishman?" The soldier continues, "Well, if you say he is an ale thief, we can arrest him and hold him for a few days as his punishment, you know, till he pays a levy for his felony, then we can release him into your care and charge." Affric looks curiously at the soldier, "You would do this for me?" She pauses a moment then laughs, "Aye, but what do you want in return, do you want to fuck me for free, is that what you really want?" The soldier gently runs his fingers through Affrics hair and sniffs at her scented locks. He gazes into her eyes, smiles, then replies, "For one as beautiful and pretty as you my sweet little doxy… I would do anything."

The handsome English soldier sits back, holds her hand, then continues, "It's plain for all to see that your anger is born out of love for this Wallace, if I can help an aching heart as much in despair as my own heart yearns for the one that I love, then perhaps I will have done something useful for another lovelorn soul, and that alone would be a just reward for me." Affric is unsure how to react; the charm of the handsome Englishman makes her smile, after all, he did say she was pretty and beautiful, so maybe it is not a bad idea if the English soldiers do place William into her charge, then she would command him to take her home. Affric enquires, "What do you really want from me to make this happen?" The soldier smiles then he replies, "Just you wait here this night and we will stay close to you. I simply want you to act as though there is nothing amiss when Wallace comes in here, and when he does, you are to point him out to us, then we will take it from there, and you—you will have your reward and we will have ours, is it a deal?" Affric spits in her hand then holds it out, "You have a trade Englishman." the Englishman hesitates then he says, "A moment before we strike our bond, I wish to show you in kind that we have no malice toward this Wallace of yours, and also, as a marked gesture that you may gain trust in me, I have a plan to demonstrate my good faith." Affric appears puzzled, "What's your plan?" The Englishman calls out, "You… Christina, come here." Christina looks at Fellows, he nods for her to go over and find out what it is the Englishman wants.

Christina walks across the inn to the inglenook and enquires, "What is it you wish from me good sir, more ale, food or a wumman' maybe?" The soldier replies, "No Christina, but tell me, this Wallace… didn't he steal some Ale or beer from you at one time not so very long ago?" Christina looks bemused by the question, "Aye sir, that he did, but it was a misunderstanding and the debt has been paid in full." The Englishman interrupts tersely, "Yes, yes. But what was the original due on his theft?" Christina continues to be baffled, but she replies, "About four silver pennies sir… but why do you ask?" The Englishman replies, "Just curiosity, now be off with you woman." The Englishman turns to Affric and takes four silver pennies out of his purse and places them on the table, "This is for you sweet Affric, when we take Wallace as a prisoner, and in good faith from the mouth of your friend Christina, I give you the dues required to free this Wallace once we have arrested him." Affric looks at the four silver pennies on the table, picks them up then looks at the Englishman for a moment, she smiles, spits in her hand again and offers it out to him, "You have a deal now Englishman." They both shake hands on their deal, then the Englishman says, "Now you go about your business here as though we are finished our time together, and be happy Affric, for if Wallace does come here this night we will have him, I promise you this." Affric, in her befuddled brain is overjoyed; she stands up and yells aloud, "Now you are mine William Wallace, now you are mine..."

Still bemused by the question, Christina walks over to Fellows and repeats what has just been said, "I don't like this," said Fellows, "This is a trap." He signals for the innkeeper to come close, "Innkeeper, you go to the outhouse and start mending ale casks and mess about, but you keep a sharp look out for Wallace. Christina, you go to the Brewster room and start making more bitter ale; if any of you see young Wallace coming, warn him that there are soldiers waiting to capture him the moment he walks through the door. At the same moment Affric comes over, full of the joys of life, excited to tell her friends of her plan. "I must tell you," she says, "I've just struck a deal with those English soldiers, when Wallace comes through that door this night, I'm to point him out and they'll arrest him... and you will get your four pennies for the ale he stole Christina." Fellows says quietly, "Affric what have yie done... it's a trap they're settin' for Wallace, he's wanted in Dundee for the killing of a young English lord called Selby..." Affric gazes open-mouthed at Fellows upon hearing his words, her clouded brain clears a moment, cautiously she enquires, "How is it that you know of this and you're only just telling me now?" Christina moans. "Oh Affric my bonnie child." Fellows says, "Quickly everyone, go and see if Wallace…." At that moment, the inn door creaks open and a tall hooded figure walks in through the door, the man is clearly weighed down with a sodden wet black friars brat. He closes the door behind him and throws back the cowl of his mantle.

"Wallace…" exclaims Affric. Everyone is stunned into silence. The English soldiers, still seated and warming themselves at the inglenook fire, are also surprised at the sudden entrance of this tall young man. They soldiers look to the senior English soldier who makes a sign with his eyes to wait, then he whispers, "If this is Wallace, the man we are looking for, then we must get some of you behind him for he's a big bastard… if he suspects anything, he may still reach for the door to make his escape and flee while we do not yet have him in chains. We must be cautious and wait for the right opportunity." Affric, Fellows, Christina and the innkeeper are helpless to warn William of the danger he is in. "Why the surprised faces?" enquires William, "I said I would come back for you ma bonnie darlin' so here ah ahm."

Affric stammers, "But…" He walks forward shaking his sodden mantle, then he pulls off the Blackfriars cape and brat and throws them over a bench bar, he enquires "How about fetchin' me some o' your special hot stovie stew Christina, ahm fuckin' starvin'?" He looks around and appears bemused by the silence. "You're all looking at me as though you've never seen me before, what's with you all?" Fellows responds, "We have some hot food in the kitchens young sir, if you would like to eat through there?" William smiles. "Naw… not with that glorious fire blazing away in the nook, and I see a stovie cauldron hanging at the fireside too… naw tá, I'll eat over there, fetch ma Ale over to the fireside where

I'll be warming up ma freezin' bones." Fellows tries to signal William that the English soldiers are waiting for him, but William completely misses the signal and walks over towards the inglenook, getting ever closer to the English soldiers who are now tensing their grip on their swords. William turns his back on them and calls out, "Christina, bring me a weight o' Fellows personal Lübeck Ale, for ah just don't think ma stomach is ready for your special ale this night."

William turns and laughs, thinking of her brew of special ale. He walks directly towards the inglenook fireplace nodding politely at the English soldiers as he passes through them. The soldiers glance nervously at each other, for William is much larger than they could have imagined, but still they make no move to subdue him. His arrival is premature and totally unexpected by the unprepared English soldiers. William stands facing the head of the inglenook fire and opens up his inner mantle to gather all the warmth emanating from the fire, blocking the heat and light from everyone else in the vicinity. The silence behind him is deafening and his heart begins to race faster as a sense of thrill and excitement courses through his body, he turns his head and smiles, then he says to the senior English soldier sitting close by, "I'm going home soon to see my love yie know."

Turning once more towards the fire, William rubs his hands for some heat. The English soldiers look at one another; then the senior soldier sitting behind William speaks while pulling his sword from its scabbard, "Scotchman, tell me, is your name William Wall…" The senior English soldier gapes as William unexpectedly spins round and brings his sword blade down on the Englishman's forearm, slicing through it with ease, leaving a detached forearm with the hand still clutching the sword falling to the floor. William instantly smashes a quillon tip through another shocked soldiers eye socket and part way into his brain, knocking him onto his back screaming in agony. William turns while swinging the sword at speed and cuts deep into the side of another soldier's head, simultaneously he thrusts his dirk down deep between the neck and collarbone of the soldier sitting next to him… Christina screams and drops a platter of stovies to the floor as blood sprays everywhere, William crashes the keen edge of his sword blade down on the skull of another English soldier, splitting him from crown to jaw, then he spins on his heels, dragging his sword with such dead force torque, the blade edge of his sword bites deep, easily cutting through forehead and brains, scalping another English skull.

The remaining English soldiers stand paralysed with fear and in a state of shock at William's swift and ferocious onslaught upon them. The two Englishmen's confidence in having the numbers is shattered when they both realise they can't move away as they are trapped in a tight corner, making them easy prey for the enraged Wallace.

William glares wild-eyed at the two remaining English soldiers, he can see it in their faces the indecision of fight or flight, suddenly he lunges at the nearest soldier who swings is sword high in defence, but William ducks under the swinging blade and rams his sword blade in low, piercing the English soldier in the groin, with the tip of the blade exiting at the rear between the unfortunate Englishman's buttocks. William shoulder charges the Englishman against the inn wall, knocking the breath out of the soldier, he wrenches out his sword from the soldiers gut and drags his dirk at speed across the falling soldiers throat. He turns quickly and can see the last soldier standing rigid in a state of fear and totally bewildered by the speed of the savage assault and sudden dispatch of his comrades. Now only one Englishman faces William. As he walks forward; the last soldier throws his sword to the floor and shouts aloud, "NO…" William ignores the plea and barges forward, simultaneously reaching out and grabbing the soldier by the throat and running him backwards until they both hit a large ale barrel, William shoves the soldiers head back forcefully till the Englishman's lower back arcs over the top of the barrel. William rams the sword down through the man's ribs with such a force, it exits between his shoulder blades and sticks deep into the wood oak lid of the barrel behind him. William lets go the sword as the soldier screams and struggles in agony to get free, he kicks out his legs frantically in a desperate attempt to pull himself away, William stands back watching as though in a crazed demented state, absorbing some strange energy as the soldier screams and writhes in a bizarre death ritual, while pinned to the beer barrel by the sword. "WALLACE…" screams Affric, "What have you fuckin' done?"

Fellows, with a sword in his hand is speechless as he observes the bloody carnage strewn all around the inn. The walls of the inglenook are awash with blood, brains and gore, the only audible sounds are the unnatural gargling, whimpering noises and death rattles of the English soldiers. Christina is hysterical and continues screaming, the innkeeper stands gazing in total disbelief, his mouth is open and gaping at the scene before him. William walks through the mass of blood spreading out on the floor and slaps Christina hard across the face, causing her to stop screaming, she slumps to the floor sobbing as Affric runs to her aid. William walks past them both and stands before Fellows almost nose to nose. Fellows, though a veteran soldier of the English army, is white with shock… he stammers, "Why Wallace, why…?" William looks into his eyes, "Why Englishman, you ask me why? You English come to our country, you torture rape and kill with impunity, sparing neither man woman nor child… and you think to ask me why I would dare to fight back?" Fellows pathetically shrugs his shoulders as William continues, "I have tried to mind my peace with you English, even after you murder my family, and when I was told of more killings by the English of my loved ones, I still had no wish to become like you… but on my way here this eve on the outskirts of Saint Johns Toun, I witnessed the most merciless of atrocities by your soldiers upon innocents of this realm."

"I don't know what you mean?" blusters Fellows. William grips Fellows violently by the scruff of his neck, replying in a fury… "I saw English soldiers herd young boys and girls, all bound with their arms behind their backs; then they were stuck deep between the buttocks with sharp lances then hoisted aloft. The English soldiers watched in a great humour as the poor wretches slowly slid down the ash shafts dying in agony while other soldiers looked on laughing, jeering and taking bets on who would succumb first. But worse than that Fellows if it could be so, while those poor unfortunate youngsters died a slow agonising death, their mothers were being raped in front of them and when their bodies were of no further use, they had their brains dashed out with axe or iron mace. Other soldiers were cutting the throats of the fathers while mere babes were flung onto blazing braziers to warm the bloody hands of your fellow fuckin' countrymen…"

Fellows stammers, "I… I must take you prisoner for this Wallace, you have left me no other choice." but William is enraged beyond all ken, "Then use your fuckin' sword now Englishman and I will surely kill you… by all that I know, I fuckin' swear that I will kill you and all of your kind with a hatred and a passion you could never imagine. Do you have enough hatred of me Englishman for you to die trying to take me prisoner?" Fellows stares at William, "I must Wallace; look at what you've done." Still half naked, Affric screams in a rage and charges at William, he turns quickly and catches her by the wrists as she tries to rein blows down on him. She shouts, "Why did you do this Wallace, why you have killed these men, why…" She screams and kicks till she loses the strength to struggle. William puts his arms around her and holds her close, Affric sobs in his arms as Fellows and the innkeeper glance at each other, Fellows speaks softly, "I'm so sorry Wallace, but what can I do? You have killed my brother soldiers, now Christina, Affric and the innkeeper here will all be hanged for this, and I will too if I do not take you prisoner."

With tears running down her cheeks, Affric looks into William's eyes, though her face is grimy and tearstained, he sees the Affric of her youth. Her beautiful almond eyes sparkle as she smiles that old smile that could melt the most hardened of hearts. Affric stands back a little while holding his hands, she says in a moment of calm, "Take me home Wallace… for I am now ready to return to the land of my birth. I long to see my sisters of the Gallóbhan, then I'm going to wash away all of this town filth in the deep clear pools of the scented Wolf and wildcat forest." She sobs and looks into his eyes, "Oh Wallace, I… I just want to go home." William sighs with relief, he tips his head back, closes his eyes and takes in a long deep breath, then feels a slight jerk, he opens his eyes and looks at Affric, she has a strange expression on her face, then he looks down and sees a sword blade has pierced through her chest, exiting between her breasts and spraying his face in a mist of blood, the needle-point tip of the blade narrowly missing his throat.

Affric loosens her grip and lightly touches the tip of the blood-covered blade; she looks up at him, "Wallace… I…" She looks down as the blade disappears back into her chest. Suddenly Fellows pushes William aside and raises his sword as an obscured long sword blade sweeps up towards him from behind Affric but strikes Fellows instead, slashing him deep across his stomach, William sees the senior soldier he had attacked earlier grinning at him while holding a sword in his left hand. Fellows drops his own blade and firmly grips the English soldiers blade. William screams at the top of his lungs, "NO…" He pulls out his dirk and launches a furious assault on the Englishman, stabbing and slashing him about the head and neck in a primeval frenzy till there is naught left but a bloody mass of skin, brains, fragmented skull pieces and clotted hair that was once a human head.

Eventually William becomes exhausted, he rests straddling above the dead Englishman like a dog on all fours, covered in blood, brains and mucus, then he hears a faint voice call out, "Please help me…" William has no idea how long he has been stabbing and slashing at the flesh of the dead Englishman before he becomes aware of a frail sounding plea nearby, he looks around to see Fellows laying against the inn wall, trying with one hand to hold on to his entrails now oozing out from a bloody open stomach wound, then he sees Affric is laying on her back being cradled beside Fellows under his other arm, with a fast expanding pool of blood oozing out below them. Affrics head topples to the side and she stares at William, pleading with her eyes. She cries out feebly, "Wallace… oh William… it hurts me so bad, please help me… I don't want to die here." William stares at Affric, he sees little bubbles of blood popping in her nostrils and at the side of her mouth, more blood is pulsing from her chest wound onto the stone flagged floor.

Realisation strikes William like a hammer-blow, he scrambles and slides across the slippery bloody floor past the sobbing witless Christina as Fellows tries to raise Affrics head. William gently catches her and cradles her on his lap, she reaches up and strokes his long hair and smiles at him then she begins choking and coughing, painfully wracking her slight body. As the coughing eases, she looks into his eyes dreamily and says to him, "My bonnie Ben an' Donner, I… I think it will be a long time till we meet at the Fionn's Fèis in the otherworld before we may ever dance again." She looks at Fellows, then she reaches out to hold his hand, in her eyes she shares a love she knows she has for him too, but has never dared show it.

As Fellows senses the true love she finally shares with him, tears begin to flow down his face. William looks down upon Affric, his emotions tearing at his very soul. She raises her hand, then with her thumb, she wipes away a tear from his cheek, she says, "I don't want to die…" William pleads, "Hang on bonnie Affric, I'll take you away from here, I will take you home darlin' for I have Warrior and Fleetfoot out the back o' the Inn just waiting for us to ride away from this place, we'll seek out true Tam and he will use his magic potions on you." The pain of seeing his young friend like this becomes too much for William, tears and emotions overpower him, "Ma bonnie woodland princess… don't go… please don't leave me, please darlin don't you be leaving me, not now…"

Affric smiles weakly, she says, "I knew you would come back for me, I'm just so sorry that I've ever been the cause of so much pain and hurt for you." William says, "No, it's me that's caused you so much hurt, I do love you Affric, don't go, ah really need yie…" William weeps openly as he tries to speak, Affric reaches up and puts her finger gently on his lips, "For so long I have been lost William… but you and your family, you were the only people who ever showed me true love and kindness…" Affric looks lovingly at Fellows… "And you too my Egyptian prince, you I shall always love…" Suddenly Affric begins to shudder involuntarily, each new spasm being more violent than the last. Affric holds Fellows by the hand, squeezing tightly; then she looks at William with fear in her eyes, "William…" He pulls her close and pleads, "Affric, don't leave me, please don't you leave us…" Resting her head on his chest, she grips his hand tightly. William feels her pushing at his shoulder in pulses, she looks up at him as a single tear rolls down her cheek.

"I'm not scared anymore William, for I see Coinach, father… my mother, sisters… I do love you Wallace… mo anam chara…" Then she looks at Fellows "And… and you have shown me kindness and love too my Ceàrdannan lover… and I tell to you, I do love you for all that you are and more…" Looking into her beautiful almond eyes, William smiles as tears blind him, he says, "We'll take you home Affric, me and Fellows here , we will take you home now, you just stay awake, don't close your eyes…" Affric stares at William with half shut eyes; she whispers quietly, "The name you seek William, but I see you already know, and you're right, It is Marmaduke de Percy… avenge us Wallace…" William replies, "I will Affric, but first we must get yie home." She turns once more to look at Fellows, "You are my man, my true guardian… I, I love you, I…"

Fellows whispers "Affric…" But she doesn't respond, he calls out pathetically, "Affric, please, don't go…" again there is no response. William looks closely into her eyes for a long time, till he sees a very faint misty blue begin to converge over her pupils, he raises a hand and gently closes her eyelids and looks up at the dark stained ceiling of the Inn, he doesn't cry out, he doesn't wail, he simply he pulls her head close to his and holds her in a loving embrace while weeping silently for his young woodland lover, his beautiful childhood friend. Fellows puts his arm around both of them and pulls them close, "Wallace…" whispers Fellows, "Wallace…"

William looks up and sees he's resting in the nurturing arms of the badly wounded Fellows, who looks back at him with tears in his eyes. He says, "She is gone from us now Wallace, our little princess of the fae has passed." William looks at Affric and thinks that now her earthly pains are finally over, she will soon be meeting with her kinfolk and his own family in a better place than this.

The pain of her loss is overwhelming him as tears blind his sight. Wiping the tears away from his face, he lifts Affric up slightly then he gently lowers her to the care of the loving arms of Fellows, then he opens up the Englishman's shirt to see a large gaping wound in his stomach, with much of his gut hanging out. Fellows says with a grimace. "I think he's killed me Wallace," William looks into the eyes of the tough looking Englishman, who speaks to him with a kindness in his voice. Fellows says, "I'll prepare our little Aicé for the shining fire of our people Wallace." William nods his head. "I so wish…"

Fellows can see that William is distraught and lost, he thinks that despite his own grief and condition to bring Williams mind to a focus, otherwise he might stay and be caught by English soldiers that are sure to coming to the inn. He enquires, "How did you know the soldiers were waiting for you?" William replies, "I just knew, I have been too long in the learning and not appreciating what comes natural to me. I now see peoples intentions by the tightness of their skin, the shape of their eyes, mouth and the slightest of body movements, it's like everyone I see, even from a distance, they tell to me a story about their intentions or about their life, their ailments and their countenance, who they really are. Before, I didn't think much about it, but if you English have taught me anything, it's how to hone that skill, beware and strike first. I know now that my very life depends on it."

"I understand…" says Fellows. William sits with Fellows in silence for a few moments amidst the carnage, then he looks into the face of his friend Fellows, "This is twice you've saved my life Englishman… why?" Fellows smiles, "You could so easily have been my son Wallace, there was something about you when we first met, and Affric…" Fellows winces in pain, William turns to Christina who is holding a cloth over her eyes, sobbing and weeping, he looks to the innkeeper who is also in tears. William calls out, "Go and fetch vinegar and as many eggs as you can; and bring some hemp line and a sharp pin, then I need you to put a blade in the fire till it's white hot." The innkeeper looks at William with a blank expression, "NOW…" commands William.

As the innkeeper rushes away to bring the requirements, Fellows says, "I think it'll take more egg skins than we have here at the inn to poultice this wound." Then he leans over and tries to pull Affric's limp body closer. "Bring her close to me Wallace, let me hold her close one more time… please, will you do this for me?" Looking at this tough veteran of war, William sees the tears in his eyes too, he looks at Affric who appears as though she's sleeping and dreaming of the most beautiful bluebell fae ring in the springtime forest. William feels more than just a kindred spirit with Fellows as he lays Affric's lifeless body in the arms of the gentle Englishman, who immediately begins to cradle Affric with great care, running his fingers through her hair as though preening and caressing her. Fellows glances at William, "I truly loved her Wallace, she's one of my kin. In her own way she showed me a joy of love that I have never known before, I… I love her so much…" Fellows sobs as he strokes her hair. William speaks, "I know you do, and she loved you too ma friend. In my life I never heard her say those words to any other man but you." William can see the obvious love and affection in the eyes of Fellows while he cradles Affric gently in his arms. "You're really a Ceàrdannan then?" enquires William. "I am," replies Fellows, "both our families came to this land after the first crusade." William sees the resemblance of dark hair and deep black almond eyes where he hadn't noticed before, now he understood Fellows and the bond between them. He is about to say something when sees Fellows sobbing with grief, lost to anything anyone could say as he cradles Affric and weeps openly for his love... his Ceàrdannan soulmate.

"WALLACE..." shouts the innkeeper as he comes rushing over, "There are many English soldiers coming this way, you had better leave now for you've only moments before they get here." Fellows looks at William, "Go Wallace, perhaps we may meet again..." Fellows pauses, sensing William's hesitation, he says, "I will take care of Affric as my very own Wallace, now you get away from here, quickly..." William nods and puts out his hand, Fellows reaches out and they shake bloody hands while looking intently at each other.

William leans forward to hold Affric, then he kisses her gently on the lips as tears once more flow freely. He stands up and looks at the innkeeper and Christina, he glances at Fellows then he says, "Forgive me..." The innkeeper looks bemused and enquires, "What..." Before he can continue, William smashes him hard on the jaw, knocking him senseless. As he falls back, William catches him and lays him gently against the wall beside Fellows, who grins, William explains, "It was the only way..." Fellows pulls the senseless innkeeper close to him and says, "You've just saved his life Wallace, now everyone will be hunting for the Brigand Chief William Wallace, who brutalized a poor innkeeper and murdered everyone at the inn." William and Fellows look at each other one last time with an understanding that men of war share, even though they be enemies, "GO WALLACE..."

orders Fellows. William nods and runs out the back of the inn and mounts Warrior, he pulls on the trail lead of Fleetfoot and canters away from the inn and up through the maze of narrow back alleys till finally, he is free of Saint Johns Toun boundaries and on to the road leading to Ceanncardine.

Upon reaching the relative safety on the summit hill of Kintillo, William gazes one last time down upon the sleepy town of Saint John's then he looks to the horizon and can see dawn will be breaking very soon. Spurring Warrior, he rides fast, hard and recklessly through the darkness, till eventually, in the early break of day, he approaches the barge river port of Ceanncardine, where he sees it is already swarming with English soldiers and patrols. He notices that everyone is being thoroughly searched and all wagons are being emptied. He decides it best to move to the high ground, making his journey far longer by skirting over the peaks of the high Ochill hills, but it will be much safer for the delivery of his charge to Wishart. As morning fully breaks, he halts in the hills above the town of Stirling, hoping to cross by the friar's bridge at Cambuskenneth priory later that night.

Deep in an Ochill fault high above the town of Stirling, William seeks a discreet bivouac for the day, he doesn't want to travel in daylight as the English patrols are too numerous and he knows they would most likely be looking for him. He also knows his skills and acute awareness as a woodland hunter will serve him best to be travelling at night, a time when most prefer to stay indoors and the opportunity of making it back to Ach na Feàrna would be so much greater. He builds a small winter obhainn with willow and hazel, covers it with his wolverine brats and fills it with great piles of dead leaves to keep him warm. When he lays down his head to rest, he reflects upon everything that has changed his life, then he thinks of Affric's passing and a great sadness engulfs him, it burns deep in his heart the great loss of his bonnie Ceàrdannan friend. Then he considers the ever-growing strife in Scotland and his own perilous situation, crushing all the youthful joy in him. All he wants to do is take Marion and hide away from the English who now hunt him as a murdering Brigand chief, he knows too that a cruel death would most certainly be his upon capture. Tomorrow perhaps, he would chance a crossing at the busy Haugh Bridge across from the Rapploch of Stirling castle... *'Hidden in plain sight...'* he thinks, as a single tear runs down his cheek... *'I must get home to Marion...'*

# Title

# ĬOP

For three long nights William remains holed up in the Ochill hills above Stirling, he avoids English patrols whilst remaining hidden throughout the daylight hours, biding his time for the right moment to move. Eventually he sees his opportunity to leave the Ochill's by using the high ground and bleak moors to travel discreetly until he reaches the outlying coppice woodlands of Glasgow's Gray rock castle. Again he heeds true Tams words, Hide in plain sight… and passes through the Castle guard-ports without incident, then down past the flesher's markets to cross saint Mungo's bridge and into the Shields forest of south Glasgow. He finally gains the familiar security within the vast Willow coppice woodlands along the Clyde, almost ten miles long, two miles wide and reaching to over twenty feet in height. The density of the willow woodlands offers him shelter, allowing a long awaited sigh of relief. By skirting west of the Ynchinnan fish landings he knows so well, he will soon be back inside his childhood home of Ach na Feàrna.

While he wanders along the secretive woodsmen's trails throughout the willow forest, Warrior and Fleetfoot become agitated, causing William to be respectfully aware of the signs coming from his equine companions. Cautiously he walks-on, knowing he's being watched, occasionally he catches a fleeting glimpse of shadows moving nearby in the dense woodland, he plays to appear as though he hasn't noticed, but steels himself for any eventually while he continues on his journey. It's not long before he exits the willow forest a few miles east of Ach ne Feàrna, partially obscured by the great hawthorn paddocks and abundant forest of Alder trees surrounding the Balloch. As he negotiates his way closer to his childhood home, his heart sinks as he detects the scent of burnt house-wood, something he's become all too familiar with since the war of the competitors and English army incursion as peacekeepers into Scotland. Clearing the last great hawthorn hedges, a sight greets him that devastates his heart. Instead of the quaint little bothies, obhainn's, great house and surrounding curtain wall palisades of his beloved Ach na Feàrna, all that appears to remain are the hulking smoldering shells of burnt-out destroyed buildings. William, almost bereft of emotion, gazes awhile at the ruins; it seems to him that the specters continually haunting him are relentless in dragging him towards the depths of despair and singling him out for a life of bitter torment.

William shakes his head despairingly, for these scenes are so far removed from the life he once knew, he feels that something ironclad is closing around his heart, for it's the only way he knows to steel his resolve and keep any semblance of his sanity. A faint cracking noise of a branch breaking not far behind alerts him, his senses that the shadows recently accompanying him on his somber journey through the willow fields are still in attendance and closing in. Cautiously he dismounts between Warrior and Fleetfoot, he then pulls his longbow from Warriors backpack, nocks an arrow, hangs three more flights in his draw hand then walks through the broken gates of Ach na Feàrna, trailing the horses on either side of him for protection, curiously, he sees something odd near the sweet ground of his ancestors.Drawing his sword as he approaches the burial mounds, he's sickened by what he sees, for wanton vandalism and desecration has been visited upon those interred. All of the graves have been opened, with bones and fragments of old shroud scattered asunder. Then, much to his disgust, he sees skulls and bones that have deliberately been smashed to pieces around the base of the great Yew trees of his ancestors. He drops onto one knee and rests on the pommel of his sword, scrutinising the scenes. Desperately he tries to understand who would do such a thing and why?

William's steely resolve will not accept this wilful and outrageous malice could be more powerful than the spirits of the departed that now protect him, therefore whoever has committed this sacrilege has not achieved anything by way of a reckless reaction from him, it only serves to strengthen his will and resolve to be ruthless in his hunt and destruction of those responsible for all his woes. His sense of shock and feelings of humanity in regards to death are all but gone, as his acceptance of the sights, sounds and scents of death that are becoming familiar and constant companions. Amidst his deep thoughts and contemplation, he hears a distinct and particular birdsong that stands out from the winter crows and rooks cackling in their treetop domain. He looks to where this particular bird sings, after a few moments he sees familiar looking characters stepping out from the dense thickets of gorse and Hawthorn.

"Torrance… Gormlaidh?" exclaims William.

His two old Gallóglaigh friends are dressed in their dark green léine's, dun-brown battle-jacks, and cloaked in bull-skin mantles greased with thick winter goose-fat, making them both virtually indistinguishable from the forested winter background, he stands up to welcome his wild heathen brethren. As they embrace upon meeting, he senses all is not well with them, William enquires urgently, "Where's wee Maw, true Tam?" Torrance looks at Gormlaidh, then turns to face William, he says, "We've her body in a wee Obhainn down by the Clydeside Wallace."

"Awe naw..." exclaims William, "No' wee Maw..." he throws his hands in the air, turns and walks away holding his head. He looks at the desecrated sweet ground and drops to squat. In his heart he half expected this news, but he had lived in hope. Torrance and Gormlaidh glance at each other, nervously waiting for his reaction. After a few moments, he looks back at them but shows no obvious emotion, he enquires, "How did it happen?" Torrance replies, "We only arrived here ourselves late last night, that's when we found your sisters with wee Maw in one of the grave pits. Ah'll tell you as it is Wallace, the English were looking for yie, when they couldn't find yie they burnt the place to the ground. It wasn't till they started tearing up the graves of yer ancestors... that's when wee Maw apparently attacked them."

Standing up and walking back over to his friends, William shakes his head trying to visualize the scene. He doesn't want to ask his next question, but he knows he must, "So, what happened, how did she die?"

There's a moment of awkward impasse, then Torrance replies, "There's no way tae make this easy Wallace, they struck her down with mace and flail then ran her through with swords." William winces at the thought of wee Maw being killed so brutally, yet fortified at the thought of her fighting to the very end with her indomitable spirit, it gives him some semblance of comfort. Looking at his friends, he further enquires, "Uliann and Aunia are they..." Gormlaidh replies "As well as they could be, but I have to tell you that the English soldiers defiled them once more, when they were finished their evil doings with the girls, they threw them into one of the open grave pits beside wee Maw and left them all for dead, that's where we found them this morn at first light, they were…" William sharply raises his hand towards their faces, "STOP…" then he turns away and stands in silence; suddenly he lunges forward and smashes his grandfather's sword into the great oak tree, breaking the blade in two. He drops to his knees facing the great oak, but no tears comes to his eyes, no grief wells up in his heart, only a black rage and melancholy descends upon his thoughts. His earthly passions and feelings have deserted him to be replaced with cold bitter hatred and vengeance surging triumphant through his mind and body. He clenches the handle of his grandfathers broken sword, knowing now that the wraiths of war have finally won their battle for his mind, but it's a battle won not to destroy him, No he thinks, it's a spiritual battle won to prepare him for a brutal war that is to come, for what he must now do… He raises himself up and picks up the other half of the broken blade then walks back over to Torrance and Gormlaidh…

"Take me to them." His friends glance at each other, with no further words spoken the two friends acknowledge in the knowing that they have never seen William like this before, not even during the worst visitations of the slaughter during the Galloway civil war, nor when they were in Ireland fighting alongside the Irish Gallóglaigh a few years ago, they've never felt such an atmosphere as this in his presence. "C'mon Wallace," says Torrance, "We're camped a few miles from here." They mount their horses and walk-on. As they enter the dense woodland, more men and women from the notorious Wolf and wildcat Gallóbhet begin to emerge from hidden places, carrying an array of their infamous spartaxe, horse-bows, evil looking ring-spears and javelins. William recognises many of the Gallóbhet dressed in their woodland green and dun-brown garb of war. The Galloway Gallóglaigh warriors are mostly tall, bearded swarthy individuals, with their unique hairstyles of hair shaved at the sides and their long cap hair tied in topknots.

The Gallóbhan women are dressed in light leather armour, also wearing their distinct hair mark braiding of eleven long beaded plaits, ornately hanging or wound around their heads, these women appearing equally capable of killing with their sinister curved blade swords, back blades, ring-spear javelins and horse-bows. William notices more unfamiliar Gallóbhet beginning to emerge from the dark woodland, though they are dressed and armed in a similar fashion, curiously, both these emerging male and female Gallóbhet also wear distinct hair styles, but shaved completely round the head above the ears, with long heavy greased frontal fringes, again beaded with finger-bones and amber beads like their Scots counterparts and hanging low below their eyes, with individual plaits of their hair specifically embellished intermittently throughout. As he passes them by, they all lower their eyes as a mark of respect for his loss, he mutters "Irish…"

Torrance overhears him, "Aye Wallace, they're here to join with us, for they've no homes or family left in Ireland. For them it's either be branded as outlaws to be hunted down and tortured to death, or be conscripted into the English army as slave levies, or in their particular case, flee their land of birth and seek freedom here in Scotland." William absorbs all the information; then he says, "It's good to be seein' them here…" They canter on in silence, with the mixed Scots and Irish Gallóbhet warriors pace running behind them towards the secretive camp.

As they approach the long shores of the Clyde River, they ride into a small bay clearing, where William sees Stephen, Fiónlaidh and Faolán sitting around a small charcoal fire.

Immediately William dismounts to meets with his friends where he embraces them all. Stephen says, "I'm sorry to be meeting wit' ya under these circumstances Wallace, but I was sent here by your Bishop Wishart fella, he said that I would be the only one you would trust." Stephens smiles, "Sure now, I also took the liberty of bringing some o' these grand folks wit' me, and Faolán here has brought a few of the Galloway-Irish Gallóbhet too."

Faolán and William glance at each other, acknowledging each other's presence, she bows her head slightly, William nods back in response. He says to Stephen, "Where are the girls?" Stephen turns his head and points, "They're in that little Obhainn over there wit' wee Maw." William enquires, "How are they?" Stephen replies, "We've taken care of them as best we could Wallace, but you'd better be preparin' yerself for what you see and hear, for the English did some terrible awful things wit them a' tell ya." Staring at the small Obhainn as though he doesn't want to enter, William puts his hand on Stephen's shoulder, then reluctantly, he makes his way over and in through the small door at the end of the Obhainn. As his eyes become accustomed to the dim light, he sees two people huddled and crouched with heavy brats wrapped around their shoulders sitting on either side of a small shrouded body. One of the individuals turns and looks at him then screams, "William…"

Throwing off her brat, Uliann stands up visibly shaking, Aunia looks round and shouts out his name too, both the young women run over to him screaming and weeping, they embrace him with such a strength, he can feel their nails cut into his flesh beneath his thick clothing. The three kinfolks stand for a long time weeping silently in pain of grief, but the girls are also greatly relieved their half-brother is now back with them. William could only gaze at the little shrouded body of wee Maw, looking so still and cold. Eventually the girls lead William forward in the obhainn where they sit together beside the body of wee Maw. In the low candle-light; William notices something amiss about the faces of Uliann and Aunia, in seeing him stare at them, they quickly cover themselves, but he pulls their hoods back to look at them in detail.

"Fuck… what have they done to yiez?"

William could see their faces are badly bruised and noses are broken, their eyes are black and swollen.

Despite their protestations, he pushes the hoods fully back and is sickened by what he sees. Both the young women's heads had been roughly shaved of hair, with large cuts and bloody gouges apparent in their scalps. The girls quickly pull their hoods back up and begin to fuss about wee Maws shroud. William looks at the shroud of wee Maw. He squats beside her body and gently pulls the shroud away from her face, fearing for what he may see. As the shroud clears, what strikes him immediately is the beauty of wee Maw's youth that shines through, her skin as alabaster and her expression is one of a seemingly peaceful serenity, she looks much younger than he remembered, and her mouth is slightly upturned. William smiles, for he believes she is smiling to let him know she is now at one with his grandfather Billy. He studies her expression for a long time, convinced he could see in her composure, a faint smile… her slumbering appearance reminds him that Affric had a similar expression when death came to her, for she too appeared so much at peace. He whispers, "Perhaps the freedom of death is more welcoming than the eternal pains we must endure in this life."

Speaking quietly as he gazes at the face of his beloved wee Maw, William enquires, "Tell me, how did she die?" Aunia replies, "Her heart more than anything I think William. The

English came looking for you, but when they couldn't find you, they threw us out of the main house and began burning Ach na Feàrna to the ground. Then the knight ordered his men to desecrate the sweet-grounds, that's when granny attacked them, but it was…" Aunia begins to sob as tears roll freely down her cheeks, she looks at wee Maw and gently sweeps a little strand of shock white hair away from her forehead. William reaches out and holds her hand as Uliann continues… "Later, the English soldiers got very drunk then they attacked us again and beat us severely."

Uliann pauses a moment and sobs, she falters as she continues, "They ravaged us William, but they couldn't destroy our spirit. We tried to defy them, but we couldn't fight back for they were too strong. When they had no more use for us, they flung us all into grandpa Billy's grave-pit then they threw our clothes on top of us and tried to bury us alive, but it was too dark to see and they left thinking us buried and dead. We didn't want to leave the grave pit in case they had left guards behind, but wee Maw, she kept us warm of body and whole of mind, it was early morn when Torrance and Gormlaidh found us." William enquires, "So when did wee Maw pass over?" Uliann replies, "She passed away peacefully just a little while ago… just as dawn broke."

Aunia says, "Before she passed, wee Maw heard the wild geese flying overhead and said that it was Grandpa Billy come to take her home, she said that you would understand… then wee Maw asked for a drink o' her favourite craitur to keep up her good spirits. We thought then that she might recover, she told us that she was grateful for such a long life and a wonderful loving caring family… and that she loved every one of us without favour." Uliann says, "William, wee Maw looked at us and held our hands, she said with a smile that we must always remember we are Wallace, be proud, and whenever we see a rainbow, it would be her looking down upon us… she smiled again then said, ae fonde cheery wains, then she closed her eyes as though falling asleep… it was a few moments before we realised she really had gone from us." Uliann holds Aunia's hand then they both embrace, holding each other tightly as they sob uncontrollably. William exclaims, "What did you say Uliann… what did wee Maw say at the very end?"

The two girls look at each other curiously; then Aunia replies, "Wee Maw said that you would understand what she meant…?" Uliann smiles and says, "No Aunia, I think it was when she said ae fonde cheery wains…" The three kin look at each other, almost in humerous disbelief. William despairingly repeats the words, "Ae fonde cheery wains…?" The two girls nod their heads and faintly smile, William shakes his head and exclaims with a smile, "Always be happy upon farewells my children…?"

He thinks about wee Maw's bizarre and almost ridiculous comment in such a time of heartbreak and crisis, then he smiles, for he knows in his heart that wee Maw was still showing them something special in her own way. Amidst all the barbarity and senseless brutality, she had left them with a smile of defiance… and a little comfort. It was then he knew it was time to tell them both about the harrowing fate that had befallen their mother Margret and also that of their uncle Alex and his family up in the lands of Kilspindie. Uliann and Aunia begin involuntary sobbing, but they too have no more tears. Both of them lay themselves down gently across the body of their precious wee Maw. William puts his arms across them and lays his head against theirs too; that they may all grieve together for the loss of the much-loved matriarch and head of the clan Wallace, their precious wee Maw, their special Aicé.

Darkness begins to fall before William emerges from the little Obhainn, followed dutifully by Uliann and Aunia. They look around the secretive camp and see that many of the Gallóbhet are huddled around the small charcoal fire. As they approach, folk move aside and make room for them to sit close by the fire, while others give them bowls of eel and wort stew, a long time passes in the somber atmosphere before anyone talks. As more of the Scots and Irish Gallóbhet begin to gather around the small fire, they all know from personal experience the pain of grief that William and the two young women are stoically enduring. Stephen eventually enquires, "Are yie all right there Wallace?"

William, staring into the little fire is momentarily lost in his thoughts, then he replies, "I don't know why this is all happening Stephen, but I am no' se' caring anymore to be looking for any answer's. I only know it is getting closer to a time when we should be fighting back… FUCK," exclaims William in despair, "I want to kill every fuckin' Englishman I see for what they've done to us." Stephen says, "Speaking of fighting back, we heard that you and young Andrew Moray had raised an army of revolt up in the north… and yiez had driven the English army into the sea from Inverness to Dun Dèagh, and now you've came back to the West to do the same down here. Now tell to me this is a fact me boy?"

"WHAT…" Exclaims William. Gormlaidh speaks, "Aye, ah heard that story too in a Paisley tavern on the way over here, that you had singlehandedly slaughtered the garrison in Saint Johns Toun, then you escaped dressed as a weavers wife…" William exclaims, "What the fuck… do I look as though I would pass for a wumman?" Gormlaidh replies, "They said the English couldn't find you for cause yie were dressed as a weaving wifey at a cotters cottage near Longforgan, busy weftin' n' waftin' behind a great stone wheel and…" William runs his fingers through his hair, not knowing whether to laugh or rage. Torrance, who is listening intently, speaks with great sincerity, "You haven't seen any English women yet Gormlaidh have yie? That's likely why the English soldiers thought that our man here was a wumman…"

For a moment there's a stony silence… William looks at Torrance and Gormlaidh almost in total disbelief, he cant hold back his emotions and laughs out loud, then everyone else begins to laugh heartily as though some manic bad spell has been broken over the small gathering, even Uliann, Aunia and the ever stoic Faolán laugh. Torrance smiles and enquires, "What did I say se' fuckin' funny? Have yie seen them Wallace, ahm no' feckn jestin' yie, English wimmin are somethin' fuckin' else?" Raising a drinking horn high, William says, "Ah think wee Maw is still with us in you Torrance, I reckon that's what she would have said too. I thank yie for yer discourse ma friends." Everyone holds up their drinking vessels to fill them with wee Maws honeydew craitur, saved from the fires of Ach na Feàrna.

"To Wee maw…" says William, "To all our wee Maws…" As one, they all toast her memory together, "Wee Maw's…"

The mood around the fire warms as the Gallóbhet begin chatting. William enquires, "Ho Stephen, where's true Tam… did the English get him too?" Uliann replies, "He's safe as far as we know." William enquires, "Why is he no' here?" Aunia says, "Uliann and I left Crosshouse with six of Ranald's best men to persuade wee Maw to return with us, when we got there, true Tam was in a terrible state, he had bad dreams and terrible signs that his home and people were aflame and needed to get back to his lands in Ercildoune. We all thought it safe enough for him to leave us, even though he didn't want to go, we thought that wee Maw would come to safety with us to Crosshouse. It took a lot of convincing for him to go to seek out his own family, for there were no thoughts or even a warning of what was to come for us, eventually we persuaded him to go see to the well-being of his family… He'd not long left when a large English patrol arrived upon us."

"Where were the men of uncle Ranald, why didn't they put up a fight?" enquires William. Uliann replies, "The English took them under threat of killing us and wee Maw, when they surrendered, they were beaten to death by the English…" Uliann falters as she recalls what happened. Stephen says, "The English cut their cut their heads off, then threw their bodies to the bottom of the main Balloch drinking well, then they piled up the heads in the old midden." William shakes his head in despair. For a long time around the campfire, silence falls once more upon the gathering, then Stephen looks at his friend and slaps him on the back…

"Then will you be tellin' to us o' great brigand chief, what really happened up in the north… did you really raise an army and attack the English?" William sighs, "Fuck naw, all that happened was an English fuckin squire wanted to kill me in Dun Dèagh for simply being a woodland hunter, I had to send him to a better place along with a couple o' his soldiers. I didn't want to do it, but I had no fuckin' choice."

William looks at his friend. He shakes his head, smiles then enquires, "And you heard that I had raised an army of revolt?" Stephen smiles, "Aye, that's the makings o' it Wallace. And like it or not, everyone around these shires is sure believin' that you are the one. Sure, the whole country is talking about ya… including the English I might add…" William glances at Stephen… "I am the one what…?" Stephen grins as he continues, "It would seem ma dear auld friend that you are the one chosen to lead the Scots forward into battle and send the English homeward to think again… for good. Wallace me boy, you're the chosen one… apparently."

William exclaims, "Fuck off… All I want to do is get back to Marion and get deep into the Wolf and wildcats till all this blows over, rest there safe somewhere where we can live in peace and raise a family…" Stephen laughs, "Are you feckn serious Wallace? And how are you going to be bleedin' doin' that me fine big simple friend, you being a notorious Brigand Chief and wanted Outlaw and all… And isn't the finest price bein' offered equal to the weight of your big head in siller… Yie do know that this makes us all here so feckn jealous of your heavenly mark of wantidness by the English?"

"Wantidness?" enquires William. Stephen replies "Aye, wantidness…" Stephen grins inanely at William, who looks back in amused curiosity, "William," says Uliann. He turns to Uliann as she continues, "Aunia and I want to sit with wee Maw awhile longer; will you walk over to her obhainn with us?" Standing up from the fire with Uliann and Aunia, they all walk over to the little obhainn where they talk awhile then they embrace, he lifts the little flap for them to enter then returns to the fire to talk with Stephen.

"I have to tell you this ma friend," says William, "When I was up in Dun Dèagh and those English bastards were doin' me down, one of them was de Percy…" Stephen exclaims, "What the fuck man, did you get him, was it the Percy we're looking fir?" William shakes his head, "Naw I didn't get the fucker, but I know it was him, there was just something in his eyes… and he knew too much about me in such a small amount of time. If it wasn't him, then he knows which one it was and I know what he looks like now. And something else that made me certain it was him; was when he saw my grandfathers dirk, that's when he panicked. Something else I have to tell yie too Stephen, our bonnie Affric is dead." Stephen exclaims, "Jaezuz naw, no' Affric too, how did it happen?" William replies, "She was killed right in front of me; it was all fucked up, for I couldn't stop it from happenin' but before she passed, she told me it was an Englishman called Marmaduke de Percy that murdered her clan, and that's who we are looking for now for sure ma friend."

"We must find this bastard Wallace, and show no mercy upon any who would keep him from us..." William and Stephen continue to discuss the possibility of finding de Percy. Eventually Stephen enquires, "So what are your intentions now then Wallace?" Looking around him, William thinks a moment, then replies, "First I'm going up to Ach na Feàrna to bring back a small cart, then I'll be taking wee Maw to the consecrated ground at Paisley priory in the mornin', I cannae be certain the English would no' return and defile her sweet ground." Stephen shakes his head, "You can't be doing that Wallace, for it wouldn't be safe. I've already sent riders to Paisley and Glasgow for Wishart to let him know what's happened and that you're here wit' us safe and well. Let him take care of wee Maw for yie, he'll be here tonight or in the early morn to meet wit' ya. And the loving of your wee Maw will no' be any lesser because yie err to caution... for the sake of Uliann and Aunia?"

Glaring at Stephen defiantly, William says, "I'm taking her Stephen, and nothing or nobody will stop me. It's sacrilege enough for me to have left Margret in an unmarked grave." Stephen looks at his friend then replies enthusiastically, "I am wit' ya big fella, and I've brought me own private army of Gallóbhet to prove it..." William exclaims, "Yie have what, an army... How many?" Stephen grins with pride, but says nothing, William repeats his question "How many for fucks sake Stephen...?"

Moments pass till Stephen proudly replies, "Twenty here, and another thirty up at our camp on the east side of Loch Lomond." William smiles, "And that's a feckn army?"

Stephen grins once more as he replies, "Of the finest dirtiest most evil murdering Scots and Irish Gallóbhet bastards a fella could ever wish for to have by his side… and another couple of hundred waiting for the call with your uncles Joannie, Seoras and MacLellan of Bombie down in Galloway as yee be needin' them. And I might add…" continues a gleeful Stephen, "Our auld fiends Conchobar and Rory from Connaught will be heading over here very soon, for they've heard you've raised an army too, they didn't want to miss out on some fine Norman black-blood hunting wit' ya."

"How could they fella's have heard so soon?" enquires William. Stephen replies with great pride and gusto, "Ach well now, didn't some of me boys here send all me bleedin' homers back to my Ireland wit' the news o' yer conquests… and of course, Rory and Conchobar got back to us immediately, saying that they'll be across the briny directly, for they miss a' hoppin' wit' their fine auld Scots cousins. Especially if it's Norman fucks that yee be fightin'." William laughs at Stephen's enthusiasm, he sighs; then with a look of almost delight in his face, he says, "One hundred and fifty Gallóbhet? And with Rory and Conchobar's Gallóbhet too… then yer right Stephen, that's easily worth a small army by anyone's fightin' standards."

Sitting down at the fireside, William says, "Maybe you should use them as yie see fit for the duration Stephen, for I'm going back to Marion after my duties are done here. I'll be taking Uliann and Aunia with me; then I'll be making sure to be keeping what's left of my family clear of all this ruination. I reckon we should build a permanent camp deep in the heart o' the Wolf and wildcats." Stephen shakes his head, and looks at William. "Yie'll have a bleedin' job there on both counts Wallace, for the girls are set on staying wit' us and joining strengths with the Gallóbhan Aicé Faolán… And where do you think you'll find peace in this foin country with a price on your head; a price that would tempt many and most?" William grimaces as he looks back at the little blue flames of the charcoal fire; he knows he has no thoughtful reply to offer Stephen. As the dark of night fully descends over their camp, William, Stephen, Torrance, Gormlaidh, and Faolán talk through the hours till dawn breaks and its time to inter wee Maw in the grounds of Paisley priory

A light dawn drizzle falls as wee Maw Wallace is gently placed in the old hay cart for her last journey on this earth. Uliann, Aunia and William sit on the bench bar of the cart as Stephen hands William the reigns, he says, "We'll be following' wit' ya along the inside of the Hawthorn hedges and willow coppice path Wallace, in the event you run into any trouble. And if yie do, we will be waiting for your signal." William smiles, "Take Fleetfoot Stephen, he's a fine friend to me and needs a good rider to handle him." William cracks the reigns and the cart trundles forward. It's a quiet thoughtful journey for the three kinfolk in the soft Scottish rain as they make their solemn journey towards Paisley priory.

After awhile on their route, William smiles… and keeps on smiling. The two young women notice, but can't understand the disrespect they feel William is showing in his humours then he laughs out loud… Aunia pulls on his reigns, stopping the horse in its tracks, "What's with the smile on your face, we don't understand?" William pauses before he answers, with tears in his eyes he looks at his sisters then he looks back at wee Maw and smiles again, "The Churn…" Aunia enquires, "What churn?" William laughs, "Wee Maw's bucket, the churn?" Uliann and Aunia appear confused as William continues, "Remember that night of wee John and Ròsinn's wedding, when granny was tellin us all about the legend o' the Aicé?" There's a moment's confusion for

Uliann and Aunia as they think back… then they begin to smile too, eventually they all laugh at this particular memory of wee Maw. They begin to talk in good spirits of the many moments that wee Maw has left them with such fond and vivid memories. "That's was just so like wee Maw's way." says Uliann, "Sayin' cheerio and leavin' us all with a big smile." They laugh heartily while they huddle together in peace and comfort as they again move along the road to Paisley, reminiscing on the many happy moments shared in their lives under the influence of such a beautiful person in character and nature as their beloved, "Wee Maw."

Nearing the outskirts of Paisley priory, they notice a large troop of about fifty English cavalry coming out of the town and heading in their direction. As the English troop approach them, William senses fear and tension from his sisters. He watches the English gain ever closer and it's mere moments before the troop closes in on them. As they meet with each other to cross paths, the lead knight of the troop brings the head of his warhorse across the front of the cart, forcing it to stop. For a few moments, the two groups watch each other in silence, then the knight notices Warrior tethered to the back of the cart. "You…" commands the knight. William remains silent as the knight circles them on his horse, Impatiently, the Knight points at William while the mounted troopers move their horses around the cart, threatening the family with lances. The knight blusters, "I said you… are you deaf, simple… or just a typical Scotch borne ignorant peasant?"

Remaining silent, William hopes that Stephen and the Gallóbhet bowyers are watching and prepared. The knight continues, "I am an honoured knight of King Edward, your Lord and master… don't you know that when you Scotch meet one such as I, you must bow your head to your superiors?" William speaks with a steely resolve in his voice, "Ahm going to Paisley priory sir knight to bury my grandmother." The English knight doesn't acknowledge William's reply, but curiously he keeps looking at Warrior. After a few tense moments the knight speaks, "No, it is most certain you are not going to do that..." William tenses as the knight continues, "You are just another piece of bloody Scotch vermin who should be walking... No, you should be crawling on your stomach before me. Now tell me, where did you steal such a fine horse as this?" The knight walks his warhorse around the little group, looking intensely at Warrior; then he changes his focus towards Uliann and Aunia. William reaches inside his léine and grips his dirk firmly, knowing he will throw it and embed it deep in the knight's face before he knows what's hit him.

"Don't bleedin' do it..." mutters Stephen while watching from the coppice woodland undergrowth, he looks to his Gallóbhet who are pulling taught on their bows, he signals, "Not yet..." The English knight notices William is flushed with anger and enquires, "What are you staring at you great ox? Did you steal this horse, and the cart too?"

Remaining outwardly calm, William feels he is only moments away from attacking the knight. The English knight looks at Uliann and Aunia once more, "Hmm, what do we have here then?" He leans from the side of his horse and pushes Aunia's hood back, "You two hounds bitches are so bloody uncouth, but you may make merry amusement for my men later this eve..." Aunia quickly pulls her hood back over her head, both girls grab hold of William tightly, much to the amusement of the English troop, then the knight's master-at-arms says, "My lord, we must continue on the road if we are to make Lanark before nightfall." The knight ignores the comment as he stares at Uliann and Aunia, then he barks out an order, "Get this vermin off the cart and bind that great ox securely, for we have a use for their horses and that cart, methinks they will not be needing them anyhoo I wager. And throw that old carcass from the back of the cart by that tree over there."

The English soldiers point their lances close to Williams chest and face, while others pull Uliann and Aunia from the cart to the ground, they drag them screaming and kicking to the side of the road where the soldiers hold daggers at their throats, making it clear they would be shown no mercy if William resists. Slowly he climbs off the cart and is quickly forced into a grassy hollow below the tree where soldiers tie his hands behind his back. He curses under his breath for being so easily subdued because of the threat to Uliann and Aunia, but now he's bound tight and unable to fight back, or protect them. He can only pray that Stephen is watching and is prepared to act…

A young knight about the same age and height as William rides up beside the older knight and speaks quietly. William scrutinises the coat-of-arms worn by both of them and shared insignia on their soldiers. He notes the older knight wears a helmet Crest that looks like a maiden's head, both knight's surcoats are emblazoned with silver and black chevrons between three green hazel leaves, he will remember these marks. The young knight enquires, "What shall we do with them Father?" The knight replies, "Hang the horse thief and hang the old hags body from that tree over there too, and bring the young whores with us, throw them in the back of the cart. If the great ox resists then cut the throat of one of those whores."

William is horrified at what he has heard. He watches the English soldiers manhandle the body of wee Maw and dump her at his feet; all the while, both he and the girls remain silent. The young knight laughs out loud; then he enquires,

"Why do we hang the old hags body too father, for she's already dead?" The knight replies, "When you're in foreign climes boy, you must always set a most severe example that all transgressions shall be met with the harshest of reprisals, or these stinking savages will think the we English are uncouth and uncivilised." Meanwhile, William is looking to see where Stephen and the Gallóbhet could be, when suddenly, the knight barks out a command, "Hang him high."

Immediately two soldiers throw a rope over the bough of the tree then place the noose around William's neck; they quickly pull the rope tight, leaving him barely touching the ground with his toes. As the rope bites into his neck, the two soldiers wait for the final command to hang him high. Uliann and Aunia struggle against their captors, the Gallóbhet strain, pulling full tension on their bows about to loose when Stephen hears a sharp whistle, he signals to hold and refrain from the loose till he finds out what the whistle signal is about. He sees Torrance pointing to another large group of mounted knights and soldiers closing in on William and the English patrol. Stephen stays the order for them to loose their arrows. The English knight is also distracted for a moment; he delays the order to hang William when he too sees the large column approaching.

Meanwhile, William is choking and struggles to breath while spinning helplessly on the balls of his feet, still straining to see if Stephen is nearby to get him out of this predicament. At that same moment, the front riders of the new column pull their horses to a halt beside the scene.

Four riders leave the front of the column and approach. William recognises Bishop Wishart and sees sitting on a grand warhorse beside him, a knight who appears familiar, but he isn't sure who he is. Wishart demands with authority, "Release this man immediately." The knight enquires,

"And who are you to speak to me thus?" Wishart replies, "I am Robert Wishart, the Bishop of Glasgow." The English Knight remains unconcerned by the reply or care less he's in the company of an imminent Bishop. He enquires in a haughty manner, "So, the Bishop of Glasgow you say. And you sir knight, who are you that accompanies this noisy prattling noisy Bishop?" The knight replies, "My name is sir Gilbert de Grimsby, personally chosen by our lord King Edward to carry the sacred banners of saint John Beverly and saint Edward the confessor into battle at the head of our army, and these good knights here are Lord Alasdair MacDubhgaill of Lorne and sir Nial Cambell of Lochawe, commanders of our King's West coast fleet."

The English knight appears shaken when he hears lord Grimsby's credentials, he looks down the ranks of Scottish soldiers and could see they are not mere provincial levies like his own troops, but hardened professional veterans of war, and they look to be in no mood to be challenged as they all grip their weaponry. "You sir knight," says Grimsby, "I recognize your armorial bearings… you are a Hazelrigg by name I presume?" The knight replies, "Sir William Hazelrigg, Lord of the Manor of Wottelslade and Yetham Corbett, at your service good sir, and soon to be appointed as sheriff of Clydesdale and Lanark by none other than King Edward himself." Grimsby replies with aggressive authority, "I think not Hazelrigg, would it not be more accurate to say that it was Bishop Bek of Durham who issued your warrant? I for one have never seen you or ever heard your name mentioned in the privy court chambers of our blessed King, Lord Edward Plantagenet." Hazelrigg flusters at this embarrassing slight, Grimsby further enquires, "And why is it that this family are stood in the ditch under guard, and why is that man there dangling from this tree? It's a curious situation to behold sir, now, release him at once." Hazelrigg replies, "But he is a horse thief, and these trollop whores with him are his gang my lord, we are simply but gracing them from their wretched existence upon this earth."

Grimsby and Wishart remain silent as they ponder over what to do next, as a tension fills the air over the situation. Wishart looks at Hazelrigg and explains, "I fear there is a misunderstanding here my lord Hazelrigg, for these are my own personal Palace workers with my cathedral horses and cart." Wishart continues, "I travel to conduct a funerary service for the Goodwife who lies at the feet of my servant, and you sir, you are in danger of committing unwitting sacrilege. These wretches do serve my precious time by using the horse and cart rather than walk. And that stallion is from my own stable. But I do thank you Hazelrigg, for your zeal and diligence may appear very true to you sir but in this instance, I assure you that everything is quite in order." Grimsby commands, "Release that man from his ordeal I say, for he is now under my protection. And you my lord Hazelrigg, I thank you for your industrious endeavour, but the Bishop is unquestionably correct. And as you may know or are soon to find out, good quality serfs are hard to come by in this depraved realm."

Hazelrigg looks at Wishart then glances back at Edwards pursuant, de Grimsby. He replies, "I accept your offer of gratitude sir… but I wouldn't trust them you know, especially that foul oaf who needs to be broken." Hazelrigg points at William, "Don't you know he had the audacity to actually look me directly in the eyes, the insolent dog?" Hazelrigg guffaws, his men laugh nervously in the presence of such a powerful looking group of armed Scots. Hazelrigg senses his humour is not necessarily shared. He immediately nods at his men holding the rope. William is unceremoniously dropped to the ground, where he gasps in great gulps of air. The soldiers release his bonds and he quickly turns over to wee Maw lying at his side and cradles her shrouded body, wiping bits of grass and leaves away. "And the women too…" growls de Grimsby.

The soldiers reluctantly release Uliann and Aunia, who quickly rush over to William and wee Maw, there they huddle together holding each other tightly beside her body. Hazelrigg glares at William awhile; then he turns to Grimsby and enquires, "Pray tell me good knight, in which direction do we travel to find a place called Lanark?"

Grimsby points due south, "Follow the road to Ruther's glen castle Hazelrigg, when you get there you may glean detailed directions from sir Archibald de Livingston, the residing commander of the garrison, he's a good friend of mine and an honourable knight of our King, and of course he is the actual Sherriff of Lanark." Hazelrigg reluctantly thanks de Grimsby then gathers his men. He mounts then spurs his horse in the flanks and canters toward Glasgow, quickly followed by his much-relieved troop. Watching Hazelrigg canter away, William vows to himself he would meet Hazelrigg again some day, satisfying himself in the knowledge that next time… Wishart quickly dismounts and approaches William while Grimsby Nial and Alasdair tend to Uliann and Aunia. Wishart walks over and kneels beside William, calling to prayer everyone over the body of wee Maw.

As Wishart closes the prayer, his men carefully lift her body and place it back on the cart. William could see the emotional impact her death has had on Wishart, as wee Maw was not just one of his flock but a formidable matriarchal influence in Wisharts younger life, she was his guiding Cruathnie Aicé and his Breitheamh mentor. Wishart glances at the shroud containing the mortal remains of wee Maw, he stammers. "Wallace I am so sorry..." William nods in understanding then thanks Wishart profusely for his timely intervention. He sees Nial and Alasdair still on the cart kneeling beside the body of wee maw. Wishart says, "Wallace, we shall take Bheitris to hallowed ground, the Gallóbhet who sought me out this morning told me of all that has happened... I have no words of comfort other than I'm so sorry this has happened at all, I truly am." Wishart, Alasdair and Nial lay their mantles upon wee Maw's body as a mark of respect; then de Grimsby takes off his mantle too and makes to cloak her body, William grabs his arm to stop him.

Grimsby looks at him curiously, William angrily enquires, "What are you doing Englishman?" Grimsby replies, "I'm resting the sacred mantle of saint John upon wee Maw." William is taken aback; he is totally surprised to hear the English knight's words and his brazen familiarity. He enquires, "How could you know who this is with your personal attendance upon her?" Grimsby looks at William, he says, "Wallace it's me... don't you remember or recognise me?" Scrutinising the knight, William is uncertain, but he sees something familiar as Grimsby continues, "It's me, Jop..." William appears baffled, then an expression emerges on his face as though struck by a lightning bolt, he exclaims "JOP...?"

A friendly smile spreads across Grimsby's face, "Aye, Jop..."

"Is it really you?" exclaims William.

Jop laughs, "None other I hope."

William is delighted, "Feck... Jop, the last time that we were together was when we were sailing little wooden boats below the Shannon falls of Sundrum, near to ma uncle Roberts fortalice. Feck me, but yie've no' changed much after all these years." Jop grins, "Aye Wallace, and what the fuck do yie mean by calling me an Englishman?" William looks on in amazement as Jop proceeds to lay the mantle of Saint John upon the body of wee Maw. For a few moments no words are spoken, as each and all of those gathered around the body of wee Maw stand in silent prayer, then they spend few moments longer in solemn thoughts and personal memories of their much-loved Aicé. Wishart speaks, "Wallace, we'll go back to the sweet grounds of your own folks at Ach na Feàrna, there I shall bless the grounds with holy water, then we'll lay to rest dear Bheitris with your kinfolk." Wishart shakes his head, "And you have my word, no one will ever desecrate your families consecrated ground again."

Wishart walks over to a company of de Grimsby's men and speaks with them awhile, after which, they immediately mount and ride off at a gallop ahead of the main body towards ach na Feàrna. Wishart turns towards the rest of the troop and issues a command… "Everyone get mounted, and you Wallace, you will ride beside me and tell to me of all that lord Moray has passed to you, I'll have one of my men attend to the driving of the cart back to ach na Feàrna." While everyone prepares to leave, Stephen and the Gallóbhet suddenly appear, sauntering carefree out of the willow coppice.

Grabbing the reigns of Warrior, William is about to mount when he feels a tap on his shoulder. He turns around to see a grinning Stephen and Faolán looking at him, William mounts Warrior then he looks down at them and brusquely enquires, "Where the fuck were you Stephen? I really thought I was done for there." Stephen grins, "Ah Wallace me boy, when we saw how yee had them there English fella's eating out of your hand, we knew that you had everything under control. Anyways, oi was waiting for your bleedin' signal wasn't I?" William exclaims, "How the fuck could I signal you when I was bound and hanging…" Shaking his head,

William smiles wryly. He turns Warrior around then calls out to Stephen, "We're all goin' back over to Ach na Feàrna." Stephen mounts Fleetfoot and replies, "We'll be seeing ya up there then, ahl be following ya wit' our very own little army." William glances at Faolán as she mounts her horse, she calls out without looking at him, "The Gallóbhan will be in attendance too Wallace." Fiónlaidh also mounts, then the three friends wave to William and canter off with their own warrior troop towards Ach na Feàrna, followed by Stephens, 'Little Army' of wild Irish Gallóbhet.

Cantering to the front of the column, William catches up with Jop, he says, "I have to thank yie Jop, I really thought I was a dead man there." Jop smiles; then a look of sadness and concern spreads across his face, "I am so sorry to hear about your family Wallace, Wishart has told me of these evil tidings and visitations that you've suffered, and wee Maw… I remember when we spent many nights listening to her stories of auld Scotland."

Thoughtful and lost in their memories of wee Maw, they both remain silent as they ride on, then William sighs, smiles and says, "Look at you Jop, you in all your fine English armour." Jop laughs, then he replies, "I've been with the Scots detachment of the English army for nigh on nineteen years. We've fought for many years in the holy land, then awhile in the Mediterranean. This is the first time we have been home since we left Scotland all those years ago." William enquires, "How long are you back home for?" Jop replies, "Only two weeks ah reckon, ah had wanted to take this opportunity to go back home and see ma mother; feck, I've not seen ma auld dear in almost twenty years now, but ma problem is that we've all been summoned back to England as soon as possible to rejoin the English army. Longshanks commands us to be prepared on a war-footing against King Philip of France, we leave from Tilbury docks near London in a months time with the English army, bound for Flanders." A puzzled and angry William enquires, "You fight for the English fuckin' King?"

Jop pauses thoughtfully for a moment, then he replies, "I was going to say how so do you ask this question with such animus, but in my travels since crossing the border marches, I've seen great pain in the faces on my fellow Scots that I have only ever seen in a punitive occupation of a subdued Kingdom." William says, "It's a bad state of affairs Jop, Comyn Brus and Baliol were at each others throats and caused a brutal civil war a few years back, now we live in a land of blood and famine under the iron boot of Longshanks and his so-called protection." Wishart, who is listening, speaks, "Ride beside me Wallace and tell me what lord Moray has pressed into your confidence." Jop says, "Go on Wallace, we'll continue with our blether later."

Moseying Warrior up beside Wishart, William tells him everything he knows about the death lists and what Lord de Moray's concerns are regarding the English forces stripping the north of all its food and grain. He also briefs him about the gathering of the young Garda Rìoghail and Ceannard Céile Aicé. Finally he gives Wishart a detailed account of the killing of Selby and the soldiers in Perth. Wishart appears ashen-faced upon hearing the detail.

"Wallace, This is extremely important, I must ask you to deliver the information you have passed to me directly to Leckie Mòr, he'll be up at Arthurslie village or more likely at his blacksmiths obhainn near Carlibar. After his deliberations, he'll construct orders for you, from there you must make haste to Crosshouse with both our writs, then relay all you know to your uncle Ranald, do not dally about, for many lives will depend on you passing this information as soon as possible, do you understand me?"

"Aye Wishart I understand you." replies William, "But after that, I am finished with all o' this politic and sweet coating with the English. I have a fire in my mind and ice in my heart for what the English have done, I'm going to Lammington to be with my Marion and leaving you all to your bloody devices." Wishart looks at William, "Then I wish you well in that endeavour Wallace, I hope that you may find the peace you seek, but all of those you meet will tell you the same thing, unless you are prepared to fight back against English tyranny, none shall escape their evil intent to enslave the people of this realm, not even your beloved Marion." William hands over the sachet of documents sent down from Lord Moray and the Northern magnates, then he says, "We'll see." Wishart spurs his horse forward to deliberate in solitude the news and the report from lord Moray.

William pulls back a little and looks at Jop, "Why do you draw bread from this English King who brings nothing but murder and famine to our land Jop? You've almost two hundred able fighting men here, I wager they too have families sorely affected by this English martial law imposed upon us?" Jop replies, "Wallace, I will tell you this and it's for your ears only, for if any other were to hear of this revelation, I and many hundreds would surely die…" William is curious as Jop continues, "MacDubhgaill, Campbell and I serve only one King… and that is King John Baliol of Scotland, but while I am still the bearer of the sacred banners for Longshanks; then I alone may gain and pass important notice to Wishart and the council of the Garda Rìoghail about the vice Longshanks has planned to close around Scotland. This information may not otherwise be gained by any other."

Glancing at his childhood friend, there's a moment of sadness that passes between them. Jop says, "Wallace, I will gladly fight and give my life if I must for your right to remain hidden away from the realities that we all now face. I would do this for you on your behalf… And many others here are willing to die protecting your right to that private discretion, but if our blood is drained away in some forsaken corner of this land, who then will protect you? And as a consequence, who will protect your sweetheart and the many children you may have?" William looks at Jop and shrugs his shoulders. Jop smiles as Nial and Alasdair, who are riding beside them, quietly nod in agreement. William feels a surge of shame sweep his mind, that these men who owe him nothing are prepared to die for his freedom, yet they ask for nothing by way of a repayment, other than an understanding of their innate knowledge of duty to their kin and homeland.

Nial says, "Wallace, everything we are born to do in this life is everything we are born to sacrifice for those we love, isn't that what Mydford used to say when he tutored us about the honours of the Grecianic cycles all those years ago, when those legends told by wee Maw and our elders amused us as children that are now our inspiration as men this day."

Reflecting on Nial's words. William remembers the stories well when Mydford taught them of the Grecian Homer's legendary Kinaethon Lakedaimon, King Amyclas, Queen Eurydice and the princess Sparta, daughter of Eurotas. "Aye Wallace," says Alasdair, "Remember when he instilled in us all about the succession of divine rulers being the origin of all our common woes and about the origin of sacrificial practice being the station of the common man, to live, serve and die protecting the lives of the ruling elite anointed by God?" Nial laughs, "Yie mean we're all fucked up then?" Wishart, who overhears them, speaks abruptly, "Enough of this blasphemy." The young friends go silent upon hearing Wishart's aggressive tone, but then they smile when they see a glancing grin from Wishart as he mutters, "Too much foolish talk…"

The motley contingent eventually arrive and enter through the broken gates of Ach na Feàrna, William could see a large grave pit has been opened up by the men Wishart had sent forward earlier, he sees too the desecrated remains of his ancestors have already been re-interred. He dismounts then walks towards the single large open graveside, where he speaks quietly to Wishart, "I want a funeral pyre Wishart, it's the old way, I know wee Maw would have wanted it so as it's the way of the Aicé." Wishart looks at his young friend with compassion, "You're Ceil Aicé right enough young Wallace, as your father and uncle were before you… it shall be made so as you wish."

The warrior Gallóbhet of Stephen and the veteran soldiers of Jop begin collecting wood from the ruined Balloch to build a great funerary pyre upon the grave pit while William speaks of his intentions and duties with Stephen, Torrance, Faolán and Fiónlaidh. "I'm coming wit ya," says Stephen, "I've instructed the Gallóbhet to be going back to our main camp near Loch Lomond and prepare everyone to move everything to the Wolf and wildcats." Faolán says, "Uliann and Aunia will be coming with me back down to Dun Reicheit Wallace, and I say this next to you my friend as is my honour, I offer to you my life in the protection of your kinfolk as my gift to you." Fiónlaidh says, "I too offer my life as my gift to you." William looks into the faces of his friends. He sees and has heard a determination and conviction resolute. He replies, "May the Aicé protect us all, I accept your offer and I thank you."

"Right Wallace," says Stephen, "I'll be comin' wit ya as far as Ranald's Crosshouse, when you've finished wit' all your duties there and we know all we need to be knowin', I need ya to tell me what yer final plans are, for then I'll head up to our camp up on the Lomond shores and get all the Gallóbhet on the move. We can meet up in a secure place later and ponder what our collective future may be from there," William thinks to protest Stephen's suggestions, for all he wants to do is to be alone with Marion and be free of this mounting responsibility to others. But he considers the words of Jop, Nial and Alasdair, Faolán, Fiónlaidh and the many folk who say that they would willingly sacrifice themselves just for his right to live as a free man.

The passion and pain shared with Stephen and everyone who now rides with him, is causing him to think about their rights to peace and freedom too. Perhaps there could be a better future in the realm if the Gallóbhet were all to rise as one and settle this blood dispute with the English once and for all, to fight and be free... or die. William says, "Aye Stephen, Jop and Wishart are leaving directly after the passing of wee Maw... you come with me as far as Crosshouse as you say, when we know what's happening after we've spoken with Leckie and Ranald, we'll find a place deep in the Wolf and wildcats that we may gain sanctuary." Stephen's eyes light up, "Now yer talkin' me boy, and while I couldn't fault your yearning for peace, there's only one way we can achieve it and that will be to be meeting the feckn Normans head on, or from the back when they be sleepin' for oi don't be carin' how we do it." At that moment Wishart comes over to the little group and bids them to attend the pyre, "All is ready Wallace, come and we shall pay our respects to Bheitris and light her path to Tír nan Óg."

Wee Maw has been placed upon the pyre, as the time has come for William, Uliann and Aunia to place broken food and other of wee Maw's cherished possessions beside her, then they light the pyre and stand back. Pipers from the troop of Jop step forward and begin playing a mournful lament, followed by the women of the Gallóbhan singing haunting Ceantra's. The funerary flames take hold and everyone stands around the pyre in a great circle in silent private prayer, paying a respectful heartfelt tribute to the last of the ancient Aicés of the Wallace family. After a while, the pyre begins to settle and the many friends of wee Maw retire. Later that night, while sitting near the Sweet grounds of their ancestors, William puts his arms around Uliann and Aunia then pulls them close in loving embrace. They sit a long time in silence till Stephen approaches them and puts heavy brats around their shoulders while they mourn and grieve in private. They are grateful to Stephen and comforted knowing that all their friends old and new are nearby, friends who would risk all to protect their right to grieve in peace.

Eventually William Uliann and Aunia raise themselves and wander over to the makeshift Gallóbhet camp amid the ruins of Ach na Feàrna. Fiónlaidh has some nourishing hot stews prepared for them. Wishart and Jop have left to go back to Glasgow with their troops, leaving William and the Gallóbhet alone to tend the remainder of wee Maws pyre. Everyone but the outlying guard sentinels sit around the glowing pyre, talking of wee Maw and her many great and wonderous legends. William Uliann and Aunia are heartened by the respect to which their glorious matriarch is held by the youth of the Céile Aicé, Gallóbhet and Breathaim Rígh Feinechan community.

As dawn breaks, Uliann and Aunia depart for Dun Reicheit with Faolán, Fiónlaidh and the Gallóbhan, Torrance and Gormlaidh soon depart with the Gallóglaigh for the Loch Lomond camp, leaving William and Stephen to tend the last of the funeral pyre. The two friends talk for a long time of everything that's happened since they first met, beginning at wee John and Ròsinns wedding, their time of exile spent in Ireland during the interregnum, to the massacre in Glen Afton and killings at Ach na Feàrna, finally, ending a momentous and often brutal chapter in their lives, the shining fire of their beloved wee Maw.

Soon the last of the pyre burns down to a fine white ash, William and Stephen kneel beside the pyre and pray awhile in silence, then they lift ash in their hands and throw it high into the air, watching as the fine white cloud drifts away on a light breeze. "Right," says William, "I'm sad at our wee Maw's passing, but I tell yie Stephen, I'm happy now she is with Billy and both our families, for it's where she yearned to be. There will be no more earthly pains for her no more and I know she'll be watching over us, telling us to keep our chins high." Stephen nods his head then replies, "She'll be watchin' to make sure we keep out o' bleedin' trouble, bless her bonnie soul." William says, "Aye, but what we set our hearts upon now will most likely bring us great shame in our old age, and it will not be for those we love to witness." Stephen sighs, "I know this to be true Wallace."

Picking up his saddle, William says, "We should start to make tracks for auld Leckie's place. We can stop awhile in at Paisley on the road through and get some fine ale and vittals, it's market day there so we can get lost in the crowds easy without getting' noticed." Stephen grins, "Sure now, ahm up for that Wallace," then he frowns, "Aye, but remember what Wishart said, *you two are to keep out o' trouble…*" William laughs and looks at Stephen, then he replies, "You know me Stephen… I never look for trouble."

"Aye… right enough," says Stephen knowingly. He smiles as he replies, "We'd best be bleedin' well ready for it then." They both laugh heartily then mount their horses and canter out of Ach na Feàrna towards Paisley town, but It isn't long before they realise there is a small troop of English cavalry is riding not far behind them. As the English troop gain on the two friends, William says, "Stephen, If these bastards start on us, have your tools of redemption ready, are you all right with that?" Stephen replies with gusto, "Ah sure now Wallace me boy, when have you ever known me not to be enjoying a little bit of bleedin' fun before me mornin' scran. And there's only about twenty o' the feckrs as well." William smiles at his Irish friends bright outlook on life. They continue onwards riding a lazy canter, knowing it will only takes moments before the English troop will catch up with them. As they prepare themselves, William whispers… "You get the leadin' knight… I'll get the rest o' them." Stephen looks at William and laughs aloud as the troop arrive and ride up beside them, William and Stephen both watch closely as the English troop canters slowly past them, some of the soldiers look at them, some don't.

As the tail of the troop pass them by, the two young friends pull their horses aside then to a halt, they're surprised as they watch the English ride on towards Paisley town. Stephen exclaims, "Would ya be bleedin' believin' that?" William watches the English soldiers ride away into the distance, he says, "It's their lucky fuckin' day…" Stephen laughs, "Right enough it is, for I was ready to be fightin' them all wit' one hand behind me back." At that moment, William glances in the direction of Ach na Feàrna, he reaches up to his neck and holds the Aicé talisman' in his hand and thinks of his wee Maw, he thinks of all his family now gone from this world to a better place. "Lets get movin' Stephen, for we've much to be doin' and little time to be doin' it."

The two friends spur their horses and ride on at an easy canter till they close on the Eastport gatehouse for entry into Paisley town. As they wander through the busy checkpoint, surprisingly, the English guards pay them little attention as they pass by and ride on into the market town. They amble through the busy streets till they eventually stop by a smithy and tether their horses for the smithy to examine and stall; then they take the time to walk through the market place buying their necessary vittals. After a while, they both agree its time to quench a well-earned thirst with a fine ale before leaving for Carlibar.

Sitting at the outer doorway the Carte inn watching the thronging crowds in the busy market and supping ale, they're about to leave on their mission when they see a disturbance and notice the clearly marked three golden leopards on orange surcoats of about a dozen English soldiers, shoving people aside and pushing others to the ground as they make their way directly to where they both are seated. "Fuck," says William, "they're coming straight towards us." Stephen grips his sword then says, "Oi'm bleedin' ready." Curiously, the English soldiers stop by the side of a blind beggar who is sitting against the wall of a drinking well, they hear an English soldier laugh out loud and say, "A blind Scotchman…" Another soldier quips, "That's because he saw too many Scotch pox whores… starting with his mother, it must have been too much for the wretches senses and he poked his own eyes out."

The English soldiers roar with laughter, then the first soldier deftly puts his hand into the beggar's bowl, but the beggar suddenly grabs him firmly by the wrist. The expression of the soldier changes as he snatches the coins and pulls his hand away, He says, "Tell me this Scotchman, is it true that you blind people have greater senses when you touch things to know what they are?" The blind man doesn't reply as the soldier continues, "Let us see if the old beggar can sense what things are by the touch?" The soldier viciously slaps the beggar across the face with such a force, the beggar splits the back of his skull open on the stonework of the well side-wall, much to the amusement of the English soldiers.

A soldier enquires, "Do you know what that was Scotchman?" The soldiers continue laughing, "That was giving a blind Scotchman a helping hand…" His friends roar with laughter. At that moment, a Flemish wool trader steps between the beggar and the English soldier to help the beggar sit upright. Infuriated, the soldier grabs the trader and topples him into the well. William and Stephen immediately stand up and look at each other, instinctively knowing each other's thoughts are they move forward to intervene, while the English soldiers gather around the injured beggar and begin pissing on him as he sits against the wall semi-conscious. William and Stephen are within a few feet of the soldiers when an English knight suddenly appears and enquires of his men as to what they're doing. The lead soldier replies, "Just having a bit of humour with the locals my Lord. William and Stephen halt when they hear the knight ordering the soldiers to follow him.

As the English move away, William and Stephen go back to their seats at the inn. Stephen says, "I thought you told Wishart and wee Maw you would be keepin' out o' trouble?" William replies, "Aye Stephen ah did, ah just went with you tae make sure that it was you who didn't get into any trouble." William suddenly remembers, "Shit Stephen, that trader is still down the well…" The two companions jump to their feet and are about to rush over when they see the Flemish trader is getting pulled out of the well by some of friends while some of the other traders tend to the injured beggar. Relieved, William and Stephen sit back down again and talk awhile longer, when they notice the English soldier who abused the trader and beggar returning to the market place with three of his comrades, pushing and shoving people out of their way and freely thieving food and chattel from stalls. The two young friends keep a keen eye on them, when curiously;

the English soldiers stop at the mouth of a wynd. (Alley) They point at something and talk furtively amongst themselves, they look around suspiciously then disappear into the wynd. William and Stephen get up and quickly move to follow the soldiers out of curiosity. Stephen picks up a small oak wine barrel and throws it on his shoulder like a trader, then he hurries to catch up with William. Upon reaching the mouth of the wynd, they turn the corner to see the English soldiers have stripped a young girl naked and they're molesting her, one of the soldiers sees William and Stephen approaching.

The Soldier immediately pulls his sword and calls out, "What do you..." William head-butts him with such a force, the crack of the Englishman's breaking nose and eye sockets sounds like a butchers cleaver going through bone. William quickly fells the second soldier with a full force fist on the side of his head, knocking him out. Stephen sees the big English soldier getting up off the weeping girl and brings the oak wine barrel crashing down on the top of his head. The fourth English soldier backs into the wall in shock, desperately trying to pull up his hose. He watches horrified as Stephen repeatedly smashes the wine barrel down on the skull and face of the big Englishman like a man possessed, blood and brain tissue splatter everywhere, with gore and bone sticking to the base of the barrel. William grabs the petrified soldier standing against the wall by the back of the neck then repeatedly smashes his head into the stone corner of a doorway till the unconscious soldier drops to the ground, nothing remains of the soldier's head but a bloody pulp.

Unexpectedly, another English soldier comes walking into the wynd and immediately sees what's happening, he raises the alarm by calling for help. William pulls Stephen off the top of the dead Englishman and urgently points to the rear gateway of the wynd, they pick up the young girl and run through the end of the wynd and back into the thronging market crowds. They hastily take the young girl back to where they had been drinking and speak to the innkeeper who knows William, "Hide her away out of sight awhile, when all this has died down, try and find her folks." The innkeeper nods in agreement and quickly shelters the distraught young girl underneath his stall. Needing to flee the scene as quickly as possible, William and Stephen run at speed to the blacksmiths corrals for their horses, there they quickly tack and mount. When pulling their horses around in the tight corral, they see English soldiers are now running in their direction and calling for others nearby to help capture them both.

Without stopping to think, the two friends look at each other, grin, then both of them charge towards the corral fences simultaneously, where Warrior and Fleetfoot easily clear the top rungs of the fences to land in amongst the oncoming soldiers, scattering them asunder. The two companions gallop through the market grounds at speed and on towards the West port gate over a half a mile away. As they close on the port gate guard point, they slow their horses down, knowing they had made good their escape from the market, now their last hurdle is to get through the guard point to reach the freedom of the outside roads. When they approach the gatehouse, they find once again that the English guards are too busy fleecing traders coming inwards, to notice William and Stephen exiting undisturbed through the final port gate.

Once through to the freedom of the open road, the pair enthusiastically spur their horses on to get well clear of Paisley town. After a few miles and well satisfied that no one is following them, they soon bring Warrior and Fleetfoot to a walking pace then rest awhile to cool and water their horses.

William curses, "Norman bastards… that wee lass couldn't have been much older than ten summers." Stephen shakes his head with an expression of deep anger and hatred etched upon his face, then his demeanour changes and he laughs aloud, "At least we know that's one fine Norman who wont be bleedin' doin' that again."

"Aye, ah know." William replies.

Stephen laughs again, "Naw Wallace, yie won't be knowing that at all…"

William looks at Stephen curiously; he enquires, "How so?" Stephen replies with a grin, "Look at these fine fellas…" Stephen holds up and dangles what looks like a pair of tiny kidneys… then he laughs, "Oi cut the big fella's bolloks off." Aghast and disgusted, William looks at the testicles held dangling from Stephen's fingers… then he laughs out loud, "Stephen ua Mac h'Alpine me mad brother, yie really are one crazy feckr right enough…" William roars with laughter while Stephen cheerfully flings the tiny testicles high into the air, as though discarding unwanted shit from his fingers. William says with a smiley frown. "Tiny wee things those for such a big fella…"

Stephen quips, "Aye, that's the English average I hear."

The two friends laugh then they mount their horses and nudge them into a canter and on towards their first destination high in the hills above Paisley town.

A little while later, as they gain near to the village of Arthurslie and the rickety olde obhainn's of Carlibar, Stephen says in a deliberate whisper, "This is too bleedin' quiet for my liking Wallace?" William pulls Warrior to a halt and raises himself in the saddle to observe the surrounding hillsides… He sees carrion crow and corbies are circling in the sky not far away, when a faint smoke wafts through from the nearby woodlands. William says, "Fuck Stephen, do yie recognise that odour?" then he grips tight his sword handle. Stephen immediately does the same, then he says, "Aye, ah sure do… that's the smell o' burnin' meat and the scent o' death in the air Wallace…" The two friends glance knowingly at each other, then William exclaims, "Leckie…"

# Labyrinth o' Carlibar

Ah don't bleedin' like this Wallace," said Stephen of Ireland, "I can still smell death in the air… yet all these little clachans and villages show no signs o' any violence, there's nobody here, not even a bleedin' hog…" William says, "Just keep yer ears and eyes open Stephen, for sure there's something badly wrong, but we cannae dally about lookin' for what it is, we've got to find Leckie mòr, deliver the message and writs, then get away from here as fast as we can for Crosshouse."

The two companions cautiously ride on in search of Leckie mòr at his renowned smithy on the Gleniffer braes, in order to deliver to him vital information from Lord Moray. As they ride towards Carlibar, Stephen nervously laughs, "It's sure been a fine morning to be having wit' ya Wallace, in me spirit wit' bonnie wee Maw's wake, and for me soul wit' you." William replies, "Aye, we've sent off our bonnie wee Maw, now ah reckon after this morns debacles, we've started as we mean to go on." Stephen grins, "Ah, sure now, that's music to me ears Wallace."

They ride on in silence till they approach the outskirts of Carlibar, where all is quiet… the cottages and obhainn's appear eerily empty of people. William and Stephen make their way down the main drag, there are no dogs barking nor birds singing. William looks around, "I hope this is no' another fuckin' slaughter Stephen…" He takes his bow from his backpack and nocks an arrow as Stephen pulls out his crossbow and lay's it across his saddle.

"Oi don't like this Wallace, the atmosphere here, it's too much like a feckn cathedral for me… bleedin' unnatural."

Eventually they pass through the Balloch and see faint thin smoke rising from the crags in the brae's above. William points at the smoke, "That's old Leckie's place up there." Stephen scans for any a sign of life around them, he says, "I sure hope he's up there Wallace, as this place is scarin' the shit out o' me for some bleedin' reason." They walk their horses slowly forward and on up the hillside track till they arrive at the blacksmith's obhainn, still feeling slightly spooked by the disturbing quietness of nature all around. The slow creaking noise of the gently swinging smithy Shoppe sign magnifies the sinister atmosphere as the two friends dismount and cautiously approach the large smithy obhainn.

Unexpectedly a voice calls to them…"Who will that be a'callin' at ma door?" Stephen whispers, "What th' fuck Wallace? That's no' a door, it's a leather feckn sheet." Suddenly crows erupt from the doorway, flying haphazard past them. A startled Stephen exclaims, "I'm out o' here Wallace. Ah cant be standing this much bleedin' stress." William grabs Stephen's arm, "Wait…" then he calls into the darkened obhainn, "It's me Leckie… William Wallace, son of Alain Wallace, hunter and Guardian to the late King and grandson to the late Bheitris Wallace, who's lineage is that of the Aicé Morríaghan. With me here is Alain Stephen ua Mac h'Alpine, son o' the chief o' Monaghan and Connaught from the Aicés o' Erinn." With sweat on his brow, Stephen whispers, "Why did you tell him your feckn life story Wallace, for fucks sake… and then yie go and feckn tell him I'm wit' ya?" William whispers, "You've met him before Stephen, yie know what he's like for tradition, especially if he's drunk, and yie know he would belt yie for just breathin' never mind makin a feckn duction mistake." Suddenly the leather bull-hide door of the smithy obhainn pulls open, the two friends jump back startled and grip their swords as Leckie walks out to meet them, looking extremely haggard and tired, much to their surprise. Leckie glares at them awhile through bloodshot bleary eyes, "Ah boys, come on in, and Wallace, yie don't need to be telling me your feckn life story."

On entering the darkened obhainn, Leckie walks over to old pitch barrels and throws a ginger cat out the small window, he sits down in a deep box chair beside a peat fire then speaks, "Ah was awfy sorry to be hearin' about wee Maw and our family misfortunes Wallace. I couldn't attend the wake o' the bonnie lass, for things here in Carlibar are no' the same as they once were, I've had my own tribulations and troubles to deal with…" Stephen whispers, "He must be feckn drunk, I've never known the wee man to ever be so amiable." William also considers their old mentor using the words, *Our family*, when speaking of wee Maw. Leckie pokes at the little fire and looks into a simmering cooking pot, "Would you fella's be liking some fine gráinneog (Hedgehog) broth?" William replies, "Naw tá Leckie, we've eaten on the way up here. We're here because we've brought you an urgent message from Lord Moray and Wishart, then we're going down to Crosshouse to see Ranald and deliver the same and anything yie may add by way o' a reply."

They sit themselves down on a large wool trussel near the fire. Leckie growls, "Did I say you feckrs could sit…?" The two friends immediately jump up, clumsily knocking over racks of swords, pole-arms, pots and pans in their panic. Amidst the chaotic noise, Leckie ladles some broth into a bowl then says, "Have a seat boyz." William looks at Stephen, who simply shrugs his shoulders while waving his hands for him to continue, William says, "I've parchment rolls here for you and Ranald from bishop Wishart and Lord Moray..." Leckie replies abruptly, "Then yie have feckn parchments for me Wallace, not a feckn message, be specific boy, its important. Didn't I drum factology into your big feckn head a thousand times when you were a wain? No wonder you needed belted se' feckn much." Looking up from his seat, Leckie glares at Stephen, "Are yie all right there wee lost boy from auld Erinn?" Stephen replies, "Oh oi'm fine Leckie sur, I'll be sitting here quiet as a mouse while you and Wallace here do all the bleedin' talkin', for it's a fine example of Scots communication going on before my very ears and eyes."

"I remember your father well," says Leckie as he stares at Stephen curiously, "you carry his canny look about yie, aye, and what a bonnie fighter too, how is yer father keepin' son?" Stephen replies, "No' se' good, he passed away earlier this year." Leckie shakes his head forlorn, "Ach ahm so sad to hear that son, for he was a fine man and better friend yie couldn't ever wish for." William smiles. Leckie glares at him, "What are you smiling at Wallace, where's the feckn rolls? And what other information do yie have for me... Fuck I don't know... the youth of today is just plain fuckin' useless?"

Moving closer to hand over the parchment rolls, William halts when Leckie notices the Aicé's amulets around his neck. Leckie reaches out and holds them gently in his hand. He says, "Wee Maw gave you these talisman' didn't she?" William replies, "Aye, she did." Leckie continues, "What a beautiful and wonderfull wee woman she was, and what a bonnie fighter too." Leckie puts his head in his hands morosely then he rubs his eyes as though holding back tears. "She was ma bonnie wee sister Wallace, not se' many folk know this, for her own protection yie understand... wie me bein' se' close to our late King. And ah might seem a bit heartless to you boys, but I'll pay ma respects to ma darlin' blood in ma own way and in ma own time, for ahm sore o' heart that ah couldn't be there to save her in her hour of need..."

Leckie sniffs, then he sits back in his chair to break the seals on the rolls, he lays them out on a barrel top beside him, next, he reaches below the box seat and pulls out a large block of curved glass and lays it on top of the rolls to magnify the text. As the moments pass slowly by, nothing is said while Leckie sups his broth and reads the writ rolls. Finally he looks up at the two companions, "I need yiez to follow me, and you Wallace, you must tell me everything that Lord Moray told to yie, make it exactly as he relayed it to yie and be sure to miss nothing out... Oh," exclaims Leckie "And bring your grandfathers sword with yie too, for I've noticed yie've broke it." William exclaims, "How could yie know that?" Leckie ignores the question, picks up a herders staff and walks toward the door to exit. Stephen whispers, "How the feck does he know your grandpa's sword is broken?" William shrugs his shoulders as they follow Leckie outside.

They walk a little distance then stopping when they near the foot of the Gleniffer Brae, Leckie points to the topmost plateau of an old volcanic plug. "See away up there boys... that's where we're going, the Devils Cauldron. Up there's the remains o' an auld Cairn chamber where no one ever goes out o' fear, for they believe it's haunted by the Demons o' the darkest Sìhd." William and Stephen look at each other as Leckie continues, "Take your saddles and tack then leave them behind the obhainn leant-to, then brush yer horses down and put them in the corral to graze, for it'll be awhile afore we get back down here, and make sure there is plenty oats left out for them too, because where we're goin' next, we might never get back out o' that place alive." William and Stephen glance at each other utterly bewildered, but they dutifully do as they are bid. Eventually they join Leckie then begin a hike up the steep winding hillside path. Leckie moves with speed, agility and the stamina of a mountain deer,.William and Stephen struggle to keep up with him.

When they finally reach the summit of the Devils cauldron, they stop to catch their breath at the highest point on the Braes of Gleniffer, where the view is spectacular. To the south they see the small mountains of Galloway, away to the west the mountains of Ceanntyre, the coast of Ireland and all the lower west coast islands. Far to the east the lush green forests of the lower Clyde valley… and to the north, the great mountains of Ben Lomond and the highlands. William feels emotional as he looks down on his childhood home, "I can see Ach na Feàrna from here…" Leckie senses William's grief, he walks up and puts a comforting hand on his shoulder, then he speaks with conviction, "Son, it doesn't matter what age you are, or who yie are, grief is a terrible thing to be dealing with. Perhaps age and experience lessens it slightly… but then, the memories are even greater." Leckie shakes his head as he continues, "Aye, we each must deal with grief and mourning in our own way, and if we are to avoid any more grief, then our wits must be whole to face the evil that's now nesting in our realm." Leckie pulls Stephen close and warmly embraces both the two young friends.

For a moment they all stand looking across the stupendous vista. Stephen enquires, "What do yie call this place o' yours Leckie?" Leckie laughs, "This is what I call an impregnable defensive location." Stephen and William laugh too, as it's not the answer they expected. Leckie continues, "And the Romans wondered how we saw them coming?" Leckie laughs again, but he stops short and stares back down at the desolate village of Carlibar, nestling on a plateau in the

Gleniffer braes. He says, "But now it's the English, and they are far wilier than any Roman general…"

The boys look at each other as Leckie continues, "Ten thousand Roman soldiers were once stationed here, and they never knew we were among them…" William thinks it best to bring Leckie back to focus on the present, "What happened down in the village Leckie, it's deserted, but there's no signs of any violence as a visitation?" Leckie replies in a somber tone, "A few days ago English soldiers came…" Leckie hesitates; then he continues, "They hung all the young men o' fighting age, for they refused to join the English army. Then they burned the old men and women to death down in Gleniffer gorge. They took away all the young girls too… they raped, tortured and killed them at the foot o the Brae, then the English soldiers finished ther' evil doing's by burnin' alive all the children in the old Kirk. Now all that's left here is a few old women and their cats hiding about these hills." William exclaims, "Fuck Leckie… ahm sorry, we didn't know." Leckie sighs, "Ach I was away down in Moffat myself and got back late last night, that's how ah missed what happened here… and at Ach na Feàrna too, it's a terrible business boys." William and Stephen are clearly affected at the blunt delivery of detail. Leckie clears his throat and resumes his steely character, "Now follow me…"

The old sword-master walks off at a fast pace, quickly followed by William and Stephen. Soon they arrive on the crest plateau of Gleniffer, where Leckie points out a little Cairn hidden by four large Hawthorn bushes and thick undergrowth at the centre of the crest. William and Stephen realise they're standing in the remains of an ancient stone circle. Leckie says, "Look around yiez boyz and yiez'll see the ring and bars of lintel stones in the long grass, can you see how they progress in sizes and different colours?" The two friends look around as Leckie continues, "Notice the stones that are larger and redder are runnin' east to west, then those smaller whiter stones runnin' north to south. If yiez are ever looking to find an underground cairn, always look for Hawthorn groves and that circular lintel stone geometry that surrounds it, and ask about the name o' *bar* from any locals thereabouts, for it identifies Royal boundaries or underground Chambers."

Leckie clears away gorse and long grass from a large flat slab, "See here, I need yiez to push away this flat stone if you fella's want to be followin' me." The two friends grip the large slab and push in the same direction, much to their surprise, the slab moves easily, appearing to spin on a pivot to reveal a tight entrance into a subterranean stairwell. "C'mon boyz," commands Leckie, "and when yiez get inside, there's hand grips on the corners o' the slab, pull hard and it'll slide and drop back into place, but mind now, it'll take yer fingers off if yiez are no' quick about it." William does as he is bid and narrowly misses getting his fingers crushed when the large slab swings back quickly and drops into position.

The two young friends cautiously feel their way down the dark stairwell behind Leckie, to where he stops and lights a small pitch torch. They then continue stepping down more wet dank cavernous stairwells deep into the bowels of the volcanic hillside, untill they come to what appears to be a dead end. Leckie pushes his hand inside a small space at head height, then a great wheelstone rolls aside, revealing a passageway just big enough to squeeze through. Leckie reaches out and grabs William, "Follow me." Stephen, still trying to see in the dim light calls out, "Where are yiez?" An impatient Leckie replies, "Hurry up Mac h'Alpine" Stephen calls out once more like a wee boy lost, "But I don't be knowin' where yiez are…" Suddenly Leckie reaches out from a darkened niche, grabs Stephen roughly and drags him into the entrance of another passageway, cursing as he leads the way. William and Stephen obediently follow Leckie down through the pitch-black tunnels while continually cracking their skulls off the lintels and low overhanging rocks of the ancient passages, all the while trying to keep up with him. Suddenly Leckie's face comes up in front of them, "Hurry up you two, for fuck's sake, and mind to bow your heads on the way through." As soon as he appeared, Leckie turns away and disappears into another passageway. Stephen mutters, "This is feckn' mad ah tell yee Wallace, bleedin' madness…" William says, "Keep up or we'll lose him down here."

They quickly follow in Leckie's direction. The panic and fear that gnaws at them both at the thought of getting trapped in this claustrophobic place almost paralyses the young friends, then they hear Leckie call out to them from somewhere in the distance, "Don't worry boyz… it only gets tighter down here." After what seems like hours stooping down giant steps and squeezing through dank wet tiny tunnels, they eventually crawl out onto a large stone platform that reveals a great underground chamber. They stand up and gaze in relieved wonderment, enthralled at the sights before them. "What is this place…?" enquires William. "This is home for me." Laughs Leckie as he lights torches and pitch-filled channels to illuminate the great Cavern. The enormity of the fabulous chamber becomes apparent as it begins to fill with a somber illuminating light, revealing a scene of almost mythical proportions. William exclaims, "You could fit a wee castle in here…"

"Would yie look at this?" exclaims Stephen. Close-by, are seemingly endless rows of ancient armour, shields and weaponry, all superbly crafted, enough of an armoury to equip and arm a small army. Looking around this place of mystical and gothic charm, giant carved standing stones are placed around the base of the chamber; ancient symbols are etched onto the walls of the amazing underground cavern. It quickly becomes obvious that at one time a whole community must have lived and worked in this fantastical cathedral of stone. Nudging Stephen, William exclaims, "Holy feck Stephen, would yie look at that…" Stephen opens his mouth, "Jaezuz…"

The two friends gaze at a monstrous horned skull sitting high and proud above blue-green lichen and a purple moss-covered base, apparently constructed with human skulls and situated in the middle of a small black-water pool. Behind the giant skull and stretching hundreds of feet up into the darkness, a sheet cascade of millions of sparkling water droplets fall in slow motion, creating an amazing sensory and emotion fulfilling backdrop to this primeval scene. They also see there are many other skulls from horses, Stag, long-horn bulls and hundreds of other beast… and eerily, more human skulls, all decorated with ancient symbols or precious jewels then placed in crevices and ledges all around the cavern, with countless numbers piled high in great pyramids. William exclaims, "What the feck is this place Leckie and what has that great big skull came off or even once been attached too?"

Stephen is amazed, "I've never seen anythin like this in me life before. Sure now, I'll be tinkin' that skull's off a feckn Dragon." William repeats his earlier question, "What is this place Leckie?" But there's no reply, he turns to see Leckie disappearing into another tunnel entrance with his torch. William bounds after Leckie, "C'mon Stephen, the auld fella is on the move again and he's heading down between those rocks going somewhere else now." Stephen quickly catches up, "Sure I don't know what's ever happened down here, but I tell yee, it must have been a good feckn night on the craitur to produce all o' this. And what was that little fella wit' the great big head bein' all about?" William, still trying to watch where Leckie has gone, replies, "Me too, ah'v never seen the likes before neither… but didn't that big head look like the dragon on me auld Dá's Coat of Arms?" Stephen replies, "Kinda… but the only bleedin' dragon I've ever seen was me auld Maw bless her, when she was applyin' herself to the leatherin' about the head of me auld Fadder when he came home wit' a little too much o' the liquid happiness in him."

William and Stephen laugh heartily as they continue following the source of the low light deeper into the bowels of the volcanic plug. They soon emerge into smaller chamber, which is also well lit with pitch channels, torches and most noticeably, by a great glowing charcoal fire in a large stone fire pit. Looking all around, they see there is even more ancient armour and weapons on great racks. At the far end of the chamber, they see four large blacksmiths forges and Leckie sitting beside them with a cask of craitur under his arm, pouring the nectar into three flagons. William and Stephen approach Leckie, whereupon he hands them each a craitur filled flagon. William exclaims. "This place is like an ancient Maze." Leckie replies, "This is the Labyrinth o' Carlibar son, the netherworld of the Aicé Sìhd o' Gleniffer. There are a few more places like this dotted about Scotland, maybe someday I'll show you where they all are. Yie've seen the one down in Glen Afton haven't yie?" William replies, "Yie mean the chamber tumulus on s' Taigh am Rígh mòr?"

Leckie laughs, "Aye son, but that's just the bung in the top o' the jug down there, there are many other small entrances around the Black Craig and the shepherd hills that leads yie intae one of the largest labyrinths in the whole o' Scotland." William is amazed, "Ah never knew that." Leckie continues, "We'll have to make sure then that both o' yiez do know that about the labyrinths o' Black Craig some other time. Why don't yiez have a look round while ah have a wee breather here?" Leckie watches contentedly as the two young friends begin to absorb the mystical qualities of the cavern. He says, "Our ancients would secrete away down here when invading armies ever threatened our realm up in the known world… Anyways, ahm wantin' to show yiez something else that's no' seen blue sky or the sun above for nigh a thousand years." William enquires, "What are yie talking about?" Leckie points across the small cavern; "Look over there and see if yiez can you tell me what yie think that is?" Stephen enquires. "Why do you auld fella's always be askin' us young fella's for answers to feckn riddles?"

The three companions laugh as they wander across the cavern and stand in front of a great white granite wheel, hanging from the rock ceiling by heavy chains. William and Stephen are greatly impressed when they see the great granite wheel is meticulously inlaid with intricate knotwork and symbols. Peculiarly, they notice the outside edge is like a great stone scabbard that has many sword hilts protruding, giving an appearance of an artistic sunburst with the swords within the stone wheel obviously pointing to the centre of the carved wheelstone. Leckie says, "This auld place here was sacred to the master hammerers of our ancestors in their fight against the Romans, then it was used again during the wars between the Christians and Cruathnie when they all fought over the land of tunnels and the entire tribal lands o' the five Island races."

William and Stephen listen intently as Leckie continues, "The Aicé's o' Gobhain' gabha, (Queen's Govan-Smithies) usually had their brionnú mòr (Great Forges) far away from townie people, but always near to clean running water, that's what's needed to be creating the magic of turning base metals into the finest o' tempered steel for the makin' weapons and armour. But these weapons made in here are no' born to life in water or pitch oil, naw boyz, they're finally tempered from the finest of live human blood that will be containing the Anam Álainn." William and Stephen sense Leckie's words are not much comfort to their humours in a place that is scaring the shit out of them. Though that thought is being eased slightly by their curiosity. "Come closer," commands Leckie. He moves forward and stands before the wheelstone. "Ahl ask yiez again, what dyie think this is?"

Scrutinising the wheelstone, William enquires, "Can we take the weapons out or touch them?" Leckie replies, "Aye, that's fine." William and Stephen step forward too and look closely at the sword hilts and pommels. Curiously, William notices the knotwork of the wheelstone is coloured a burnished ocher red in the depth of the channels. They both pull out the swords and run their fingers over the blades, they can feel the edges are still keen despite their ancient looking condition. Stephen notices that five particular slats amongst the array of weapons is blank, Leckie sees his curiosity. "Well, have yiez worked out what this is yet?" Stephen replies, "These swords look really old Leckie, yet they could still be used today. Feck, these blades are bleedin' fantastic. They appear to be fold forged metals, but they're too short for a modern sword." William says, "I have never seen such beautiful designs in a blade ever before Leckie… and the way these gemstones are set into each of the quillons. Wait… these blades remind me o' my fathers claymore and ma dirk…"

A moment of realisation comes to William when he notices something on each sword that also looks very familiar, "Ah," he exclaims, "This is the same forge mark on my fathers dirk." Stephen says, "It's the same with this sword, but it's near three times the size o' the others… like a little fella's claymore. Is this a giant sword for the little people Leckie?"

"What did you say?" enquires Leckie, he laughs aloud; then Stephen notices something else that's very familiar at the centre of a sword, where the handle and quillons meets with the blade and tang. He looks at his fathers ring; then he looks back at the sword and sees the same symbols embedded in both. William looks down at the symbols on his weapon then at wee Maw's amulets, "It's the same marks on these too." William sees Stephens gaze then he realises … "These swords and weapons are our ancestors brands aren't they?" He continues, "This place is of the Aicé Sìhd, the home of the ancients and the Guardians armoury o' legend… this is the armoury o' the Fianna Mòrna and Aicé Garda Rìoghail isn't it?" Leckie replies, "Right yie are there on all counts Wallace. And this wheel here is the great tablet of the Artur's and Aicés when they used to meet to settle their differences, it was taken away from the auld Stanehoose overlooking the Forth River in the East." William exclaims, "Naw Leckie, surely yer jestin' us… is this the actual Tablet of Adoration?" Leckie grins, "Aye, it sure is." William and Stephen are both in awe. William blusters, "Naw, then all o' those legend stories o' wee Maw's are true?"

Running his fingers gently in the channels of knotwork, William exclaims, "This really is the Tablet of Adoration?" Leckie laughs, "Aye son, and there it was that you fella's thought fairy stories were no' true… shame on yiez." Stephen holds up a sword trying to catch more design detail from the light of the forge and torches. He enquires, "Why are they here, and why is this sword marked wit' the same symbols of me fadder's signet ring, where are we Leckie and what is this bleedin' place?" Leckie replies, "I know that your elders have been telling you ever since you opened your tiny wee eyes and your tiny wee ears, all about the legends of the Cruathnie and the warrior Aicé's… am I right?"

Both William and Stephen nod in agreement. Leckie continues, "Then I'll no' be repeating them, but what I will tell yiez is this, always remember that somewhere between the legends that your families have told yiez to that o' the fastidious academic, you'll find in your heart the real truth, and that reality is now before yie both for a brief moment in time… for you're both blood descendants from great warrior Guardians of our blood." The two young friends sit down on a plinth beside the Tablet of Adoration, completely in awe and almost disbelief.

Leckie takes a swig of his craitur then he continues, "You there young Wallace, you're from the bloodline o' the Britonic Aicé o' Strathclyde, Morríaghan and her first Artur, Àrd Goibhéan Rígh. And you young Mac' h'Alpine, you're the blood o' the Aicé na Éirú Dannu and their famed Artur, Àrd Céthur h'Gréine Rígh… both of whom carried a Claiomh Solais (Sword of Light) into battle to protect their own folks. You Wallace and you Mac h'Alpine, are both blood of the original Artur's and Aicés of the Tuatha Dé CruinnèCè and spirits o' the Aicé, Ánnan Sìhd of these islands."

William and Stephen are speechless, they had heard these legends many times and often differing, depending on how much craitur had flowed into the auld folks doing the telling, but this time the story before them is shockingly real, this time of telling feels to them like it's the last piece of a faith puzzle they always knew and questioned. This time they both know it, for now they are standing before the fabled Tablet of Adoration. Seeing the amazement and look of wonderment on William and Stephen's faces, Leckie continues, "In this chamber there once lived the ancient Féine Mòrna s' Breitheamh Rígh, who Christian historians mistakenly call warrior Druids, for the Christians know not the melodies of our tongue. But these Christians penned the earliest history of these islands and wrote many manuscripts, including the ancient Bonedd Gwŷr y Ystrad Cluid,(Descent of the Men of Strathclyde) and Leabhar Ríoghachta nan Alba (Book of Royal Scots) and some even skreeved the first Leabhar Gabála Érenn Stephen, (The Book of the taking of Ireland) Aye, they recorded these stories of our ancients for the amusement of minstrels, poets and clerics. And all of that effort simply to reconcile their Christian faith with our ancient beliefs and deities… Anyways, the ancients referred to our land as Henn Ogledd, 'Old North' where the thirteen Treasures of the ancients are laid away from those who would corrupt and kill for their own avarice. When the Artur's and Aicés invoked the spirit of the divine Tri-Aicé in these weapons, they're only ever to be used for the protection o' innocents from the ravages of conquest from those of evil intent. It's then the inspiration of these legends becomes a reality in the hands of true warriors, those who in turn become immortals themselves…"

As Leckie pauses for a moment, the young friends pick up on his faltering demeanor.

"What is it that's botherin' yie Leckie," enquires Stephen, "for ya sure have me worried wit' something there?" Leckie smiles feebly, he shakes his head, rubs his eyes then he continues, "Ah'll tell yiez… with the passing of ma son, I'm now the last keeper of the labyrinth o' Carlibar, few have entered here in my lifetime, only King Alexander, the fathers of the Guardians and theirs before them, Malcolm and your father Wallace… and your father too Stephen, True Tam and then ma son…" Leckie falters again. Giving himself a shake, he continues, "Aye ma son… he who would have been the next keeper had he not been murdered a few days ago by English soldiers sent to search for me…" The two friends are shocked to hear Leckie's words. Before they could say anything, Leckie continues, "In giving up his life, the English who murdered him mistook his life's passing for that of mine, that's why I could not attend Bheitris boys… even though I wept sorely for her when I saw the smoke arise from the pyre of ach na Feàrna."

The normally stoic Leckie falters again as he relives his pain, "I couldn't save ma son so cruelly treated… glory be to him, but he never did reveal where our relics of antiquated Treasures lay hidden in safety, for that English King is savage and merciless in his search for all things related to the great kings called the Artur." Leckie pauses, then he walks over and sits on a boulder-seat beside a glowing forge. He looks at William and Stephen, "That sword your holding master Stephen… that's the legendary Claidheamh Soluis, the sword of light o' Céthur h'Gréine Rígh, the first Artur of alt Cluid, it was he who first pulled the sword from the Tablet o' Destiny upon the royal hill of Clach Mhanainn. The one you're holdin' Wallace, that's the brand of Artur, Goibhéan Rígh, crowned on Doomster hill down by the smithy village of auld Gobhain. Aye, those fine moments forging our history, they all started here with the master hammerers, creating the great swords of Carlibar."

"The Dragon head down in the Black-pool chamber…" utters William, "Is it the emblem of the original Artur?" Leckie replies, "Aye son, if any good-born man or woman draws the brand of Carlibar from the Tablet of Adoration, then their combined Anam Álainn instinctively knows how to get it to sing with pride and honour. It will appear to onlookers as though the blade is white hot from its pommel to its tip, it's then that the sword of light does surely deliver without malice the precious gift of sending wrongdoers away to a better life… that they may be born again with a greater hearts intent." Stephen holds the magnificent sword aloft and gazes at it in wonderment. Leckie sighs, "Ach then the Christians arrived here and the old ways were eventually discarded. Those pious people are mostly good and peaceful souls, but believing with such a zeal in a single God they're blinded from seeing their masters are naught but a gaggle of greed-infested evil bastards, who have the guile to elevate themselves into untouchable positions of power by the quill, something they could never have achieved by a sword of honour."

Looking at the detail of a large claymore, William enquires, "How could men of the quill subdue a realm of the sword?" Leckie spits in the fire, "Ach son, for hundreds of years through intrigue and terror, these weasels have acquired power over others, simply by nurturing peoples darkest fears and their desperate need to believe in a better afterlife." Stephen enquires "Then you're saying that these weapons are religious relics of our ancient faith, like pieces of the cross are to Christians? Is that why the Christians set their stall upon the religious sites of our ancestors, to destroy everything not of their own bleedin' faith?"

Leckie replies, "Aye Stephen, more or less, but like my son, the old seers of the ancient faith did not let them have any of the Thirteen Treasures of the Cruathnie, both here in Gleniffer and in the Glen of Adoration in Ireland, for that's where the great wheel before you was created. These Treasures will rest here till warriors of the true faith return, for as the Norse once believed in many Gods like we do, that's something now deemed heretical unto death if yie ever question the Christian faith. Believe me this boys, there will come a day well beyond our lifetime, when folk will look back on this cult of the one true God and think it sustained by primitive madmen and power-hungry fantasists." The two young friends observe Leckie, who appears as though he's a broken man. Stephen enquires, "So why do you be tellin' us all of these wonderous things Leckie, and why do you show us these fantastical old weapons? Though I have to be tellin' ya straight, I do understand in me heart what yie tell to us, more than I could express in all the words and languages I've ever learned." William said belatedly, "And me."

Smiling, Leckie explains, "There are many reasons ah suppose, but mostly because you're both surviving seed o' the original Guardians, for they are few left alive now, and this situation in our realm with the English, it has never been known before, not even from the Romans, the Norse, Danes, Saxons nor any other who has ever thought to conquer this land of our birth. But these are different days with different needs, and those Ragemanus Rolls fuck... the Nobles and clergy have taken bribes and sold their souls to serve this Norman usurper called Longshanks. Most of the fuckin' nobles here are of Norman blood and care little for our people nor the ancient faith of this realm, they only care for title and their land holding revenues in England and France, they are fuck all but privileged self-serving bastards who rule by fear and conniving self-entitlement."

William and Stephen listen intently as Leckie continues... "This realm o' ours is becoming little more than a slave backwater to feed the ambitions of a cruel English King, for he has done this great evil successfully in many lands, including Cymru and Eire. Now this Longshanks fella is spreading his evil stench into Scotland and none of note is prepared to stop him... but I tell yiez this, I and other elders have watched you Wallace, and you too Mac h'Alpine, you've both trained for the church and absorbed much as good and learned students, particularly in history and languages. But your training in the arts of war with the sword and the goose-wing broad are exemplary. Yiez both have the eye of the Warrior architect. I've known yiez both since yiez were wains, I knew you that you both owned the geometry of the blade." Leckie smiles then he says, "And against ma better judgment, I really do like you boyz, even though on occasion I may have had to give yiez the occasional friendly belt about the head when visitin' your establishments of joy and enlightenment. Though it was always for yer own good mind, never was it for ma own pleasure… Well, sometimes it gave me pleasure, often if the truth were to be told."

The two young friends laugh as Leckie continues, "Seriously though, me'self and few others know that a bloody and merciless war is coming, but as our nobles have stood down our army and most of our bishops seats are warming English arse's, we know this war will be impossible to avoid with the English, and if we hold back too much longer, it will simply be a desperate stand against an unstoppable slaughter of our people. So, with those writs from Moray n' Wishart and what you have told me of the death lists, I'm now even more convinced that you both have an important part to play in Scotland's future. But only if you have the courage to stand against murder and tyranny imposed upon us by this English king, blessed be he by the so-called Holy Church o' fuckin' Rome."

"Oi'm feckin wit' ya Leckie," exclaims Stephen eagerly, "Sure now, we'll fix Scotland proud, then we can free my Ireland next." William thinks about his family and everything that has passed, then he replies, "I'm with yie too Leckie, to the bitter fuckin' end, whatever and whenever that may be." Leckie smiles, "Good boyz, we will sure be talkin' a lot more about this another time, but for now, we'll be staying here this night as its likely dark outside. In a wee while I want it that we should be building up the fires o' the great forges and fillin' the channels and torches wie more pitch, for there is much for me to be doin' afore yiez leave this place. And if you two poor wee souls are too tired for work later, there's plenty o' places for yiez tae crib down." William enquires, "Is it all right to look at the weapons again and have a wee wander about the place?" Leckie stands up and stretches his weary muscles, "Go ahead, you please yourselves, but mind this both o' yiez, it's at your own risk if yie disturb the spirits down here. Now, am goin' tae sleep awhile, so make yer peace with yer own Gods and maybe ahl see yiez if yiez are both alive later." Leckie lifts a pair of thick Wolverine and Bear brat's and drags them along the floor of the cavern, then he makes a deep crib beside a glowing forge fire, climbs in and lay's his head down to rest.

For a while, William and Stephen sit looking round the vast forge chamber thinking of Leckie's words, then Stephen nervously whispers, "What the feck did he mean *IF* we are still alive later?" Thinking of the underworld spirits, William replies, "Ah sure do hope that it was just his humour?"

They both sit talking awhile longer, then William says, "C'mon Stephen, lets go and look at these auld weapons set out for us to be examinin.'"

They wander through the many caverns, looking at the fabulous collections of their ancestor's ancient weaponry and armour. Stephen enquires, "What is it you'll be makin o' this day Wallace?" William replies, "I really don't know what to make o' it Stephen, this morn we surely blessed and gave wee Maw up to the four winds, next we find out an auld sorcerer is related to us both, and then he invites us into this underworld to tell us we're special... Feck, ah hope if ahm awake in ma crib in the morn that this has been some mad feckn dream and it's been too much nippin o' wee Maw's wake craitur that's got to me, either that or we're both dead and we don't yet know it?" Stephen laughs nervously, "What d'yie mean *IF* yie wake up? And what do yie mean we might be dead already?" William sighs, "We'll find out soon enough ma friend." Stephen looks around the underground forge cavern with big staring eyes; then his gaze falls upon the sword pommels of the ancients protruding from the Tablet of Adoration. "Well, if we really are bleedin' dead already, then we may as well have a wee look about our new home then…"

Wondering around their potential new home in the underworld, Stephen exclaims, "Would yie come and look at this Wallace, it's feckn amazin." He picks up the Claidheamh Soluis of Céthur h'Gréine then they walk over to the fabled round tablet of the Ancients. William pulls a short sword of the Aicé from the stone tablet and studies its exquisite beauty. He pulls out another four, each one different from the last. He studies them and shakes his head, for he's never seen anything of its likes before, so beautiful in craftsmanship, not even his grandfather's great claymore. They continue exploring the chambers and caverns for many hours, completely in awe of the craftsmanship of the weapons and armour they keep finding. Suddenly the gruff voice of Leckie startles William and Stephen, who are totally immersed in the magical underground realm of antiquated armour and relics from their ancestral past…

Leckie stands before them over-wrapped in wolverine brats, appearing like an ancient sorcerer of legend. The flickering lights from the flames of the cavern torches create shadows that dance ominously across his wizzened face, though his dark piercing eyes remain completely focussed. "When yiez wake up young Wallace, I want you and Mac h'Alpine here to be firing up all four forges for the remakin' o' your grandfathers broken brand, along with the iron from five swords o' the Aicé's and the brands of Artur

Àrd Nuadha. I'll be forging them all together to be pleating yiez both two refreshed Treasures. First, the Claidheamh mòr Cainnel, the Great Sword o' the bright flame from the fourth forge of A'nnan, as though it were brought to you Wallace from the divine Aicé herself. '*For none shall escape the gift of Fragarach the Retaliator once it is drawn from its sheath, none will resist its sweep, no shield will be a defence and no enemy shall recover from the wrath of its deliverance.*"

"And for you Mac h'Alpine, the next Treasure… I will forge for you Lúin fàinne mòr, 'the great Slaughterer.' A leaf-head ring spear o' many fine blades, worthy o' the four ancient forges o' Falias, Findias, Gorias and Murias. It was once said by the ancients o' our past, '*No foe shall ever be sustained against it, nor shall woe be brought against the warrior who wields Lúin fàinne mòr tried and true.*"

Leckie continues, "The Anam Álainn in both o' yiez with the spirit o' these Treasures, will all be imprinted with honour and justice, welded together by the most delicate, perfected craft my lives worth will create. And they shall be forged together in the black blood o' our enemies. The purest spirit of our ancients will be embodied in the forging of Treasures. Scotland will need the leadership o' Retaliator and the Slaughterer if we are to be free from the yolk of tyranny that now threatens the end of our race. It is for you young men of the Aicé that destiny does offer the power to wield such weapons. It shall also be the last known brands and blades cast from the great forges of Carlibar, for we of the Tuatha Dé Céile Aicé, believe that you two are the blessed ones to release them from the stone forges." Leckie turns his back on them both and returns to his crib, where he lies back down and resumes a deep sleep. The two friends both stare at each other with open mouths. William gasps, "What the fuck was that all about?" Stephen replies, "Now was that not a real spooky feckn story to be tellin' us; maybe we are dead right enough like yee said Wallace and that there old bastard is too? This is getting' bleedin madderer than before, ah tell yee." William says nothing by reply; he simply stares in the direction of Leckie's crib. He shakes his head bemused as Stephen whispers, "Wallace, we should get the fuck out o' here right now if we are still alive, for I be wantin' to see your beautiful rainy Scots heavens and freezin' sunshine at least one more time in me bleedin' lifetime." William shrugs his shoulders, "We can't leave Stephen, even if we knew how to get out of here, which we don't. Ah'd rather work with Leckie in this underworld than be having him in a wrath lookin' for us all over the feckn' middleworld." Stephen nods sympathetically, "Aye, maybe yer right, so what do we do now then me dead brother?" William replies, "C'mon, lets get the forges started for Leckie and get all our duties done… if he's going to make us each a brand o' the Treasures, then it doesn't matter if he's off his feckn head or dead, there's no other that I know that could make us weapons like this man could."

Rolling up his léine sleeves, William walks over to the great forge and lights it. Stephen wanders over to help, he quips, "At least if we be busy doing all o' this, we'll still be awake if we're dead in the mornin…" he rolls his sleeves up and grabs the handles of the great bellows to help bring to life the ancient fourth forge of Carlibar. The two young friends work for many long hours, bringing all the forges to a semblance of heat they think would be right for Leckie to begin his crafting. But at some time during their labours they both fall asleep, for in the great cavernous labyrinth of Carlibar; they could not know if it was day or night… Stephen wakes with a start, thinking he can smell frying bacon. He looks up and sees Leckie with a great skillet full of spitting bacon and sizzling eggs on the great forge, Leckie says, "So yer awake then?" William stirs too and can smell the glorious aroma of frying bacon. Stephen says enthusiastically, "Ah'll have a quick wash a piss and be right wit' ya." Leckie replies tersely, "We'll feed now, piss later. Once everything is in order for the creation o' the Treasures, yiez can leave here and continue on your mission." A relieved Stephen whispers, "It looks like we're no' dead after all Wallace." William replies, "Thank feck for that Stephen, jaezuz, Marion would sure no' have been very happy at all if ah had been dead." Leckie, shouts at them, "Get the fuck over here right now you two wasters and get some fine and tasty scran in yer bodies, for yiez will need it."

Leckie, with authority in his voice and the threat of a big breakfast ensures the two companions are more than happy to obey his commands.

Later, Leckie prepares Big Billy's broken brand for smelting while the two friends collect the five ancient brands of the Aicés and that of the great sword of the legendary Artur Àrd Nuadha. They remove the pommels, quillons, tangs and all metal pieces to prepare for the forging. They also remove from each brand a unique and precious stone. William enquires, "What are these wee gem stones for Leckie? Ah'v never seen these before, and look… they seem to glow in the dark?" Leckie smiles, "They're called Reul na Madhainn… the Morning Star. Flemish traders call them Peridot or Moldavite son, diamonds from the heavens, brought to us by the followers of Scotia. They're magical gems o' many great qualities, for when a blade has them affixed in the quillons, the pleated blades are kept forever sharp. And don't be asking me how or why, it just is…" Stephen says, "They're emerald and sapphire beautiful whatever they may be for sure." Leckie wipes his hands on a rag. "Right me boyz, we need the Tablet of Adoration settled now, I want yiez to pull on these chains attached to that big frame, then lower the tablet till its face up resting on the corners of the four forges." The three companions hook up the large stone Tablet of Adoration, then after much careful maneuvering; they eventually bring it to rest upon the corners of the four forges. "Its like a giant round fancy feastin' table," says Stephen, "yie could lay two bulls head to head right across it." William says, "Ah don't think there's going to be much feasting offa' this table Stephen." Leckie laughs, "Ah reckon that once upon a time the Duine lighiche and Bean míochnú would beg to differ…"

William and Stephen both remember wee Maws legend of the Cruathnie medicine people and how they used to feast from the gifts upon the Tablet of Adoration. Stephen shudders at the thought; then he enquires. "Why do you be wantin' the Tablet set like a table then Leckie, are we goin' to be eatin' again? And ah sincerely don't mean eatin' folk." Leckie smiles then lifts a torch from the cavern wall and walks towards a small hand-hewn tunnel entrance. He turns and looks at them, "There's one more thing we need for the creation o' the treasures… now follow me."

The two companions look at each other but say nothing as they follow Leckie down a wet and slippery moss covered stairwell. Finally they enter a small dark and dank cave, what greets the two young men shocks them to their very core, for this particular little cave resembles a hellish prison and stinks of urine and excrement. They stand and gape at Leckie almost in disbelief, for there are heavy-set iron cages hanging from the cavern ceiling, but one in particular makes the two young friends recoil, for it imprisons a dozen naked men, all firmly bound and gagged. Upon seeing Leckie and the two young friends approaching, the prisoners express sheer terror in their eyes, but no sound could be heard other than muffled screams of primeval fear from behind their gags.

"What the fuck…" exclaims Stephen, They gasp at the sight

before them. William enquires, "Who the fuck are these poor bastards, and why are they here…?" Leckie replies abruptly, "Show them some respect Wallace." Then he continues, "These men are the very essence of the great Treasures life force, now give me a hand here." Leckie lifts a small smithy hammer and knocks iron rivets from outer clasps to open the front grid on the iron prison containing the men. He begins to manhandle the petrified men out and onto their feet. Confused at this sight, William enquires, "What are yie doin' Leckie, what's going on, ah mean, who are these men?" Leckie replies tersely, "These men are our enemies by their own making and choice. Now nature herself has gifted their souls to me for my blessed work."

Leckie forcefully drags the first man forward and binds him by a rope to the neck of another. Stephen watches dumbfounded, he mutters quietly, "This setup is playing badly wit' me brains."William does not know what to say. Leckie shouts in anger at William and Stephen as he roughly pushes the two men towards the stairwell.

"Now you know where they are, when I require each gift, I want you to bring him to me by the side of the first forge." William reaches out and grabs the first petrified man, which halts Leckie in his tracks,"Wait Leckie… I mean yie no disrespect, but what the fuck are yie doin'?" William speaks with an attitude of resistance to the scene. "I will tell yie both just the once," growls Leckie, "These are the Englishmen who came through my village raping, murdering and slaughterin' ma people… and do yiez see the one at the end there…?" Leckie points at a man who looks a different class or cast from the others, "He's the one who mutilated, disemboweled then slit the throat of my son, then the bastard impaled ma sons head on the gate of a hog pen. And if you need any further inspiration, then you should know they are also part of the troop who visited Ach na Feàrna a few days ago." William spins his head round to look at the terrified prisoners; some drop to their knees as though crying for forgiveness through the look in their eyes.

Grabbing Leckie, William demands, "What are you going to do with them?" Leckie grips William by the wrists with his immensely strong smithy hands, "I will send them to a better place for a new beginning, for it was their own Gods of war who sent them to us Wallace. And tenfold will be their reward in pain and suffering for their efforts, blessed with the experience of having met me. Then perhaps they will live and lead a much more beneficial and benevolent life should their souls ever return to this earth."

The eyes of the two men waiting bound are bulging; their muffled screams could barely be heard. Leckie says, "When we release each of their gags, their screams of joy will enhance the power of the life-force in their blood, we require this for the purification of the brands. This is the true song of the blessed that will also encourage the others to sing heartily when their time comes."

His mind in turmoil, William enquires, "You would seek revenge on these men?" Leckie replies, "Naw, not at all boy, that would be a bad thing and wrong my own faith, but I will be sending them forth to meet their own maker well and truly blessed. For if it were not my duty I now set in motion, these men would feel much more pain before they depart, aye, be sure o' that Wallace. But as destiny has led them here to stand before us, they will feel naught much other than a slight sting, then they may never to wake again in this lifetime." William and Stephen are confused, Leckie says, "You should both know that one o' them told me the personage you seek for the killing of our Malcolm is a Lord Fenwick. For the murder of both your kinfolks at Glen

Afton, you must seek out Lord Cressingham and his squire, Marmaduke de Percy…" William and Stephen struggle to rationalise what Leckie has just said to them. William says, "Marmaduke de Percy, that was the last words uttered by Affric before she passed." Leckie says, "She knew Wallace, she knew that by her speaking those words, you would bring an end to this evil man, for she was a Gallóbhet Aicé. You are now her weapon of choice." Stephen says, "Those bastards boiled me family alive…"

The two companions now stand bereft of any feelings for the prisoners; their personal thoughts are interrupted when they hear Leckie command, "Now bring to me the blessings as I require them." William and Stephen instinctively know now they must follow Leckie and do his bidding, for he has the right as a man and father to exact at least satisfaction upon his son's murderers, for they too had experienced first hand the cruelty of the English.

Both now feel great satisfaction, knowing for certain who they will seek out for the slaughter of their loved ones, and it was through Leckie's faith and guidance they found this out. Leckie looks at a tall prisoner for a moment, then he says, "All except that tall one there…" He points at the one who looks a class above the rest. "For you sir Knight, your voice in your song of death will complete our task, and I will surely savour your wails of departure; your tortured cries will harmonise with the very sinews of resilient steel we must forge. For you sir Knight, you have had sustenance when the others here have not, you must feel all that you have ever delivered upon others tenfold, for that's the way of what must be done, purifying and make good those you've wronged."

Something in Leckie's words make William and Stephen feel a soul satisfaction to help. The cruelty and barbarity of the English has meant simple revenge could never recover their own innocent senses, but Leckie's delivery of his life's ancient and eternal faith makes sense to them, where words could simply never explain.

Reaching the forge cavern, Leckie takes a firm hold of the first man and stands him beside the forge, he grips the young man firmly by the shoulders, lifts him high; then forces him into an extreme squat position in the centre of the Tablet of Adoration. Leckie then chains him to iron rings on the side of the Tablet, securing him firmly, now any movement from the man is impossible. Leckie enquires of the prisoner, "Is it the English that yie speak son?" The terrified young man, about the same age as William and Stephen, nods in the affirmative. Leckie continues as he sharpens what appears to be a butcher's skinning knife, "Then by my faith in Magda Mòr… mother-nature to you son, I must be telling you of what I will do to you before you depart this life to enter your own spirit world. What is about to happen will form the memory of your last few moments here with us, and these memories will stay with your diseased soul to give you a better demeanor should yie ever choose to return yer cleansed soul to this earth in another life."

Gazing into the young mans eyes, Leckie continues sharpening the blade, subtly torturing the young man's wit. He says, "Son, do yie have a mother where yie come from?" The prisoner nods affirmatively. Leckie continues, "Then I would want yie to think of her, can yie see her son, what's she like, is she crying and worried about her wee boy do yie think, does she weep for yie boy?" The prisoner, with tears welling up in his eyes, nods. Leckie continues, "Do yie think she can feel yer fear right now son?" Again the prisoner nods affirmatively, Leckie says; "That's good, for that's the kind of spirit ah need if yie be thinkin' that, then the next wain yer auld maw delivers will be carrying that same message through your departin' spirit, and that message is for you and yours no' to be ever coming back to Scotland with such evil intention and doin's ever again." The muffled screams of terror from the young man are indescribable as Leckie continues, "You son, you have brought what's about to happen to yie upon yourself, yie have come by yer own choices to be in my land, you have cruelly taken innocent souls away that I loved without ceremony nor any mercy, and you've done these things with a violence and a hatred in your heart. But I have no hatred for you, nor any violence to offer... Yet it is I who will return you to where your mother and father plucked your soul from the heavens and gave you life."

Standing close by, William and Stephen both watch and listen intently as Leckie continues with his terrifying faith recital, all the while slowly and deliberately sharpening the skinning blade in front of the unfortunate young Englishman. He moves closer to the Englishman... "You will no' feel very much pain, well maybe yie will because ahm a wee bitty out o' practice... So ma son from a different god, soon yie will fall to the final sleep, but untill that moment comes, I want you to look at that great simmering vat over there and know that it's waiting for you. Once we have your life force near drained from your body and you can still feel pain, we'll slowly boil you alive in that cauldron and strip all the flesh from your bones... and then son, your bonnie skull will adorn these ancient cavern chambers, just like the Romans, Saxons, and Jutes before yie, and for your precious gift of life... we here will be thankin' yie."

Resolutely, William and Stephen observe what looks to be a religious scene, but Leckie shows no emotion when speaking in a fashion designed to unleash unthinkable terror upon the prisoners. Yet the two friends know it was by this Englishman's own choices and deeds that brought him here.

"Ah know what yiez are thinkin' boyz," says Leckie, "That this young fella in some naïve way has brought himself here against a force transcending anything he could ever have imagined. All o' these Englishmen have selected themselves as gifts for the Treasures o' the Aicé. They have gambled with the power o' their own deity against the faith o' our beautiful Aicé… and their deity has lost. Now, I want yiez to fetch the next gift for me, for I cannae be starting on one gift without the next gift here to watch and hear all of what his short-time future will be by the fate another." The two young friends quickly disappear back down to the prison chamber while Leckie continues to use purposeful words to torment the young Englishman, causing him a greater intellectual pain that any physical torture could ever inflict.

William and Stephen soon return with the next gift and secure him exactly where Leckie wants him, in a place where he can specifically see and hear everything and miss nothing. Leckie turns his attention back to the young man, bound tightly and squatting above the ancient Tablet of Adoration.

Suddenly and deftly, Leckie reaches out and grips the young mans penis and testicles, the young man screams out in pain and terror, Leckie proceeds to squeeze the testicles firmly till the pain causes sweat to pour from the young man and his skin goes deathly pale. Leckie takes his razor sharp blade then slowly and methodically, he cuts the penis and testicles away from the base of the prisoner's stomach, releasing blood that flows and spurts into the ancient knotwork runnels in the Tablet of Adoration. As the blood pours from the young mans body, it fills the knotwork channels, turning the channel furrows a dark crimson red, while the ridges of the channels remain alabaster white. At the foot of the Tablet, a great trough catches the bloody life force and begins to fill up. Intently watching the flow of blood run in certain channels, Leckie shakes his head and mumbles, "Hmmm that's not good news…" Leckie removes the Englishman's gag, allowing him to scream, instantly William and Stephen put their hands over their ears, trying to block out the chilling screams of a terrified dying young man. It's a long time before the young man stops screaming. Hanging in his hunched position, he looks with pleading eyes at the three companions. It's then that William and Stephen notice his tongue has been cut out.

Meanwhile, Leckie is examining the last of the young man's blood running freely through the tablet channels as though he is reading a book, then he says, "Aye, that's better, that's a good sign." Leckie whispers to the terrified young man, "Before yie fall to the final sleep son, I'll be thankin' yie for your gift of blood, for it's with the essence of your life-force that we will temper the treasures of the Aicés. Aye, there's nothing finer than the life force of our enemies that will suffice to be forgin' all o' the forces required to weld together these blades for their fine new caretakers." Leckie pauses for a moment then he unties the young man from his bonds and gently cradles him in his arms like a babe; curiously, Leckie nods in a particular direction… "Now do yie see that big vat over there boilin' and steamin' son, we're goin' to place yie in there, it's a special place where you may bathe awhile as we boil the meat from your bones…"

On hearing Leckie's words, the petrified gaze of the young man heightens, then appears to subdue slightly, the grip of terror in his eyes begins to fade as a hazy state of sleepiness takes over his spirit. Leckie then walks slowly towards the boiling vat when the wretched young man's head lops to the side. His eyes lift as he looks over at the great boiling vat, instantly he revisits his terror at the thought of being slowly boiled alive, but becomes less each time he glances over, as his life-blood ends, so will his life. Leckie reaches the vat and sits the Englishman on a stone throne, loops a rope attached to an overhead pulley under the wretches arms then Leckie hauls the Englishman into the air and maneuvers him over the simmering vat. Once in position, Leckie slowly lowers him into the vat. As his feet enter the vat, the Englishman's screams are so pitched; they reverberate around the tunnels and caverns of the Labyrinth. As his cries of pain fade to searing groans Leckie says, "Son, never fret, for soon yie will be reduced to the original force that gave yie life… water." Leckie turns to William and Stephen, "Right boys, I made it easy for that young fella' during the boiling in the vat, for he was just a servant and he has now served out his three deaths. For the final pleasures o' the Treasures I will be reserving those rites for his knight commander, for him, aye it will sure be much more entertaining, so bring him up here next to witness all o' his minions demise…"

"Leckie," enquires William, "Is this no' simply revenge?" Leckie laughs, "Naw son, the terror the gift feels makes their blood much stronger for our needs, the song they sing harmonises the pleats of steel with the purest of natures vibrations, simple revenge is wrong. Yie must always treat kindly with the gifts, tell them the truth without malice, any other way will bring failure for the Treasures and a curse upon the one who would use them under such eternal and base pretences." Leckie looks at Stephen, "Ah know that the cauldron and boiling vat brings yie back terrible memories of the bonnie Katriona and your wains Stephen, and we sorely share that memory with yie son, but yiez both must understand what we do now and why we must do it? Without the force of terror set tenfold upon those who would murder us, then there is no Anam Álainn more powerful for the forging of the Treasures. Yiez both once questioned who is there to save us? Well, it is men like you two, for there is nothing else may stop this great and evil creed." William and Stephen nod in understanding, confirming the bloom and innocence of youth has departed the young friends. As it is with the nature of men who feel no emotion for the demise of an enemy, they commit to do as Leckie bids them, for they know they do not wrong their beliefs in fulfilling their chosen labour for this wise old man.

Leckie says, "I'll be letting one o' the Sudrons leave this place alive to be telling their story… One must live to be telling his masters and friends of his experience. Some day soon the chosen Sudron will wake up far from here to retell of what has happened, that's if his wits are still in tact. Right boyz, now yiez know the why for, I want yiez to bring the Knight and the next gift up here while I get another forge ready for the tempering. Remember this for when you gift a life o' an enemy, whenever yie can, another gift must always be brought to witness, for it's the way of the gift, meaning, the greater the terror of the mind, the more powerfull the spirit in the blood." Leckie turns to William, "Wallace, I need yie to stand before me, for I must measure you up for the makin' o' Fragarach the Retaliator." As William stands before him, Leckie says, "A Claymore must be accurately measured for the particular user, so here, hold this staff a moment and place the bottom end between your two big toes. Now I want yie to clasp your hands over the top end so that you're looking straight across your knuckles, resting your front knuckles against the bridge o' yer big nose." Leckie squints his eyes at the measurement…

"Hmmm… Ahl cut a wee bit off the top then ah want yie to try that again." Once again William clasps the staff on top, this time as he leans his thumbs and clasps his top knuckles firmly against the bridge of his nose, he can see directly down his knuckles like a line of sight, "That's it…" says Leckie, "Perfect… how does it feel young Wallace?" William replies, "Excellent."

Smiling as he takes the staff away, Leckie says, "Now that's to be the length of your Claymore son, for each guardian is a different size and this is how we gain perfection in fit and balance for the gift giver." William enquires curiously, "The gift giver?" Leckie replies, "Aye son, when yie dispatch someone who stands before yie with a guardian brand, both you and your enemy should be happy that the gift you deliver by Retaliator, ends the conflict between yie both and gifts your enemies demise quick and fast, for which your enemy should be eternally grateful, that's called a gift Wallace." William grins as Leckie continues, "When yie stand guard, rest your knuckles on the pommel, for then yie have a core of steel running down the centre of your body like a guard of iron, for that there is the finest guard yie may ever have." Leckie continues, "Always remember this Wallace, a centre strike is a kill, a side strike hmmm, it will hurt yie sore, probably… but yie will survive, that is why yie must always stand attentive with the Guardian blade down yer centre." William nods, amused by Leckie's care and description.

Engrossed, William listens intently as Leckie continues, "And from that guard rest position, such is the torque that it only takes a slight forward motion pushing against the brand with yer knee to spring the claymore up in defence. And the giftee for whom the great sword rises, cannae tell the distance it travels as yie shove it forward direct and centre toward them." William understands the simplicity of the instructions, as he has he's practiced it many times with his fathers claymore. Leckie enquires, "Yie are understanding the geometry, the arc and the motion o' yer blade?" William replies, "Ah do." Leckie scowls, "Ah should think so, it's feckn simple enough. It's no' like it's a great feckn secret or anythin'." At that moment, Stephen returns with another petrified man, bound and gagged. He has not forgotten the pleasure it gives to be *nice* to an enemy, and the reason for the pleasantries. Stephen says politely and with a big smile in attendance, "Good sirs, here's another gift for the cutting off o' his bollocks then boiling him alive." Leckie replies courteously, "Why thank yie young Stephen ma boy," Stephen replies, "Gu failte… Your welcome." The three of friends laugh at the bizarre courtly manners of the occasion, for thoughts of their loved ones deny any sympathy for the 'Gifts.'

"Oh Fuck…" exclaims Leckie, "I near forgot, that other wee bastard on the tablet has near bled out up there. He scrambles onto the Tablet of Adoration to carry his gift to the cleansing cauldron.

A few moments later he returns.

"Right…" says Leckie, "I'll get this next gift here secured, and you Wallace, you fetch me another one while ah measure up Stephen here for Lúin fàinne the Slaughterer. Then ah'll smelt some separate blades to make yie both a fine pair o' side brands. Now, ah want yie both to be watchin', for every time we fold the steel and temper the separate blocks, we must have the blades ready to be dropped in the gifts life force before it cools below the Tablet of Adoration." Leckie continues, "When we separate the different metals for the brands o' the Aicés require, we'll take a small piece from your grandfathers sword for both the Treasures." Looking at Stephen, Leckie says, "And for you young Stephen, I'll re-forge Nuadha's sword befitting an excellent son and true blood of Erie. Are yiez with me boyz, are yiez ready to get started?" William and Stephen reply with great zeal in their temperament. "We are."

"Then fire up the forge Mac h'Alpine," says Leckie "and you

Wallace, you keep shuffling our gifts as required, and select yourself the special one that will be released, he wont know it yet, but he will be telling this story one day. And yie might as well fetch up the Knight commander too, for ah want him to see everything, but ahl be dealing wie the knight last, for it's his voice that will make Fragarach and Lúin fàinne perfectly tuned, for the more the gift sings, the greater the temper will be drawn from him… and no brand could be finer made ah tell yie." Leckie continues, "The application o' the final temper will be very different from the rest o' the gifts me boyz, for this man commanded the actions of the previous gifts and he must feel the pain of what he has done before his own gods come to collect him. And ah must take great care to make sure that his departing is a long and joyfully delicate occasion."

Pausing for a moment Leckie smiles… "Yie must enjoy yer work too yie know, and ah'll not be give him up lightly, every fibre of his soul must know that we are exacting a hundred-fold what he has delivered to others before we send him on his way. Now bring the knight commander up next. It'll be good for his spleen to witness all that goes before him. We'll secure him close to the Tablet of Adoration, for there is nothing that's coming for him that I would wish to be a surprise." The three companions work feverously in their underground haven, oblivious to time or the middleworld, the world that rests above them. The four ancient forges of the Cruathnie Aicé A'nnan once again smelts to protect the people of Scotland.

"At last, we're almost done…" says Leckie. He looks at many thin sheets of metal, all separated into groups of soft, medium and hard metals, ready for the forging and folding for two of the most beautiful blades the Labyrinth of Carlibar will ever have borne to this world. Stephen is curious, "How long is it do yie reckon before the blades are complete and ready for gift givin'?" Leckie laughs, "Ah cannae be faulting your zeal young Mac h'Alpine, but a reckon a season will be time enough to spend on these brands." Stephen exclaims, "Yie mean a few months?" Leckie replies, "Och aye, that it will be, and then the Treasures will surely last a lifetime and beyond." William enquires, "What do yie have in mind for the knight?" Leckie replies nonchalantly, "The delicacy of this fella's gifting is to keep him alive while he is slowly flayed. He must endure a great deal till all that's left is his hearts beatin' and brain's a' thinkin' for the pot. Ah must work him ever so finely till there are no more sounds that may exhale from this songbird."

Completely oblivious to the terror going through the mind of the English knight, Leckie continues, "Now boyz, I need yiez tae be getting' ready to be going back to Carlibar and speeding on your way to Crosshouse, for the song this man must sing is for me alone and not for such bonnie young ears such as yours, maybe another time though, for there will be plenty more gifts a' comin'." Stephen quips, "I don't mind hearin' a foin tune on a Norman harp Leckie."

"Well ah do thank yie once again for your enthusiasm Stephen," says Leckie with a smile, "and ah also believe yie to be truthful too, that's good for a master hammerer to be, but yiez have worked long and hard boyz and yiez must get some rest and a good sleep too, for the urgency of matters regarding the state of the realm above us must now be foremost in yer minds to conclude." The young companions shake their heads reluctantly, for they had taken well to their tasks in the underworld, but lost all track of time. Work and sleep in an underground realm provides no awareness of normal time and Leckie knows when they surface, it must be night, for there can be no risk of them being seen as they exit the underworld of Gleniffer. "Go and get some sleep boys." says Leckie, "It's a full moon later this night and that's when I require yiez tae be leavin' me to ma craft. Now here, drink this, for it will help yiez get a good sleep, and when it's time, ah will lead yiez back to middle-world." Leckie hands them each a drink laced with honey, whisky and something tasteless that he fails to mention. They make cribs in the topmost cavern and quickly fall into a deep sleep.

William stirs and rubs his eyes, something feels wrong. He sits up to see that Stephen is already sitting up and staring wide-eyed. William, though still half asleep, enquires, "What are you starin' at Stephen?" Without looking back at William. Stephen points and replies, "Him… ahm starin at bleedin' him." William enquires, "Him who?" while vainly peering in the direction so keenly keeping Stephens attention, "Who the Feck is him? I Cannae see a feckin' thing…" Then William sees to whom Stephen is pointing at, and sits bolt upright, for standing still in the shadowy mouth of their cavern, is the shadowy outline of tall man covered by a thick crow-feather cloak and stag-horn helmet, with only his piercing eyes to be seen. Clearly he has been observing them awhile.

The tall stranger points at them and speaks, "Cuiridh fiacail nan caoraich an' crann air an' sparr." Stephen exclaims, "What the Fuck did he just say there Wallace? I don't think I be liking so much this feckn strange world you feckn Scots have got goin' on over here, too many unnatural bleedin' surprises." William translates in whispered curiosity, "The teeth of the sheep will lay the plough on the shelf…" William mutters, "It's the Galloway Gaelic he speaks." Stephen jumps up and grabs his sword, "Oi don't give a Fuck if it's welsh mountain poetry spoken in forked fuckin' tongues… What the feck are we goin to do about him…"

The stranger speaks with familiarity, "Co'nas Wallace óg?"

William enquires tentatively, "Is that you true Tam?" The stranger walks forward. "It is I…" replies True Tam, "I'm here to help Leckie honour the Treasures." In a sleepy stupor, Stephen attempts to front true Tam, but William catches him and pulls him back. "Don't Stephen, this fella will kill you before yie blink, he's a seer and another great sorcerer." Stephen puts his hands on his head, "Awe fir fuck's sake, ah can't be takin much more o' this magical madness." William laughs and slaps Stephen on the shoulder, "Ahm only jesting with yie Stephen, True Tam is all of that right enough, but a greater more genuine friend to us we couldn't wish for." True Tam comes over to the two friends, lifts their drinks to his nose and sniffs the aroma.

"Ah…" says true Tam, "So Leckie is freeing you two young sorcerers apprentice's from the underworld?" True Tam gazes with piercing eyes into the hearts of the two companions. Suddenly William feels cold and wet, he jumps up with a start; nearby he sees Stephen is sleeping blissfully unaware, it's a black night and they're outside the Cairn of Gleniffer underneath the stars, he is totally bewildered.

Aggressively, William shakes his friend, "Stephen wake up, wake up for fucks sake…" Stephen wakes with a start from a deep sleep, he lazily looks around then exclaims, "What the fuck… Whoa… this is not bleedin' right, what the bleedin fuck ahm I doin' outside in the rain?" Stephen jumps to his feet while pulling at his sword, then he scratches his head, "Wallace I've had the most crazy feckin dream, did we get blootered in some bleedin' flea tavern last night?" William replies as he scans the night-time vista, "Ah don't think so, not that I can remember?" Stephen shakes his head in bewilderment, "Well ah'v just had one mad bleedin dream ah tell yee." William is equally bemused, "Was yer dream with me and auld Leckie down in some mad underground

Cavern wie Dragon skulls, auld weapons and some gifted Englishmen goin to sing songs at the forge o' A'nnan… and finishing with true Tam speakin' in some riddle about a toothless fuckin' sheep?" Stephen looks at William, "Right that's it; oi'm goin back home to fuckin' Erinn where it's much safer on me brains fightin' feckn Normans." William says with guarded humour in his voice, "I think ah might go with yie." Stephen enquires, "What's that at yer feet?"

Looking down, William sees three parchment rolls on the ground beside his crib brat. He picks them up and sees Leckie and True Tam's seals of the crossed Hammers and a Raven and Swan stamped on each of them. William replies, "One's for us, this one's for Ranald and the other one is for Bishop Wishart?" Stephen looks across at the dark Clyde vista, "We better get off this feckn hill Wallace, ah see that the dawn is breakin' soon and to be tellin ya the truth brother dreamer o' mine, I really need a strong feckn drink likely more for that dream has me bleedin' rattled."

The two friends wander down the Gleniffer brae, still trying to fathom out what had just happened. They collect their horses and tack where they had left them behind Leckie's obhainn. As they prepare to they make their way towards Crosshouse and complete their task, they are still in a great quandary about their seemingly shared dream. Stephen enquires, "Wallace, tell me, did all that shit really bleedin' happen…?" William replies tentatively, "I think so…" After a few moments pause, William considers the deadly reality of the situation. His demeanour suddenly changes, "C'mon Stephen. Every moment we waste, someone innocent in our country feckin' dies at the hands of the English."

"So where are we going then?" enquires Stephen. William replies, "We're going for blood..."

Coming Soon

**The sixth thrilling instalment in**
Wallace: Legend of Braveheart